Behind him the early evening wind rustled the richly embroidered floral curtains on the open window, rustled one of two papyrus scrolls that lay on his bedtable. He half-turned, looked fondly at the scroll, read the title, "The Gospel according to Mark."

There was a soft rustle behind him. Just the curtains or perhaps... He half-turned to look.

A hooded figure was framed in the window, silhouetted black against the last fading afterglow in the sky. Instantly Odysseus understood. *So, he thought, you climbed up the vines on the outside of the house to attack me from behind!*

A javelin hurtled through the air to bury itself in the old man's back.

The killer stepped toward him.

Odysseus twisted, looked up, recognized in the flickering lamp light a familiar face. His last words were a strangled whisper:

"I knew... I knew it was *you*."

Other books by Ray Faraday Nelson

TimeQuest, Tor Books (1984)
Prometheus Man, Donning/Starblaze (1982)
Murder Among Friends, Harlequin/Ravin House (1979)
In the Footsteps of Jack London, Self-published, nonfiction (1979)
Arthur the Celt, Corgi (1978)
Arthur the Roman, Corgi (1978)
Revolt of the Unemployables, Anthelion (1978)
Dimension of Horror, Pinnacle/Blade Series (1977)
Ecolog, Harlequin/Laser (1976)
Then Beggars Could Ride, Harlequin/Laser (1975)
Blake's Progress, Harlequin/Laser (1974)
D.A.'s Wife, Greenleaf (1970)
How To Do It, Greenleaf (1970)
Agony of Love, Greenleaf (1969)
Ganymede Takeover, Ace (1966)

Mr. Nelson's short fiction has appeared in such publications as: *Weird Tales, Fantasy and Science Fiction, Science-Fiction Review, Harper's Weekly, Amazing Stories, Fantastic Adventures, Gallery, Parade, Dude, Nugget, Gamma, The Miscellaneous Man*, and many others.

Special note: The 1988 science-fiction action thriller, *They Live* (John Carpenter/Universal), is based on Ray Faraday Nelson's short story, *Eight O'clock in the Morning*.

Dogheaded Death

Ray Faraday Nelson

Copyright © 1989 by Ray Faraday Nelson

Strawberry Hill Press
2594 15th Avenue
San Francisco, California 94127

No part of this book may be reproduced by any mechanical, photographic, or electronic process, or in the form of a phonographic recording, nor may it be stored in a retrieval system, transmitted, or otherwise copied for public or private use—other than for "fair use"—without the written permission of the publisher.

Edited by William E. Johnston

Proofread by Elizabeth Lohse Hession

Cover painting by George Barr

Cover by Ku, Fu-sheng

Designed and typeset by Cragmont Publications, Oakland, California

Printed by Edwards Brothers, Inc., Lillington, North Carolina

Manufactured in the United States of America

Library of Congress Cataloging-in-Publication Data

Nelson, Ray Faraday, 1931-
    Dogheaded death / Ray Faraday Nelson.
    p.   cm.
    ISBN 0-89407-079-7 : $8.95
    1. Egypt—History—30 B.C.-640 A.D.—Fiction. I. Title.
PS3564.E4745D6   1989
813'.54—dc20
                                                      89-11428
                                                         CIP

Veritatem cognoscentis et veritas vos liberabit.
John 8:32

Table of Contents

Cast of Characters   9
Prelude   15

Book One

Chapter One   21
Chapter Two   33
Chapter Three   47
Chapter Four   58

Book Two

Chapter One   75
Chapter Two   92
Chapter Three   102
Chapter Four   113

Book Three

Chapter One   125
Chapter Two   133
Chapter Three   147
Chapter Four   162

Coda   177

Cast of Characters

CENTURION GAIUS HESPERIAN; a reflective and compassionate member of Emperor Nero's palace guard with a knack for detective work. He's considered rather odd by his fellow officers because he doesn't torture witnesses.

ODYSSEUS MEMNON; a Greek-Egyptian shipping magnate, the Onassis of the First Century Mediterranean, who is found murdered in his Alexandrian mansion after announcing his conversion to an evangelistic cult to which he plans to donate all his worldly goods.

ADRASTIA MEMNON; old Odysseus' young, beautiful wife. Nero had her father murdered. Now she spies for Rome's enemies.

DEMETRIUS MEMNON; Odysseus' brother: cruel, gaunt, and old. As Odysseus' business partner, he's made a fortune smuggling weapons and supplies to the Jewish rebels, to the barbarians, to any subversive group plotting against Nero.

OCTAVIA MEMNON; Odysseus' divorced first wife, mother of his children. She lives in well-heeled exile in Rome, secretly idolized by her son.

SERAPION MEMNON; Octavia's son. He has the face of a young philosopher, but the hard, muscular body of a gladiator. After captaining his father's ships, not only merchant vessels but fighting and racing craft, he enters the temple of the ancient gods of Egypt, Isis and Serapis, to study for the priesthood.

HATHOR MEMNON; Odysseus' beautiful tomboy daughter. Odysseus gave her as good an education as if she'd been a boy, but now she has become distant. She won't even reveal the name of the lover she meets secretly in the Alexandrian slums.

SABELLA; a sixteen-year-old black slave girl in the Memnon household. She calls Adrastia "Mama", and Adrastia loves her far more than she loves either of her step-children.

ROPHOS and **WAKAR**; eunuch slaves in the Memnon household. Rophos dies of poisoned soup intended for Odysseus. In the investigation,

Waker is tortured by the authorities and crippled for life.

SUCHOS, **HORUS**, and **BUBO**; Adrastia's hunchbacked dwarf clowns. They laugh, joke and turn handsprings, but nobody knows what they really think and feel.

SIMON BAAL; a Parthian spy as well as a rich ship owner. Baal backs the Memnon enterprises from behind the scenes, and his friends in high places have gotten Odysseus his prized Roman naturalized citizenship. In return, the Memnons do his bidding.

OPTIO MANNUS; Centurion Hesperian's ambitious second-in-command, a powerfully-built soldier of forty. He's tough and loyal, of good simple farm stock, but a little slow of wit.

LIBRARIUS DAPHNIS; Hesperian's clerk and secretary. Vain, clever, aristocratic, Daphnis delights in outwitting Mannus, his superior officer.

The Apostle **MARK**; founder of the first Christian church in Alexandria, author of the earliest canonical gospel, eventually a martyr in Alexandria, all according to church traditions.

BISHOP ANNIANUS; also according to church tradition, appointed first Bishop of Alexandria in 61 A.D. by the Apostle Mark. A Jewish shoemaker by trade, he also was martyred, for protesting the worship of Serapis, in 84 A.D., during the reign of Emperor Domitian.

BASILEIDES; a rich, powerful friend of the Memnon family, his parents were slaves and he was made a freedman by the Emperor Claudius. Now he is the secret pawn of Simon Baal.

REMUS; Captain of the Guard at the Alexandrian prison, a tall, heavy-set Roman. He can read, but not without moving his lips.

Old **HECATE**; Hathor Memnon's observant and talkative landlady in the slum neighborhood of Rhakotis, the Egyptian quarter of Alexandria. It is at old Hecate's that Hathor meets her mysterious lover.

T. VINDAIUS ARIOVESTUS; fat "compounder of panaceas." He and his equally fat wife **Livia** sell all manner of medicines and drugs, including poison.

Cast of Characters   11

Old **KISSINGFISH**; Adrastia Memnon's sensitive, fastidious hairdresser, above suspicion, it would seem.

DIONYSIUS; head librarian at the vast Alexandrian library from 67 to 117 A.D., a student of Chaeremon, the previous head librarian, and a secretary to ambassadors and Emperors.

TIBERIUS JULIUS ALEXANDER; governor of Egypt from 67 to 71 A.D. He is a native-born Alexandrian Jew with naturalized Roman citizenship, nephew of Philo the Philosopher, and formerly (46-47 A.D.) Procurator of Judea.

Prelude

"Master, you awake?"

The heavy door muffled the voice of the young girl.

"Master, you in there?"

She knocked lightly.

"Master, please . . . I got to talk to you." She sounded desperate, on the verge of tears.

An early evening breeze rustled the richly embroidered floral curtains at the open bedroom window, set the flames in the gold and silver oil lamps to dancing and flickering and sending out tenuous streamers of acrid black smoke.

Even here in Egyptian Alexandria there were few bedrooms furnished as lavishly this one. A niche containing a small greenish-bronze bust of an adolescent girl; a vast many-pillowed bed draped in green silk, with a bedstead of bronze formed by a master craftsman into the shapes of women, gods, flowers, animals and birds all blending together into ornate grotesque hybrids that in the moving lamp light seemed to breathe with quick nervous gasps; murals depicting in painstaking detail the progress of a dead man's soul through the Western Land, the Land of the Dead, and past all sorts of trials and monsters to the foot of the throne of Mother Isis and Father Osiris-Serapis, monarchs of the underworld; a modest altar on a low table where a statuette of a seated, bearded Osiris-Serapis (in the realistic Greek style) seemed to bless anyone who stood before him; a bed table where two scrolls lay, one of them partly unrolled to reveal the title in Greek, "The Gospel according to Mark"; a green desk bearing writing tools—a stylus for wax tablets and a pen for papyrus scrolls—and equipped with compartments for current reading matter; three green glazed earthenware jars, each half as tall as a man, where, carefully encased in leather sacks, other manuscripts were stored; a white ceiling slightly grayed by lamp smoke; and a floor of pink marble edged with a Greek key design in mosaic. All these combined to give an impression of relentless opulence, of a luxury that defied all restraint.

"Master! Why don't you answer?"

Distant dogs barked, then were silent.

Two things marred the perfection of the room.

The first was an unsheathed knife with a curved, polished blade and with emeralds, rubies and diamonds set in the handle; a knife that seemed to have been carelessly tossed on the floor where it now lay, its jewels reflecting the restless lamp light.

The second was a corpse.

He was—or had been—old, gaunt, skeletal.

He was—or had been—rich.

The rings on his bony fingers could have, by themselves, paid for a ship and the slaves to row it. His green silk robes and tunic were worth a year's wages for a centurion, and a prostitute from the Egyptian quarter might sell her body for a lifetime and not earn the price of his silver-trimmed and bejeweled sandals.

"Master! Please!"

She knocked again, louder.

His eyes were open.

They were dark brown, almost black, and now that they were motionless seemed made of clouded glass. From the way his body was twisted as he lay there on the floor beside the bed, he must have been trying very hard to see something when he died, something behind him. Except for that twist in his body, he would have been lying face down, spread-eagle. His features were frozen in an enigmatic grimace. Could that be some kind of tortured smile? Could that be a look of triumph on his face?

His face . . .

It was not a rich man's face.

It was not the face of a man born to softness and ease, but was, rather, the face of a poor man, a merchant, a man who had early learned and never forgotten the art of squeezing a coin. That bald, beardless, head was made to poke itself out of the folds of a camel driver's cloak, not from these slippery silks for which men had no doubt given their lives to bring them all the way from China.

"Master!"

She tried the door, found it was unlocked.

She opened it a crack, letting a sliver of light into the room from the more brightly lit hallway.

Jutting upward from between his shoulder blades was a spear or javelin with a wood shaft and an iron head and point. The twist of his body made it tilt at an acute angle to the floor. The point of the spear had passed through him and protruded slightly from his chest, almost touching the marble floor, and was caked with drying blood. There was more blood on the floor, an amazing amount of blood to have come from such a small, thin old man.

The door swung open and she stood there, framed in the doorway, silhouetted against the brightness of many-branched petrolabrums behind and above her. She was a black girl, about sixteen-years-old, clad only in an unadorned grayish wool shift that barely reached her scrawny knees.

"Master?"

She stepped into the room, unable to see clearly before her eyes adjusted to the light. Something was there on the floor beside the bed, but she couldn't quite make it out. She took a few shuffling steps toward it on the cool stone. Now there could be no mistake.

It's him, she thought. There was no feeling of shock yet. She stood over the corpse for a full minute at least, looking down with round eyes and open mouth.

Finally, she thought, *They did it. They finally did it.*

She closed her eyes, opened them again.

The old man was still there.

"No!" she whispered, stamping her bare feet. The panic was rising now, but she wanted to stay calm, wanted to do the right thing, the smart thing, the safe thing.

"No!" she screamed, and the loudness of her own voice startled her. She backed out of the room, began to run down the hall. She continued to scream, unaware that she was doing so. She tried to block the image from her mind of what she had just seen, tried to concentrate on simple physical sensations.

She was going down the great marble staircase.

She could feel her bare feet slapping on stone, felt her small breasts bouncing on her chest as she leaped down three steps at a time. At the foot of the stairs a man was looking up at her, eyebrows raised, a man who looked very much like the man she had just seen crumpled on the bedroom floor . . . old, gaunt, hairless, richly-robed. He stepped into her path and grabbed her by the arm, then slapped her across the face so hard that she was afraid for an instant he had loosened her teeth.

"Sabella!" he shouted at her, shaking her violently. "Stop that screaming!"

She tried to pull away from him, screaming all the louder.

"Do you want me to get the whip?" he demanded.

"No! No!"

"Then quiet down, you hear me! Tell me calmly what's bothering you, or I'll . . ."

"He's dead! He's up there on the floor dead! The Master's dead!"

"What? You're lying! You're lying, Sabella!"

He raised his hand as if to slap her again.

"No!" she howled up at his contorted face. Partly from fear and partly from dizziness caused by his first slap, she fell on her knobby knees at his feet. "He's there! Go look!"

A woman's voice called out angrily: "Let her go! Sabella's no liar!"

He released her, after a moment's indecision, and Sabella scuttled away from him on her hands and knees.

"A slave only tells the truth under torture," he grumbled, wiping his hands on his silk tunic as if he had dirtied them by touching Sabella.

"Get up, Sabella," the woman commanded, firmly but kindly.

Sabella obeyed.

The woman was pale, slender, and young, with black hair that hung to the small of her back. Sabella had often thought, when she saw her Master's wife like this, dressed in fine embroidered linen gowns and wearing rings and necklaces, that she was the most beautiful woman in Alexandria.

"Come here, Sabella." The woman opened her arms.

"Yes, Mama Adrastia."

Sabella called Adrastia "Mama" all the time. She'd never known her real mother.

Adrastia held the black girl in her arms until the trembling stilled. Sabella liked to be near her. She smelled so good.

"Now, Sabella, do you think you could take me with you and show me whatever it is you saw?"

"Yes, Mama Adrastia."

"You're spoiling that slave . . ." began the man.

"Not now, Demetrius," snapped Adrastia.

They left him behind as they went up the stairs.

Adrastia stood over the corpse even longer than Sabella had. Finally she sighed, shook her head slowly and said, "By the gods, I wish there was some way we could keep the authorities out of this. *We have so much to hide!*"

Book One

Chapter One

THERE WAS ONE SEAGULL, all white with some of his tail feathers missing, who had stayed with the ship when, off the toe of Italy, the others had turned back. As a reward for loyalty, Mannus had given him a name: Charon.

The Roman officer stood, elbows resting on the rail, watching Charon glide over the wake, a dark spot against the cloudless, blindingly-bright sky. Though it was hours before the thin dark line of Africa would appear on the horizon, other gulls had now appeared, hoping for a share of the sparse garbage the Romans dumped overboard after each meal.

I wonder . . . thought Mannus . . . *will Charon stay with us all the way to Alexandria?*

There was a burst of laughter from below decks where the rowers, Mannus knew, were casting dice in their interminable game. They were an inexperienced crew, assembled at the last moment and without training. (Mannus suspected that this was the first time some of the younger ones had been to sea.) Thus it was fortunate indeed that the wind was behind them, strong and steady in the great square mainsail. They had scarcely needed the oars since they'd left port.

The commanding officer, Centurion Gaius Hesperian of Nero's Imperial Praetorian Guard, was also below decks in his cabin and had left orders that he was not to be disturbed. Mannus, then, was now in command. He was an *optio*, something like an apprentice centurion, and some day, if he served Hesperian well, he'd have the rank himself and eighty men serving under him. Mannus smiled, thinking about it.

I'm thirty years old now. I wonder if I'll get my command before I'm forty? Hesperian would certainly make the recommendation, but there was always a wait for a vacancy, a wait that might last for years. Mannus frowned, thinking about it.

Hesperian was forty and had already served as a Chief Centurion, with sixty other centurions under him; but, Mannus decided, that was probably too much to hope for. Rare indeed was the man who became a Chief Centurion before the age of sixty. Mannus ran his blunt, powerful fingers through his short-cropped brown hair . . . hair that was beginning to turn gray and recede at the temples.

Charon, seeming to hang for a moment motionless just out of reach, squawked raffishly. Mannus laughed. "What are you, eh? A clown? A rascal? Or a philosopher?"

The bird did not answer but, with a few arrogant beats of his wings, swooped up to perch on the yardarm. Mannus, turning to follow his flight, caught sight of another Roman officer approaching with uncertain steps across the shifting deck.

"Daphnis!" called out Mannus. "Where are your sea legs?"

Daphnis came weaving up and leaned on the rail beside him. "You're a swine, Optio Mannus. Did anyone ever tell you that? You're a filthy swine." The tone was delicate, disdainful, aristocratic; not really angry. "Sea legs indeed!"

In spite of a muscular soldier's body, there was something almost feminine about Daphnis. Mannus, out of the corner of his eye, studied the officer's handsome, hawk-like profile. Daphnis was five years younger than Mannus, and it showed.

"It's the wind," complained Daphnis. "It does nothing at all for my hair." Short hair was the prevailing fashion for soldiers, but Daphnis had long blond hair, as beautiful as any woman's. "I think I'd love the sea, really, if it weren't for the wind." He rolled his eyes heavenward in mock despair. The wind was, as he said, whipping his golden locks like a banner, tangling the strands, drying it out.

Hesperian had once described Daphnis as being in philosophy a rigorous skeptic and in love a rigorous homosexual. A rigorous homosexual! As usual Hesperian had summed things up perfectly. *Damned boy-lover*, thought Mannus disgustedly, but he kept his thoughts to himself. These days it was considered old-fashioned to be shocked by what was coyly referred to as "Greek love."

Daphnis was a *librarius*, a sort of clerk or scribe to Hesperian, and though he was of a lower rank than Mannus, he had, as usual, not bothered to salute; yet another cause for Mannus' irritation.

"When do you think we'll reach Alexandria?" asked Daphnis absently.

"Tomorrow morning." It was a stupid question. Daphnis should have already known the answer.

After a pause, Daphnis put another question. "You wouldn't care to give me a teeny tiny little hint about the nature of our mission, would you, Optio Mannus, sir?"

"You know it's confidential. That's all you need to know, Librarius Daphnis, sir."

Daphnis shrugged. "With such a third-rate crew and only eight fighting men it can't be very important."

"A man like Hesperian is not sent on unimportant missions!"

"Well, it's obvious we're not going into battle. But it is, you say, important. Will we be transporting some high official? No. there's not enough comfort on this tub for that. Well, we all know what Hesperian has become . . . Nero's trouble-shooter, Nero's investigator, Nero's watchdog and bloodhound. There's going to be an investigation. Right?

But no ordinary crime would bring Hesperian all the way from Rome. Is it treason? No, then there'd be more troops on board, to fight possible rebel armies. Murder, then! Ah, I see by your face I've guessed right. A murder in Alexandria! And the victim would have to be someone of wealth and influence."

"If Hesperian finds you in possession of state secrets..." began Mannus angrily.

Daphnis finished the sentence. "... I'll say you told me, my dear Mannus." He smiled archly. "It's the truth; isn't it?"

"I've said nothing!"

"But your face... it's blabbered everything!" He laughed delightedly and slapped Mannus on the back. "But how did Nero hear of this murder? Thanks to the war and the winter storms, there's been next to no communication between Alexandria and Rome since last autumn. The murder took place last autumn, didn't it? Ah ha! Again your simple farmer's face tells me 'Yes'. But why didn't Nero leave the investigation to the local authorities in Egypt, to Praefectus Tiberius Julius Alexander? Well, we all know the character of our beloved Emperor. He sees traitors everywhere, and not without reason! The Jews in Palestine are in revolt, and Tiberius Alexander is a Jew. Does Nero suspect this murder is part of a plot against Rome? Ha! I'm right again! Nero thinks Alexander may have deliberately allowed the murderer to escape detection, so our beloved Emperor sends Hesperian, a high-ranking official from his own private Imperial Guard, to look into the matter. Mannus, with that eloquent face of yours, you should be on the stage! A bet, Mannus! A bet!"

"A bet?" muttered Mannus suspiciously.

"Wine! I'll bet you a jug of wine, a gurgling amphora of the finest vintage Falernian!"

"What's the bet?"

"I say Hesperian will fail!"

Mannus' hand went to the pommel of his shortsword.

"By the gods, I'll..."

"No swordplay, handsome!" He patted Mannus on the cheek. "If I lose the bet, don't you think that will be punishment enough? But I won't lose. How could I? This time your precious centurion will have only two days to solve a mystery that has baffled all the local authorities for months... provided they haven't solved it already before we get there."

"Two days?" Mannus was dumbfounded. "Why two days?"

"If we drop anchor tomorrow morning, we'll be in Alexandria two days before the Festival of the Ship of Isis. During the winter all the suspects have been effectively sealed up in the city, unable to escape by land because of the war in Palestine and unable to escape by sea because the port of Alexandria has been closed during the winter storms. The Festival of the Ship of Isis, March fifth, will celebrate the opening of the port, and regular shipping will resume for the spring season. All the suspects will then be able to sail away and . . ." He made an airy gesture with his hand. ". . . vanish into the vastness of the Empire."

"Two days," said Mannus softly. He hadn't realized . . .

"Is it a bet?" demanded the librarius.

Mannus glanced at the smiling Daphnis, so cool, so superior, so young. Who was this sneering effeminate clerk to doubt a man like Gaius Hesperian?

"It's a bet!" shouted Mannus. "If Hesperian doesn't find Memnon's killer, I'll buy . . ."

"Memnon?" broke in Daphnis, impressed at last. "You mean the murdered man is Odysseus Memnon, the Greek grain merchant and ship owner?" Odysseus Memnon was one of the wealthiest and most powerful men in the Empire.

"So now you know it all," said Mannus dejectedly.

Daphnis shook his head in wonder, repeating the magic name in a whisper. "*Odysseus Memnon!*"

■ ■ ■

Odysseus Memnon never dreamed; when he first became interested in the obscure Jewish heresy called Christianity, that he was setting in motion a chain of events that would eventually result in his death.

A week before his murder, he had stood in the dewy grass of the Jewish graveyard, beyond the city walls in the Eastern Necropolis, singing hymns to Jesus Savior (*Yeshua Soter*, they called him) and waiting for the sun. All around the old man had stood the Christians, mostly poor Jews, with a sprinkling of Greeks, their numbers recently swollen by an influx of ragged refugees from the war in Judea, all raising their arms skyward in unison. Some were singing the words, some simply humming the tune, some only uttering half-hysterical cries, as if they were on the verge of "getting the Holy Spirit."

A slowly moving mist obscured all but the nearest Christians, and all but the nearest tombs, statues, gravestones and sepulchers; further away, all that Memnon could see were vague shadowy figures and the occasional flickering glow of a torch or oil lamp.

The Apostle Mark led the singing. Odysseus could hear him but could not see him because of the mist and dimness. Because of the distance, he could not make out the words, but he could hear and join in on the chorus, which was always the same:

"*Glory to thee for ever and ever!*"

It was cold in the cemetery, though there was almost no wind. Memnon drew his richly embroidered maroon cloak tightly around his bony body and shivered. This meeting in graveyards was one thing he found hard to accept, but the Christians had told him that their "brothers and sisters under the earth" were not dead, "only sleeping." One day soon they would awake and walk.

An old woman called out in the midst of the singing, "Come soon, Jesus! Come soon!" Her voice was cracking with anguished longing.

The morning sun, when it came, came suddenly. The sliver of light on the eastern horizon was so bright that Odysseus could not look at it.

Odysseus gestured to his slaves, who came with an elaborately carved and gilded sedan chair to carry him away on their shoulders.

After the singing in the graveyard, the Christians, led by the Apostle Mark and Annianus, the old Jewish shoemaker Mark had appointed first Bishop of Alexandria, filed in solemn procession back into the city, back into the slums of the Valley-by-the-Tombs that bordered on the thriving Jewish quarter. Odysseus Memnon, riding in his chair, went with them, the only one there who was not on foot.

Odysseus, glancing out, saw a young Jewess kiss an older woman on the lips. The Christians, though they were a chaste lot in most ways, often kissed each other like that. *None of them*, Odysseus realized, *has ever kissed me*. But then, how could they kiss a man in a sedan chair?

He chuckled at the thought. Ahead lay a crowded inn yard.

It was the custom of the Christians, after these morning ceremonies, to share a meal together, a meal they called the Love Feast, or *Agape*. Odysseus had watched them eat before, but today, for the first time he climbed from his chair and shuffled over to take a bite—just a bite—of the food himself. His teeth were bad and the bread was hard, but he managed. As he took a sip of wine he saw his slaves staring at him in open-mouthed astonishment and chuckled again. The Christians smiled at him. A fat, bearded old Jew embraced him and kissed him on both cheeks saying, "I wondered how long you'd be content to merely watch us."

Odysseus' eyes grew moist and he impatiently wiped them with his tunic sleeve.

"Come," said the Jew. "Come and meet Mark and our Bishop." He pulled Odysseus along by the arm, leading the way through the crowd. Odysseus wrinkled his nose at the stench of unwashed flesh. He tried to avoid brushing against some of the more unsavory of the Christians, but the old Jew, intent on the task of locating his leaders, took no notice, let alone offense. Odysseus clutched at his purse, thinking, *What a paradise for cutpurses!* Yes, his money was still there.

He caught a glimpse of a man in the toga of Roman citizenship. That was the thing that fascinated him most about these people, the way men born lowly Jews, Greeks and even Egyptians could mingle here on a seemingly equal basis with high-born Roman citizens. That, somehow, was more impressive than all the claims of miraculous cures, eternal life for the faithful, and a raising of the dead by a Savior who, they had told him, was expected to himself return from the dead at any moment.

"Bishop Annianus!" called the old Jew, waving.

A hawk-nosed little old man with a bald, sunburned head and hunched shoulders turned and, with a toothless smile, returned the greeting. From the rough gray wool tunic Annianus wore, it would have been impossible to tell that he was any sort of high official; many in the crowd were better dressed than he.

"Bishop Annianus, I want you to meet . . ." Here the Jew faltered.

"My name is Odysseus."

"Brother Odysseus," said the bishop, and Odysseus received a second Christian kiss.

"This is the Apostle Mark," said the old Jew.

"Brother Odysseus!" Mark had a deep, reverberant voice. A third time Odysseus was kissed.

Mark, smiling down at him, seemed tall, athletic, and dark, but no longer young. Even this man, of whom all the Christians spoke with awe, dressed more simply than a peasant, though at least his grayish linen tunic and brown wool cloak were clean. His only overt sign of rank was a wooden cross, a cross with a loop on top which represented the Egyptian hieroglyph for Eternal Life, worn on a leather thong around the Apostle's neck.

"Brother Odysseus has a question," said the old Jew.

"A question?" said Mark.

Odysseus was flustered, embarrassed. He had no question. He hadn't said he had one! But after a moment he began haltingly, "Tell me, sir . . ."

"Yes?" Mark was patient, attentive.

"Could you tell me . . . How can I become a Christian?"

Mark's eyes traveled over Odysseus in a quick, calculating glance, taking in the rings, the jewels, the fine robes. "Go," said the Apostle. "Go, sell whatever you have and give the proceeds to the poor." He gestured toward a group of ragged, half-starved war refugees that stood nearby, a little apart from the others.

Bishop Annianus added, "We who believe are together in having all things in common."

"But . . ." began Odysseus, raising a skeletal hand in protest, but someone had come up, insisting on speaking with Mark, and Odysseus found himself shoved aside into the crowd. The old Jew, who was still with him, said triumphantly, "You see? Isn't he wonderful?"

Wonderful? Insane! Subversive!

Odysseus broke away from the Jew and half-ran, half-shoved his way back to the sedan chair. Safely seated, he commanded his slaves, "Get me out of here! Trot!"

They lifted him and, exchanging knowing glances among themselves, set off.

Their pace did not slacken until they reached a place more comfortably familiar to their master; the Agora Diplostoon marketplace, where jostling crowds of buyers and sellers made rapid progress impossible. Odysseus, chin in palm, contemplated the bustling multitudes, the crude stalls and tables where street merchants displayed a bewildering selection of food, clothing and luxuries against a backdrop of stately marble buildings with colonnaded facades in the Hellenistic Greek style. Here men like Odysseus bought and sold whole shiploads of grain and whole fleets of grain ships as casually as the street merchants bargained an apple for a skein of yarn.

Give everything to the poor?

Hold all things in common?

Odysseus shook his head in incredulous wonder.

Suddenly he remembered one of the popular sayings of Epictetus, the joyous slave of Nero's court: "What else can I that am old and lame do but sing to God?"

What indeed!

And he remembered the prophecy, in the poet Virgil's Fourth Eclogue, of a boy born to be a world-savior.

And he found himself perversely drawn to this outlandish Jewish heresy, in spite of the high price it seemed he must pay to become a Christian.

He toyed with the idea, savored it, examined it from all sides. He wondered finally how his brother Demetrius, who was his partner in business, would react to the idea of giving everything to the poor. And how about his son and daughter, who hoped to inherit his fortune? And what about his lovely young wife Adrastia, who could have had no other reason for marrying him but his money?

He thought, *They'll all be insane with fury!*

"So much the better!" chuckled Odysseus Memnon.

■ ■ ■

The universe was red.

She opened her eyes, blinking in the shaft of afternoon sunlight that had awakened her.

She closed her eyes again, and again the universe, now limited to the light that filtered through her eyelids, was red.

She turned her back to the light, tried to go back to sleep. It was no use. Eyes open, she sat up, yawned, stretched, her slim bare young body half in light and half in shadow. The moist heat in the room was overpowering, and she was glistening with sweat. The dirty linen bedsheet stuck to her back. The nauseating stench of sweat, rancid olive oil and hot, fermenting camel dung filled her nostrils, making her faintly ill.

She turned, rested her weight on her elbow.

There was a man sleeping beside her, his face to the wall.

She smiled, and tenderly touched his hair with her fingertips.

She listened to the sound of a heavy oxcart passing in the street below her shuttered window—the rumble and grind of its wheels, the clip-clop of the oxen's hooves—and heard also the shouts of children playing and, somewhere, a cat fight. There were so many cats in this neighborhood!

She sighed, then she shrugged.

She swung her legs over the edge of the bed, rested the soles of her feet on the rough unpainted wood floor, and stood up. A swarm of flies took wing, angry at having been disturbed.

She swatted ineffectually at them.

She slipped her tunic over her head, tried to shake some of the tangles out of her shoulder-length light brown hair. The tunic was torn and dirty, little more than a rag.

She let her eyes travel around the room. It was a shabby filthy little hole—an upstairs room over an inn, fit only for camel drivers and prostitutes.

She smiled with satisfaction.

On the chair was the armor and shortsword of a Roman soldier. Against the wall was a Roman soldier's javelin. She looked at these things, still smiling enigmatically, as if thinking of some private joke.

She crossed the room on tiptoe, picked up a wood-backed wax tablet and stylus, and began to write out a shopping list in quick graceful, elegant Greek characters, softly humming a bawdy Roman drinking song.

This done, she glanced once again at the sleeping man, then put on her threadbare cape and, with sandals in one hand and wax tablet and moneybag awkwardly clutched in the other, made her exit, carefully pushing the door closed with her slender buttocks. In the hall she put on her sandals, balancing first on one foot, then on the other, then climbed down a ladder and passed through a short passageway into the street.

The street was narrow and, here and there, quite crowded, but she walked quickly in the direction of the nearest marketplace, threading her way effortlessly through the masses of fat Egyptian and Arab housewives, gaunt beggars and naked, dirty brown children, leaping with experienced ease over the occasional piles of camel and ox dung that lay in her path.

She reached the corner at the end of the blocks turned . . .

And stopped dead, eyes widening.

Coming toward her, so close that they might have collided, was the young black slave girl, Sabella. Sabella glanced up, gasped, almost dropped her bundles. For an instant the two girls stood motionless, staring at each other; then Sabella called out in astonishment, "Hathor!"

But Hathor, face quickly hidden by her cloak, pushed past the skinny black girl and hurried on and, when Sabella followed her, Hathor broke into a run.

"Hathor!" called Sabella again.

Hathor sprinted, face still hidden, sandals almost flying off, cape swirling behind her and, an instant later, vanished into the crowd.

Dumbfounded, Sabella stood in the center of the street, heedless of the passing eyes that gazed at her with curiosity.

"Was that really Hathor?" she murmured to herself.

She shook her head slowly. "No, no. That ain't possible."

It couldn't have been Hathor. What would the daughter of Odysseus Memnon, one of the richest men in the Empire, be doing here in the Egyptian quarter, Rhakotis, the most ancient and decaying slum in Alexandria?

■ ■ ■

At the front door, as it were, of Alexandria was the Mediterranean Sea; at the back door was Lake Mareotis. It was here, in the neighborhood of the "back door" of the city, in the ruddy glow of the setting sun, that Odysseus Memnon's brother and business partner, Demetrius Memnon, made his way, alone and unattended by his customary retinue of slaves and flunkies.

He crossed the drawbridge over the Nile Canal, his footsteps sounding hollowly. A heavily-loaded camel blocked his path and Demetrius paused, stepped to one side, biting his lip and swearing under his breath. The camel driver glanced down at him, glanced down at the bald, emaciated little old man who returned the glance with such impatience. The driver spat, narrowly missing his target. Demetrius ducked back not a moment too soon. The driver was not fooled by the rough dirty clothes Demetrius wore; this was clearly a rich man pretending to be poor. Only the rich are in such a hurry.

The camel passed.

Demetrius, almost running, continued on his way.

All along the street yawned the great shadowy mouths of warehouses. There was cargo here, cargo from all over the East, sometimes from as far away as India and China. He was only dimly aware of the busy slaves who labored all around him. They were no more than moving patterns of darkness and red light in the corners of his eye, but he could smell the tea and spices, hear the rumble of barrels on the floor, the shouts of habitually angry overseers. Never mind all that. Here was the dock of the Port-of-the-Lake, and there, masts and rigging a black spider web against the sky, were the merchant ships riding at anchor, vessels of every size and shape almost motionless above their reflections. Beneath his feet he could hear the whispering lap of waves against heavy timber piles as he paused, panting and wiping the sweat from his forehead with his sleeve.

He thought, *What if I'm late?*

He hastened onward, frightened eyes darting from one ship to another, searching for a certain one.

There it was! Ah, the gods are merciful!

It was a trim forty-eight oar Arab felucca with lateen rigging instead of the Roman great square sail, almost too trim to be a merchant vessel. She could have been a fighting ship if she'd had a ram. High up on her prow she had a figurehead, a woman, naked to the waist, wearing an angry expression. Demetrius leaned out over the water, trying to read the Greek characters inscribed on the ship's ornately carved bow.

"Ishtar,' he whispered. It was the right ship. He sighed with relief, then glanced around to make sure he was not being followed. *All clear!*

He mounted the gangplank, gave the password to two sullen black guards, and found himself on board.

"Demetrius!" called out a voice, an oily baritone with a thick foreign accent.

Startled, Demetrius spun around to face the man.

"Simon?" asked Demetrius uncertainly.

"Of course."

Simon stepped out of the shadows, smirking. He was a short, dark, middle-aged man in the clothing of a well-to-do shipowner. Rings and necklaces glittered in the dying sun, and he wore his long black hair in braids. He crooked his finger, beckoning almost playfully.

"Come, Demetrius. We can't talk out here."

Demetrius followed him through a doorway, down a short flight of steps, and, after a pause for Simon to unlock the door, into the captain's cabin, a windowless little room dimly lit by a few smoky oil lamps. The smoke made Demetrius' eyes water.

"Won't you sit down?" Simon gestured toward a handsomely carved wooden chair next to the table. The furnishings were few, but of the highest quality.

"Thank you." Demetrius lowered himself into the chair. Simon sat down across the table from him. The two studied each other in the flickering lamp light, and Demetrius thought: *It's hard to believe this is Simon Baal, a secret agent of King Vologases of Parthia.* The Parthian Empire was Rome's rival to the east, now at uneasy peace with Nero but looking for some way to turn the rebellion of the Jews to Parthian advantage.

"I have something for you," said Simon Baal. He disdainfully tossed a bag of coins on the table. Demetrius clutched it instantly. "Aren't you going to count it?" added the Parthian.

"No, no, I'm sure it's right."

"Such faith! Such trust! It's rare anywhere, but particularly in our line of work." He began absently playing with one of his braids. "But then, King Vologases has always been generous with you and your brother. Right?"

"And we . . . we have been loyal to the king."

"Yes, you have performed a few little services. I won't deny it."

Demetrius thought about the "little services." Smuggling weapons and supplies to Rome's enemies, to the Jews, to the barbarians, to any subversive group that, for one reason or another, aimed to overthrow the government of Nero.

"And we continue, as always, to place ourselves at your service, and at the service of your gracious monarch."

"Of course, yes."

"Is there anything we can do to prove once again our loyalty to his Royal Majesty and to you? Perhaps some information?"

Demetrius had often passed on information to Simon from the Parthian spies in Alexandria, and had occasionally uncovered a few things that even these spies had not been able to find out.

Simon shook his bead. "No. Demetrius. Not this time."

"What then? There must be something . . ."

"Or I wouldn't have summoned you here? That stands to reason, doesn't it?"

Demetrius nodded mutely.

"It's about your brother, Demetrius." Simon Baal leaned forward, eyes glittering in the feeble light.

"Odysseus?" Demetrius suddenly felt ill.

"Yes, the great, the one and only Odysseus Memnon. I have heard reports. Very reliable people have told me your brother has been acting strangely, that he's starting to take an interest in some insane Jewish superstition. I don't like that, my friend. The king must be assured of absolute loyalty."

"Certainly. This is only . . ."

Simon lowered his voice. "There is too much at stake to tolerate the unfortunate whims of a senile old man."

"Well, we all understand that." Demetrius could not meet the Parthian's gaze. "But I assure you, sir, that my brother's wife—you remember Adrastia, so young, so beautiful—she is deeply loyal to the Parthian cause. Her father, you know."

"He is one of the many Nero has had murdered. So what?"

"If Odysseus wavers, Adrastia can be trusted to put him back on the right course."

"Really? Does she go with him to the meetings of this Jew cult?"

"No, I don't think so. She wants nothing to do with such . . ."

"This cult has a certain ceremony, a ceremony in which a man gets up in front of a multitude of fellow fanatics and confesses all his sins, tells all his dirty little secrets."

"What harm could there be in . . ."

"Imbecile!" Simon Baal's fist struck the table with an angry thump. "This man's secrets are not his alone! They are mine, and yours, and the king's!" Demetrius cringed as Simon, calm again, reached across the table to touch him on the back of the hand, murmuring almost gently, "I will not let the fate of nations rest on the alleged fidelity of a woman, or on the discretion of a lunatic. If Odysseus Memnon does anything, or threatens to do anything, that will hinder our plans, it will be your duty, Demetrius, to kill him!"

Chapter Two

IT WAS THE EVENING of the following day.

The flesh-toned paint on the naked statues that surrounded the mansion of Odysseus Memnon had faded slightly, but in the waning afterglow they still seemed as they had seemed when new; almost alive in their disquieting realism, or better, like corpses frozen in a multitude of lifelike postures. The Hellenistic sculptors had aimed at magnificence but had hit instead a dreamlike quality, a feverish imitation of the decor of our nightmares. They had aimed at an impression of life and hit instead an overwhelming and oppressive impression of death.

The light dimmed.

The statues grayed, here a group, there a couple, over there a single figure striking a heroic pose next to a bending palm tree. There were stretches of lawn between them, trimmed hedges in geometric patterns, flowerbeds full of blossoms brought down the Nile from unknown Central Africa, blossoms so exotic they had, as yet, no names.

This vast park, with all its sculpture, greenery and broad mosaic walkways, was surrounded by a high, spike-topped stone wall. In the center of the front section of this wall stood a massive wood gate, now closed and locked. To one side of this gate was a smaller door, the only other entrance to the estate to be seen.

Metal clinked against metal.

The small door opened.

A rustle, a soft footfall, then the door closed again behind a tall cloaked figure who turned and bent over to lock it with a key on a chain attached to his belt.

Inside the gate he straightened and glanced around, absently pulling back his hood so it fell loosely to the small of his back. His hair was cut fairly short, sandy-colored and somewhat unkempt; perhaps in imitation of Nero he wore bangs across his forehead. His face was triangular, with deep-set brown eyes and pronounced cheekbones, and his thin lips were curled in a habitual aristocratic half-smile. It was the face of a young philosopher, a young gentleman of wealth and ease, but his body was as hard and muscular as a gladiator's.

His sandaled feet took a few steps on the serpentine mosaic of the walkway, then he stopped, listening.

A dog barked, then another, and another.

In a moment the pack was in full cry, pounding toward him from the direction of the house.

He stood motionless, waiting for them.

They bayed and yelped like wolves as they came, for they were half-wolf and barely tame, trained for only one thing—to kill intruders.

Still the tall young man, without a sign of fear, stood his ground and waited.

Now, suddenly, they were upon him, springing up to lick his face with great rasping tongues or to nip playfully at his arms, and he laughed, fending them off, though they were so heavy they occasionally almost knocked him down.

"Hey there!" he cried. "Hey, now! Don't you recognize me? I'm only Serapion."

Of course they recognized him! Serapion, Odysseus Memnon's only son. Of course they knew his scent; the smell of the sea with a trace of burning incense. Of course they knew his voice; deep, faintly mocking.

Surrounded by the milling dogs, Serapion continued on his way. He looked around him as he strode along, shortsword bouncing on thigh. He thought, as he had thought so many times before, *Beautiful!*

The statues, the walkways, the lawns, the hedges, the palm trees—even the great looming bulk of the mansion that now crouched ahead of him, typically Egyptian—that is, tomb-like—in spite of the token touch of Greek Doric columns around the entrance; it was all, in Serapion's eyes, beautiful.

He loved all these things, not because he would someday possess them, but because they represented to him the spirit of Alexandria, the finest city the world had ever known. Because he had always had them, possessions meant nothing to him. But Serapion, whose very name had been taken from that of Osiris-Serapis, his city's patron deity, loved Alexandria—her history, her science, her philosophy, her mongrel gods—part-Egyptian, part-Greek, and sometimes, part-animal—and loved, finally, even the taint of madness, cruelty and subtle evil that had always clung to her.

He heard a breeze stir in the palms, smelled, for an instant, the salty Mediterranean, sucked the air deep into his lungs.

For he loved the sea, too, and ships.

Unlike his father, who only made money from ships, Serapion was a real sailor, and had captained not only merchant vessels but racing biremes and, in fights against pirates, large combat rammers. Unlike his father, he felt not the faintest desire to imitate the attitudes and customs of the Roman conquerors, and much to his father's disgust, he turned his back on money matters and instead interested himself in intangible things like philosophy, the world's religions, in particular the mind-straining complexity of the religion of ancient Osiris-Serapis (which, in this age of scientific unbelief, he perversely persisted in believing in), and, above all, the poetry and beauty of the sea.

With the good stench of the Mediterranean in his nostrils, he thought, *When a man dies, his spirit does not go skyward, but to the sea!* That, he believed, was where Amenti, the Western Land of the Ancestors, was actually located. That was where you were guided when the time came to leave your body and go away with the dark god Anubis, Dogheaded Death.

He shooed the dogs away, mounted the short marble staircase, and entered the house.

"Master Serapion!"

"Good evening, Sabella."

He removed his cape and handed it to the little slave girl. Under it he wore a bleached linen tunic with a narrow blue stripe on the border and a leather belt with a gold buckle in the shape of a demonic face from which hung his moneybag, dagger and keys. His shortsword was on another belt loosely slung from his shoulder.

"Wait, Sabella . . ."

"Yes?"

"Are the others here yet?"

"Your mother . . ."

"My *step*mother!" he corrected her.

"Your stepmother, yes sir. She in there." She pointed a skinny finger. Adrastia was not his real mother. It was important to him that no one make that mistake. His real mother, Octavia Memnon, lived in well-heeled exile in Rome. Odysseus had divorced her when she got too old.

Adrastia was young, almost as young as Serapion.

They were both in their early twenties, as was Serapion's sister Hathor, who was a little over a year younger than her brother.

Old Odysseus had been too sickly since his remarriage to father any children by his second wife, a fact that often led Serapion to say to himself, *The gods are not without humor.*

He stopped in the doorway. She had her back to him, examining herself thoughtfully in a hand mirror. Her green silk robes and glittering jewelry were, as usual, breathtaking.

"May I come in?" he asked softly.

"Of course, Serapion," said Adrastia.

She turned and came toward him.

They embraced coldly, perfunctorily.

"My hairdresser," she said, by way of introduction.

The hairdresser, a thin, well-groomed white-haired Greek, bowed. Serapion had seen him before but could never remember his name, so he called him—to himself—Old Kissingfish, because of the man's habit of always puckering up his lips.

Adrastia seated herself and gossiped with forced gaiety while Serapion, still standing, nodded politely. Kissingfish, with an air of intense artistic absorption, set to work on her elaborate coiffure.

"Oh Serapion, whatever shall we do about the Jewish problem?"

"I leave such matters to the proper authorities..."

"And have you noticed how the prices are going up? I can't understand it! We live in a decadent age, my dear. It was different when Cleopatra was queen, before the Romans came."

"That was before you were born. How do you know..."

"Well, I can read, can't I?" She pouted. "Everything is becoming such a bore, don't you think? Everybody says so."

"Please, Madam." said Kissingfish. "You must try and hold still."

"I want my dwarfs," she said.

"Dwarfs?" said Serapion.

She clapped her hands and Sabella appeared at the door.

"My dwarfs, Sabella!"

"Yes, Mama Adrastia."

The black girl left at a run.

"Why don't you ever call me 'Mama,' Serapion?"

"You're too young, my dear."

"Hmm. I suppose so."

A huge white cat padded in and, without hesitation, leaped into Adrastia's lap, settled down, blinked a few times, and went to sleep. Adrastia's wiggling, which had been upsetting the hairdresser, now ceased. She did not, of course, want to disturb the cat.

She continued to chatter about this and that until Sabella returned with the dwarfs.

"Ah. Serapion, I want you to meet Suchos, Horus and Bubo," said Adrastia.

Serapion bent over and shook hands with the little men, one at a time. Sabella giggled.

"You may go, Sabella."

"Yes, Mama Adrastia."

The slave girl backed out, bowing, trying not to laugh.

Instantly the dwarfs, all three hunchbacked and ugly as toads, began doing handsprings, cartwheels and little dances, making faces all the while. Bubo, their leader, did an imitation of Alexander the Great, head cocked over to one side.

"Bravo, Bubo!" cried Adrastia, delighted.

"Madam, please," pleaded the long-suffering hairdresser.

Bubo did a deep, sweeping bow.

Serapion was more annoyed than amused.

"Adrastia, have you any idea . . ."

"Why old Odysseus has called us together tonight?" She shrugged. "He's got something important to announce. At least he *says* it's important."

"Give me a hint."

"A hint? I don't know a thing about it myself. The whole Memnon family is invited, that's all I know—you, me, your sister Hathor, old Demetrius. That stubborn old goat who calls himself my husband—you know how he is! He's said he won't tell what it is until after supper, and that's that!"

Serapion sighed, then said, with real concern, "I've felt for a long time that he was headed for a crisis—a spiritual crisis."

Adrastia looked at her stepson with raised eyebrows. "Spiritual? *Him?*"

Serapion flashed her a worried, distracted little smile.

■ ■ ■

Odysseus Memnon lay on his bed panting as the room came back into focus and the pain in his chest subsided.

"Another attack." He was whispering, though there was no one else in the room to overhear him.

A pain. A dizziness. A shortness of breath. *Nothing*, he decided, *to worry about*. It would be better not to tell his doctors about such a minor matter, and besides, they might bleed him, and he was sure he needed every drop of blood he had!

"I'll rest a moment," he murmured, shifting into a position where the pain was less—where it seemed almost to vanish altogether. There was no hurry. This confrontation with his family could wait. In fact, it would do them good to stew a bit before he threw his secret, like a handful of mud, into their faces.

He laughed softly, wheezing, but he did not laugh long. There was something frightening about that wheeze, something that smacked of death. He thought, *I never was too healthy, not even as a boy. Odysseus the sickly, Odysseus the little guy, the runt*. His father's face materialized in his mind with an expression of mingled pity and contempt. Croton Memnon had been a muscular man in his time, like Serapion but without Serapion's cultured airs. Croton Memnon had worked very hard all his life as a shipwright, but had never been able to get completely out of debt. He'd told Odysseus time and time again, "That's what a man lives for—to work!" What pride there was in old Croton's voice when he said those words!

Then, when Odysseus was twelve, Croton was imprisoned for debt.

Odysseus had a good memory.

He remembered his father's face, on the other side of the bars. The pity and contempt were gone. That face, that always before had been clean-shaven as the divine Alexander's, was now hidden behind a tangled graying beard, but nothing could hide that new expression, the look of frozen surprise, the look of a man whose gods had departed. He did not talk that way. He did not talk much at all about gods or abstract things, but it was there in his face, the clear message, *My gods have betrayed and abandoned me.*

Such abject despair! Such unconcealed unhappiness!

A child can forgive his parents anything but unhappiness.

Odysseus had looked up into that tortured face and said with controlled anger, "Whatever I do, I swear I'll never be like you!"

Croton wept, but Odysseus the runt was at that instant transformed. There was no pity or love in him, only the ecstasy of sudden freedom, of rebirth as a new being, of an awakening from a kind of walking sleep. In a single leap he had become what he was to be as an adult; in a single instant he had changed more than in all the years before or since, and his mother and brother were shocked to see him, as they left the prison, singing and dancing in the street.

The next day Odysseus marched fearlessly up to his father's employer and demanded—not asked for, but demanded—a job, and the astonished shipmaster had given it to him, in spite of the youth and small stature of this ugly boy who stood before him, fists on hips like a young Julius Caesar.

That night Odysseus said to his mother, "I'll take care of you now."

Odysseus worked like a gnome and schemed like a Herod, and two months had not passed before Demetrius, his younger brother, was also working at the shipyard, much to his own surprise.

Two years later the boys were able to buy their father out of debt, and thus out of jail.

Croton did not thank them.

Odysseus had not expected that he would.

He understood his father now, looking down on him from a great height, and it did not matter to him whether his father was grateful or not. When Demetrius said blissfully, "At last we've got a little security," Croton had looked up from his bowl of meal with all the hate of a dying animal in a gladiatorial spectacle, and only Odysseus really knew why.

His mother said, "Now, Odysseus, you can relax and have a little fun, like a normal boy."

"Not yet."

"Then when, I ask you?"

"When I'm a Roman gentleman."

Of course they all laughed at him then.

They went on laughing for days, telling all the neighbors, whispering, glancing at him out of the corners of their eyes.

Then, quite suddenly, the laughter ceased.

Odysseus had caught his overseer embezzling and exposed him. Before Odysseus had had a few friends, but now that was over. He and, because of him, his whole family were no longer members of the community of the working poor. Everyone was stealing, some on a large scale, most on a small. Not one of them could risk the danger of a friend who was too honest.

The embezzler—one of old Croton's best friends—was tried, found guilty and sent to the mines where, it was said, he lasted all of a year and a half.

Odysseus went into the office, almost as an adopted son of the boss.

At the age of twenty-two, Odysseus became overseer, and everyone under him was older than he was except for his brother Demetrius and a handful of the rawest apprentices.

His father had been drinking heavily for some time now. Drink had cost him his job. Drink had kept him from getting another. When he heard of his son's promotion he waited for him in the evening, singing in a bitter, off-key voice and drinking unwatered wine right from the camel skin flask, chasing everyone else from the room.

"Is that you, Odysseus?" he called out as his son entered.

"Who else?"

"They say you do the hiring now, down at the yard."

"That's right."

"Well, now . . ." He gave Odysseus a wink. "Here's your own father looking for a job, as hard a worker as ever swung an adz. What do you say, boy?"

"I say no."

"What? I don't believe it!" Croton dragged himself to his feet and stood there, swaying.

"You're not a good risk."

Croton screamed wordlessly and kicked over the table, then came at his son with a drawn kitchen knife, still a head taller and fifty pounds heavier than Odysseus the runt.

Odysseus had a knife too, a beautiful thing with a jeweled pommel and floral designs embossed on its long curving blade. Just once he plunged it into his father's stomach, all the way to the hilt, then as quickly jerked it out again. Croton did not fall immediately, but when he did Odysseus stood over him for several minutes, watching the light fade out of his father's eyes.

When he was dead, Odysseus finally spoke, very softly.

"You gave me no choice, old man."

Odysseus was not brought to trial, thanks to the intervention of his powerful employer.

He saw less and less of his mother.

When she died, a few months later, neither Odysseus nor Demetrius was present, but they gave her the finest funeral the neighborhood had ever seen.

On the night of her death Demetrius had been in a whorehouse and Odysseus had been visiting an old Jewish rabbi who was teaching him how to read and write Greek like a gentleman. (He was teaching himself bookkeeping and mathematics, and all the texts were in Greek.)

He learned the ways of money so quickly it was as if he'd learned it all in some past life, and now was only brushing up. Clever men began to fear his cleverness, and stupid men feared him even more because they thought he was demon-possessed. Odysseus encouraged their fear. It made everyone eager to please him. It kept the workers under him from giving him any trouble.

He heard them whispering behind his back, "A man who'd kill his own father . . ." and he smiled.

When he asked rich but superstitious men to lend him vast sums of money, they hastened to oblige.

"Yes, Memnon. Of course, Memnon. We know your reputation . . ."

Odysseus leased a cargo ship.

The established shipping companies temporarily dropped their rates, after consulting together in secret meetings in dockside inns.

Odysseus was forced into bankruptcy.

One step away from debtor's prison, he sought out a Parthian agent and made a deal.

"Yes, Memnon. We pay your debts, give you another loan, provide you with steady financial backing."

"And I smuggle slaves, arms, money, information—anything that will either bring a high price or help the Parthian cause."

"Exactly."

There was an unlooked-for bonus.

Parthian agents in high places arranged for Odysseus to be granted Roman citizenship.

Before he was thirty Odysseus was able to buy out, one by one, most of the established companies that had conspired to ruin him in his earlier venture.

He sailed to Rome—his one and only visit to the Imperial capital—and when he returned his brother met him at the gangplank.

"Odysseus! What's the meaning of that medallion hanging from your neck?"

"I've earned the honorary title of 'Caesars Friend'!"

"But that's impossible!"

"Not if one foots the bill for one of the Emperor Caligula's gladiatorial games."

He was so Roman now.

Osiris-Serapis? Ignorant superstition! Jupiter was a god who stood for something, even if it was only the power of the Roman army.

He had learned the paradoxical Roman morality, too—so permissive in some ways, yet so puritanical in others.

He smiled and slowly shook his head, remembering.

He remembered his first wife, Octavia.

He still was not sure it was true, but he'd been told she was distantly related to the Ptolemaic dynasty and the dead but still famous Queen Cleopatra.

True or not, the claim had gained him some measure of acceptance into upper class Alexandrian society, a colony of displaced bluebloods who lived in the glorious past before the Romans took over Egypt. Such social connections were useful but expensive—the bluebloods were often in need of financial aid to help maintain their facades.

"Parasites," muttered Odysseus Memnon, lying on his green-draped bed.

Octavia had borne him one son, Serapion, and one daughter, Hathor, then a number of stillbirths, and he finally divorced her and sent her to Rome so he could marry the young and beautiful but shallow Adrastia. Adrastia was, perhaps, the greatest mistake he'd made.

"Bitch," muttered Odysseus Memnon, on his bed.

His frown passed quickly.

He thought, *I've done it. I'm a Roman gentleman.*

That, at least, was good.

But it was no good to be old.

It was no good to have a son who made light of the hard-won Memnon financial empire, no good to have a timid brother who kept trying to maintain the status quo and protect what they had by never taking risks, no good having a daughter who no longer confided in him the way she had when she was a little girl. He'd spent a small fortune bringing her up almost as if she were a boy, giving her a boy's education in Greek and rhetoric, even allowing her, when she asked for it, to be given training in arms, in the use of sword, horse and javelin. Now she acted as if she were a complete stranger! Sometimes he suspected her of having a secret lover somewhere, yet she'd always shown little interest in the opposite sex.

No, these things weren't good.

They weren't right!

But the worst of it was the way his wife Adrastia treated him, like some sort of idiot. She spent his wealth without the slightest understanding of the lifetime of effort it had taken to amass it.

"Parasites," he growled under his breath. "They're all parasites."

But this strange new religion, Christianity—it might prove to be the ideal weapon to put them in their places. What blame could attach to a man who, like a holy Pythagorean philosopher, renounced all worldly goods to become a humble mendicant? And that would certainly put the religious pretensions of Serapion in a different light!

With this thought bolstering him, he rose, chuckling, from his bed and shuffled off to preside at the supper table.

■ ■ ■

"Hathor?"

"Yes, Father?"

Odysseus Memnon, reclining on the couch at the head of the table, cast a calculating glance at Hathor on another couch to his right. Serapion, lying beside and slightly behind her, concentrated on nibbling the date he held delicately between his thumb and forefinger, but Hathor met the old man's eyes with perfect composure.

"Sabella told me."

"Told you what, Father?"

"You know."

Adrastia, who shared Odysseus' couch, gave him a peevish little shove. "Don't tease, dear."

"Sabella told me she saw you in the Egyptian quarter. Is that where you're hiding your lover?"

He studied her reaction, but she gave nothing away.

"Sabella was lying," she said, still meeting his eyes squarely.

"Sabella does not lie," interrupted Adrastia with mild indignation.

"All slaves lie," said Demetrius gloomily. His couch was on the opposite side of the table from the one shared by Hathor and Serapion.

"Well, if she didn't lie, then she must have been mistaken, Father. Whatever would I be doing in a place like that?"

"Ah, Hathor, that's exactly what I was going to ask you!"

An uneasy ripple of laughter passed around the table. There was no joy, Odysseus realized, in their laughter, just a momentary release from tension. *They're afraid*, he thought.

He was enjoying himself more than he had in years. "We're finished," he told the two eunuch slaves, Rophos and Wakar, who stood at ease nearby. The two began unobtrusively clearing away the remains of the long and delectable supper, and Odysseus noticed that his family had apparently not been very hungry; there were so many leftovers.

"And you, my fine young man—what are you doing to protect your sister from handsome thieves and fortune hunters?"

Serapion replied curtly, "She needs no protection. She's as good with weapons as any man, and twice as cunning."

At any other time Odysseus might have been angry, but tonight he had a secret of his own that undoubtedly dwarfed any possible secrets his children might be keeping from him. He turned his attention to his brother Demetrius.

"And you, what—or whom—have you sold lately?"

"Whatever I've done," said old Demetrius stiffly, "I've done for the good of the family."

The family, thought Odysseus. *Anything for the family.* That was what everyone said. That's what he'd said himself up until quite recently, but now . . .

Last the old man turned to his wife, the beautiful Adrastia. The hairdresser, it seemed, had produced a masterpiece, but none of the Memnons gave it more than a fleeting glance.

"I'm afraid you'll have to spend somewhat less on your hair in the future, my dear."

She paused, then said coldly, "Indeed? How much less?"

He let his gaze travel slowly around the circle. All were trying to pretend indifference, but even proud Serapion was hanging on his father's words. They knew him. They knew this was the moment when he would tell them his secret, and they sensed that it would be something unexpected and . . . unpleasant.

"Nothing at all," said Odysseus Memnon.

"What kind of nonsense . . ." began his wife.

"Not nonsense." He was gloating now, triumphant. "You see, I'm going to join the Christians."

They looked at him with stunned astonishment. He noticed that only Demetrius was not completely surprised, only horrified, like a man who sees a nightmare coming true. "Odysseus, you fool . . ."

"Yes, my dear brother, you heard me correctly. I'm joining the Christians, and when I do I plan to hand over every last drachma to their leader, the Apostle Mark. Then I'll sell every ship, every bit of real estate—everything I own, and give the proceeds of those sales, too, to the Christians."

A voice piped up from the doorway. "Sell everything? Even me?" It was Sabella.

"Even you," he told her gently, "but I'll see you get a kind master."

Slave and master contemplated each other for an anguished moment, then, abruptly she burst into tears and ran from the room.

Odysseus turned again to his family. "All my life I've been looking for something. You know that's true, don't you? Rejoice, then, that I've found it at last! Rejoice, if you love me!"

Still they did not speak.

"What's this? No cries of joy? No happy hugs and kisses for old Odysseus? But perhaps that's because you'll miss me so much when I've left you. Then listen, my little brood. You can accompany me into the brotherhood of the Church!"

The silence that followed was broken only by the rustle of silk as Adrastia, holding herself stiffly erect as if balancing her elaborate hairdo on her head, stood up and looked down at her husband with a cold contempt warmed with only the faintest trace of pity. It was he, not she, who first looked away.

She said, speaking not to his face but to the bald dome of his bowed head, "So this is your little surprise, darling. You don't give us much choice, do you? Now, before you have a chance to change your will, one of us will simply have to do you in."

■ ■ ■

"The Blues!"

"The Reds!"

The hysterical shouts were faint in the distance.

"The Greens! Go! Go, Greens!"

Almost everyone was at the chariot races. Their cheering echoed through the deserted streets of Alexandria as they hysterically screamed out the colors of their favorite teams. The flies and seagulls went about their business, paying no attention.

The sun was hot and bright, the dung plentiful.

Livia closed the shutters, tired of gazing into the empty street below, tired of the sun and the heat and the smell. She sat down on a keg with a deep sigh, grateful, at least, that she could take the load of her great bulk off her feet. She had no use for the races. Neither did her husband. He was at least as fat as she was. He agreed with her that on a day like this the racetrack was too far away to walk to.

So, even though there were no customers, they kept the little shop open, telling each other that it helped to build a reputation for reliability. It was important to build-up a "name."

His name, as the sign above the entrance to his shop proclaimed, was "T. Vindaius Ariovestus, compounder of panaceas, including Chloron, the Unbeatable Green Salve." In smaller letters, it added, "A preparation of aniseed."

His name was there on the sign, but it was she who labored in the upstairs room mixing everything. Vindaius was just the "front man."

She heard the ladder rattle. He was coming up.

A moment later his round pink head appeared in the open trapdoor, glistening with sweat. "Livia! Livia! We have a customer!"

"So?"

"He wants poison, Livia!"

She shuddered in spite of the heat. Why did they have to deal in poison? Didn't the regular medicine and drug trade bring in enough money? But he'd told her there was a demand for it, and it was their duty to . . .

But at least she had convinced him it was not wise to advertise this darker side of the business. Only a few people knew, and those few were not fond of publicity.

"What kind?" she asked him dully.

"The most powerful you can make!"

With a grunt she heaved herself to her feet. "Let me get the recipe." She opened a dusty trunk and rummaged around in a pile of yellowed papyrus and parchment scrolls.

"Hurry, dear!" Vindaius was excited. "This customer . . . he's a rich man. I can tell by his clothes. He keeps his face hidden by his cloak and speaks in whispers."

"In whispers, eh?" Some kind of disgusting pervert. All rich people were perverts, as far as she was concerned.

"I have to go down now," he said apologetically. "We wouldn't want him to get impatient and take his business elsewhere!"

"I suppose not."

The ladder rattled, and when she looked over at the trap door he was gone. A moment later she heard his high-pitched laugh, sounding very nervous, somewhere down below.

She was afraid, as she always was when she had to touch the collection of jars and bottles she kept in the back of the room—in a separate cabinet. She was afraid—and not without reason—that she might one day find she had accidentally poisoned herself.

Nevertheless she set to work pounding, mixing and stirring, now and then consulting a recipe on a scroll she could barely read in the dim light. It wouldn't do to disappoint the customer!

The customer!

As she worked she became more and more curious. In these cases it was generally best to know as little as possible about the client, but still . . .

Was he a disappointed lover? Or perhaps an ambitious politician? In spite of herself she was consumed with curiosity.

It showed in her voice a moment later when, crouching on her hands and knees by the trap door, she called down, "It's ready."

The ladder rattled again, and she reached down, carefully placing the small stoppered vial into her husband's pudgy hand.

After hurriedly using her pitcher and basin to wash her hands, she hastened to the shutters in hopes of catching a glimpse of the customer—but a glimpse was all she did get as the heavily cloaked figure strode away down the street.

A moment later she had climbed down to join her husband in front of the shop, bombarding him with questions, but he was no help. The best he could say was, "The rascal overpaid me, so he must be up to something, but he kept his face so well hidden in his cloak he could have been a woman and I wouldn't have known it."

Chapter Three

SHE LOOKED AT HIM ANXIOUSLY from behind a wayward lock of her shoulder-length light brown hair.

"Father—you've always been a reasonable man."

"I like to think so, my dear."

His face a mask, Odysseus Memnon thought, *When, little Hathor, was the last time I heard you praise me, even insincerely?* She bit her lip nervously while he waited for her to go on. Her hair was swinging now with the swaying of her gilt-trimmed white sedan chair and Odysseus, his own chair moving beside hers, felt a sudden tenderness, an impulse to reach over and touch her, but he remained frozen, immobile. There were too many people around—the slaves who bore the sedan chairs on their padded shoulders, the crowd of dusty sweating Jews, Greeks, Arabs and Egyptians who flowed past in the savage noonday sun, the eunuch Wakar who marched ahead shouting "Clear the way there! Clear the way, you lowborn dogs!" Odysseus hated to make any sort of public display of his feelings, particularly before those he considered his inferiors.

As the silence lengthened, he self-consciously arranged the folds of his long green silk tunic. Why didn't she speak? What was she waiting for?

When she finally began, her voice was so low he couldn't make out what she was saying above the din of the streets.

"What's that?" he demanded, leaning toward her.

"I said, I hope you will continue to let reason rule your life."

"Of course I will!"

"I hope you will continue to be open-minded and willing to listen to rational appeals, if those appeals come from those who love you, who have only your best interests at heart."

Rhetoric, he thought with disgust. Perhaps it was a mistake to educate females—if this was the result!

"Sometimes," she went on, choosing her words with care, "when a man reaches a certain age . . ."

"Go on, girl. Spit it out."

"When a man reaches a certain age, he allows hope to usurp the throne of reason and . . . "

"Yes! Yes!"

"And he becomes a willing victim of liars, of liars who promise him anything—even eternal life—in order to lay hands on his money and property."

"Those are the Christians you're talking about, aren't they?"

"I'm not talking about specific cases."

"At least not yet, eh?" He chuckled, grinning at her candidly.

"The wise man, Father, the philosopher, does not act this way," she continued doggedly. "The philosopher continues in his old age on the path he chose as a youth. As the noble Socrates demonstrated by his example, even certain death does not sway the Man of Reason. The Man of Reason has spent his life building something; he does not at the end tear it all down. His heart..." She faltered, gripping the arms of her sedan chair so hard her knuckles turned white.

"His heart...?" he prompted.

Suddenly her composure broke. "You fool!" she screamed. "You damn fool! Don't you see what they're doing to you? You can't do it. You just can't!"

"Oh, can't I now?" He leaned back in his chair, smiling with satisfaction.

She gestured toward the crowd. "Do you want to see me out there among those people, hungry, filthy, sick? Don't you know what will happen to me without the protection of your money and position?"

"Full circle," said the old man, almost to himself. "I began out there, you know. There was a time when I was lower than the lowest of them. There'd be a certain justice, a certain poetry..."

"Justice? Poetry?" She half rose, then fell back in despair.

She did not know—how could she—how close he was to being swayed by her appeals, but there was something missing still. If only she could reveal to him by some clear sign that she still loved him as she did when she was small, he thought. If only she would confide in him!

"About your lover..." he began slyly.

She stared at him blankly.

"You can tell me Hathor. I can keep a secret. Only the gods know all the secrets I've got locked away in here." He touched his hairless head with a long bony forefinger.

"Don't try to change the subject, now..."

"Why won't you tell me, eh? Are you ashamed of him? Can't he support you properly? Or perhaps he is, as they say, less than a gentleman."

"He's as rich and well-bred as you are!"

"In that case you *must* tell me his name. I'd like to meet him."

She turned away without answering.

"Well?" he insisted.

"You know him already." Her voice was almost lost in the clatter of a passing wagon.

"What? What's that you say? I know him already? Then tell, you witch! Tell! I must know!"

She faced him, pale and frightened. "By Isis, I hope you never do. It would kill you... and me too!"

■ ■ ■

The following morning, before the heat of day, Odysseus Memnon visited the temple of Osiris-Serapis, patron deity of Alexandria. Was it a lingering trace of belief, or at least respect for the god his father believed in? Odysseus himself could not have said, but there was a feeling in the visit, a sadness that stuck in his throat, pained him in his chest.

He was saying goodbye, once and for all, to an old, old friend.

He left his slaves behind him at the foot of the great marble staircase and, sandals in hand and with bowed head, he slowly mounted the hundred steps up to the entrance, then paused at the head of the stairs, panting and slightly dizzy.

He thought, *What if the heart attack comes here?* If he died at the entrance to the temple, everyone would take it as a sign that he'd returned to the True Faith.

"I can't let them think that," he muttered under his breath. "I've got to stay alive just a little longer."

Beneath him lay Alexandria, the White City, spread out under the blue morning haze. There was the harbor, split by a long land bridge out to the island of Pharos, where the immense lighthouse towered, impressive even at this distance. There, beyond the lighthouse, was the sea.

He turned and continued on his way, pulling his cloak tightly around him, though there was no wind.

He passed between two rows of massive red granite columns, crossed a wide stone-paved courtyard, and entered the Hall of Worship through a pair of huge bronze doors whose carved panels told the story of the birth, death and resurrection of Osiris-Serapis. Above him was a high dome of dark green basalt displaying the twelve signs of the zodiac and the celestial history. Ahead hung a broad tapestry which represented with breathtaking artistry Alexander the Great dressed as Pharaoh Osiris-Serapis, with the combined crown of Upper and Lower Egypt. Beneath Memnon's shuffling bare feet stretched a glittering mosaic of many-colored glass, jewels and precious metals portraying the mythical history of Egypt, its kings and queens, its gods and goddesses, from Osiris and Isis, who brought culture to Egypt from the fabled Western Land, to Cleopatra, last to rule before the Roman conquest. The mosaics felt cool and smooth under the soles of his feet.

He lifted the corner of the tapestry and stepped into the semi-darkness of the Holy of Holies.

He stood swaying, blinking, letting his eyes grow accustomed to the dimness, then looked around. There was nobody else in the room. Odysseus was alone with the god.

At the end of a long broad aisle that passed through a forest of carved and painted pillars, Osiris-Serapis sat enthroned, faintly illuminated by flickering oil lamps and tiny candles set in red glass containers.

Odysseus approached him.

When at last Odysseus halted, the god loomed over him, majestic and beautiful. Serapis' body was carved from blue-black marble and his ornaments were of precious jewels set in gold, but his face was made of delicate polished ivory and wore an expression of calm, fatherly concern. His long hair and full beard looked almost real, for the art style was Greek, lifelike and flowing, not rigid and stylized like the style of the Pharonic Egyptians.

Serapis was not a statue, it seemed, but a giant man—a kind, sad, giant man.

Looking up into his face, Odysseus said softly, "I could have loved you."

The god did not answer. So it was just a statue after all.

Odysseus waited, giving the god every opportunity to speak, then said mockingly, "You never should have let the Romans win" and with a cruel, blasphemous snicker he turned his back on the god and stumped away.

He was still smiling as he emerged from the darkness and, squinting and shading his eyes with a bony hand, recognized the figure of his son Serapion strolling toward him in the company of three shaven-headed priests.

■   ■   ■

"Are you surprised to see me here?" asked the younger Memnon as they reached the head of the Stairway of a Hundred Steps.

"Why should I be? You're always hanging around here in the temple, wasting your time on ancient scrolls and endless fruitless argument with baldies like that." Odysseus gestured contemptuously toward the three priests behind them in the courtyard, now too far away to overhear.

"Well, I must say, my honored Father, that I was surprised to see you here—surprised and pleased." As he beamed down on Odysseus, the old man looked away, annoyed.

"Don't try to read any profound meaning into it, my boy." Old Memnon leaned against a granite sphinx and slipped on his sandals, then started down the steps, his son following.

It was already warmer than it had been when Odysseus had gone in, but a slight breeze had sprung up. *I won't even work up a sweat*, he thought, *if I take it easy*. In the back of his mind somewhere was the thought of a heart attack. It would still give the wrong impression if he died here on the temple steps. To die leaving the temple, in fact, was even worse than dying while entering.

The father dawdled along, and the son, humoring him, dawdled with him.

"It's beautiful, isn't it?" asked Serapion in a hushed voice.

"Beautiful? What do you mean?"

"Alexandria." He gestured toward the panorama that stretched out before them. "Alexandria is the most beautiful city in the world, and I've seen them all."

"More beautiful than Rome?" Odysseus had not "seen them all," but Rome, the only foreign capital he had visited, had impressed him greatly.

"Rome is so gross. All those apartment buildings." Serapion wrinkled his aristocratic nose.

Something, Odysseus realized was wrong, but at first he couldn't figure out what. Then, quite suddenly, he knew what it was. Serapion had not mentioned Christianity, let alone attempted to argue with him about it, and Serapion was the one in the family he'd most expected— even hoped—would be furious.

He glanced at the boy over his shoulder, frowning. He'd never been able to figure Serapion out. Was this really his son, this tall soldier-like youth with the face of a holy ascetic? Or had his first wife Octavia had some lover visiting her while Odysseus was spending night after night in business conferences? No, that was impossible. She'd been too good for such things. In fact, she'd seemed at times to have been too good for any vulgar sexual things, even with her husband.

Serapion, his voice distant and impersonal, had begun an impromptu oration on the glory of Alexandria's past, of Alexandria's traditions and cultural sophistication. Odysseus had heard it all before. Angrily he turned and snapped, "Don't play with me, my boy."

"Play?" The slightly disdainful eyes looked pained.

"Tell me now, and tell me frankly—what do you think of my becoming a Christian?"

Serapion, a few steps higher than his father, looked down and said gently, "I too have been going through a religious crisis, but now it's resolved. The Temple of Osiris-Serapis has accepted my application to study for the priesthood. You will serve your god, *and I will serve mine!*"

■ ■ ■

"I'm sorry to interrupt your reading, Master, but . . ."

"Yes, yes, spit it out!" Odysseus laid the scroll he had been reading on the bed table and looked up at Rophos, his eunuch, thinking, *What now?*

"Your brother Demetrius has been here since early this morning, Master, waiting to see you."

"What time is it now?"

"Around noon, Master."

The old man grimaced.

"Tell him to come back tomorrow."

"He says he won't let you put him off again, Master. He says he absolutely insists on seeing you today, if only for a few minutes."

Odysseus thought, *He's been here every day since that damn dinner party. I suppose the only way I'll get him to leave me alone is to give him a few words.* With a sigh, he motioned to Rophos to show his brother in.

Rophos left the room, bowing.

Odysseus stole a longing glance at the scroll on his bed table. The Gospel of Thomas! It was not like the other scroll the Christians had given him, not like the Gospel of Mark. The Gospel of Mark told a strange story, but a clear one. The Gospel of Thomas, supposedly the older and more authentic document of the two, seemed to contain only disconnected sayings of Jesus, without story, context or explanation, and some of the sayings were so obscure Odysseus could only guess at their meaning—but he'd always been fond of puzzles.

"Demetrius Memnon!" announced Rophos from the doorway. Bald, emaciated, wild-eyed Demetrius stumbled in, white tunic rumpled and disheveled, claw-like hands clasping and unclasping each other. "Odysseus! I must see you!"

"Here I am. Look your fill."

"No, no. Alone." He glanced meaningfully at Rophos.

"As you wish," sighed Odysseus.

Rophos departed with a low bow.

"You're sure we're alone?" Demetrius was glancing around with suspicion.

"Of course."

Demetrius leaned over the bed on which his brother was reclining and, controlling himself with some effort, assumed a low serious tone. "It's a joke, isn't it?"

"A joke?"

"You becoming a Christian." He forced a strangled laugh. "I must admit you almost had me fooled, but you're a Greek-Egyptian and a Roman citizen. Christianity is only for Jews and slaves. Everyone knows that!"

Odysseus shook his head. "It's no joke."

"But how . . ."

"In Christianity there are no separate Romans, Greeks, Egyptians and Jews, no separate masters and slaves. These ranks, nationalities and separations belong to this world, and we leave the things of this world behind us."

Demetrius brightened slightly. "Business is a worldly thing, too. Isn't that right? So why don't you turn the business over to me?"

"Never!" Odysseus' eyes narrowed.

"Why not?"

"Because it was I who built it up. It's mine to do with as I please."

"At least give me half!"

"No! If it weren't for me there would be nothing. Why don't you build up your own business from scratch the way I did?"

"I can't do that! You know I can't. I'm not like you. I never was. And now . . . and now I'm no longer a young man." For a moment he broke off, unable to continue, then added bitterly, "I always wondered why you kept everything in your own name. I always wondered. You were planning, weren't you? All these years you were preparing for this moment!"

Odysseus considered the suggestion with surprise, though he gave no outward sign. It was possible. A man never knows all that is in his own mind, and it could give such a meaningful pattern to everything, from the very beginning, a pattern that would be complete and beautiful when he finally took the step of joining the Christians. He smiled.

Demetrius, noting the smile, changed his tack. "What about Simon Baal?"

Odysseus snorted derisively.

"Don't you know how dangerous it is to cross a man like that?" Demetrius demanded. "The whole Memnon family could be murdered if he felt it was . . . expedient."

Odysseus dismissed this threat with a wave of the hand. "So? Death is always not far away, but if the Christian promises are kept, one can buy eternal life with one's death in this world. That's a good bargain, as any businessman can see."

"Bargain? Bargain?" cried Demetrius. "A gamble, you mean. An impossible gamble!"

"What's one more gamble, old friend, after so many others? I've gambled my life and fortune again and again for prizes far more trivial than eternal life. Unless you gamble, you can't win! But you don't understand that. Only a few do. I was born understanding it, and that's why I have what I have. That's why I am what I am. Don't you see? The same gambler's spirit that made me rich now drives me to Christ, now drives me to throw the dice for immortality!" As Odysseus argued, his own doubts began to vanish and he found himself, for the first time, believing his own eloquent words. He paused, astonished, and considered what he'd said.

Demetrius burst out, "Have pity on me! I'm your brother."

Odysseus answered gravely, "I have so many brothers now."

Demetrius was about to protest, but the sight of his brother's otherworldly expression stopped him. His shoulders sagged. He looked at the floor, saying, "I'll come back, after you've thought..."

"You'd be wasting your time."

"I see... Well, I guess I'm leaving then. I have things to do. My work, and yours too now. We're pretty busy, you know, what with three grain ships in dry dock and all."

"I know."

"And the war."

"The war. Yes."

Demetrius halted by the doorway and, before departing, called back defiantly, "If I get no pity from you, you can expect none from me!"

Odysseus Memnon, already reaching for the scroll of the Gospel of Thomas, did not bother to answer.

■ ■ ■

In the cloudless sky the light of day was fading as Odysseus strolled arm in arm with Adrastia through the gardens of his villa, Sabella leading them with an earthenware oil lamp and Rophos following with a huge feathered fan. The air was hot, humid and sluggish.

"I've let my hair down, darling," said Adrastia.

"Oh? Yes, so you have. I didn't notice."

"You didn't notice," she mocked. He heard the trace of despair in her voice but ignored it, only glancing at her briefly, without curiosity. She was, he noticed, examining a lock of her long black hair as if trying to determine why it had lost its attractiveness. Her smooth, fine-cut features wore a puzzled frown, fitfully illuminated by Sabella's lamp.

"You should have seen the dwarfs today, dear." She waited for his answer, but his attention seemed to be on something else. She continued brightly, "I never saw anything so funny in my life! You know how mischievous they are, but they're so cute one can't stay angry at them long. Bubo is the ringleader, because he's the boldest. You know Bubo?"

"They all look alike to me."

"Bubo is the one with the biggest hump on his back. Now do you remember him?"

Odysseus shrugged.

"Well, today—you won't believe this, Odysseus—today Bubo stole some of my clothes from my room and dressed up like me, and Suchos dressed up like you, and the third, Horus, pretended to be a Christian priest, and they stood on the table in the kitchen and presented a little play that they made up as they went along. The kitchen slaves were screaming with laughter! They didn't know I was standing in the doorway, watching it all. You should have seen them! There was the one that was supposed to be me pulling on your right arm and there was the Christian priest pulling on your left arm while they both squealed, 'He's mine!' 'No, he's mine!' It was easy to see by the gestures that the priest was a homosexual. It was so funny! By the gods, it would have done your gloomy old heart good to see them!"

Odysseus grunted politely, and Adrastia went on with a gaiety bordering on hysteria. He looked up at a statue of Anubis, the dogheaded god of death, a looming silhouette against the sky, and thought, *What if I suffer a fatal heart attack before I become a Christian?* His wife's chatter faded away in his consciousness, and there was only Anubis, a faint trace of a smile on his ebony canine lips, gazing down at him. *Will I really go to that place of eternal torture the Christians have told me about?* He turned abruptly and grasped Adrastia roughly by the shoulders, stopping the flow of her monologue in mid-sentence. "I've no time for talk of dwarfs and pranks!"

She was startled. "What's this, my dear? What's this?"

Haltingly he began, "I may die soon . . ."

"Oh no, darling! Don't say that!" Her tone was false.

"Listen. I'm serious. I'm sick, Adrastia, sicker than I've ever allowed you to know. I've had a few attacks already. The next one, that could come at any moment, might finish me. Can't you understand? Can't you see? My body is finished—so I must turn to those who tell me there is another part of me that will remain after my body is gone."

"I can tell you that! You should have asked me. Listen—there *is* a part of you that will remain after your body is gone."

Surprised, he let go of her arms. "What part?"

"Your money."

He did not join her in her laughter, but muttered, "I can't talk to you," and turned away. "Money, pranks, dwarfs—that's your whole universe." He gathered his cloak around him, though it was still quite warm in the garden.

From behind him her voice came to him as if from a great distance, though he knew she was close. "Our foolishness is holy if it amuses the gods, and isn't that what they made us for? I can't think what else we can do for them. Gods are to men as men are to dwarfs—isn't that right?—both men and dwarfs live only as long as they amuse their masters—and you, you've become a bore, not only to me, but to the gods—and everyone else!"

He sighed and turned again to face her. "I can't talk to you," he repeated softly, then took her arm. "Come, my darling. Let us join the family at the supper table. There will be gossip and wit there, I'm sure, enough for even you."

They returned to the house in silence, each lost in private broodings, and allowed Sabella to lead them to the dining room.

The others were already there, reclining around the table—Serapion, Demetrius, Hathor, and a few serving maids. Odysseus scanned them with disgust as they turned to him their smiling mask-like faces—or was that just the effect of the smokey, flickering oil lamps?

He took his place at the head of the table, and Adrastia settled down beside him. Hathor, sharing a couch with her brother Serapion, looked at Odysseus with puzzled curiosity. *Ah, little Hathor, if you knew what was in my mind . . .*

Wakar the eunuch served nuts, cakes and fruits—just an appetizer.

As usual the others politely waited until Odysseus had taken his first bite before they began. Chewing, he watched them with a speculative eye. Was there danger here? He could feel it, as if one of the gods was whispering a warning in his ear. He'd learned to heed such feelings; they'd saved his life several times before.

The appetizer course was soon over; now it was time for the soup.

Rophos entered the smokey, lamp-lit room pushing a little red wooden serving cart on which sloshed a large silver soup tureen. Stopping next to the table, he removed the cover and inhaled the savory steam that billowed forth, his lips curved in a dreamy smile, his eyelids drooping in a pantomime of gluttony.

He bowed and began ladling soup into bowls. It was chicken soup. Odysseus could smell it.

Was it the steam? Or was it the hot humid air in the room that made Odysseus break out in sweat?

Hathor, spoon in hand, raised her eyebrows at him questioningly.

What were they all waiting for? Oh yes, they were waiting for him to take the first sip of the soup. The host must always take a sip first before the others can begin. That was just good manners—or was it, this time, something more?

His eye moved slowly from face to face in the dimness, searching for . . . what? Fear? A hint of guilt? Anxiety?

All dinner table gossip had ceased.

Silently, without expression, they returned his gaze.

He cleared his throat. "Hmmm . . . well . . . With so much resentment around us—we live, as everyone knows, in a decadent age—perhaps I should adopt the habits of our beloved Emperor Nero and have someone taste the food for us . . . Just in case."

He gestured to Rophos, who hesitated, then stepped forward to bravely play the role of "royal taster." Rophos took a sip, frowned a moment in concentration, then swallowed, smiled and looked around at the guests. "Very good!" he announced, then licked his lips as if making sure not to waste one precious drop.

Everyone was watching him intently, but he seemed perfectly all right.

"If you're quite finished . . ." Adrastia began impatiently.

"Wait!" warned Odysseus, raising his hand.

Still the eunuch stood there smiling, pleased to be the center of attention.

Finally Odysseus picked up his spoon and dipped it in his soup, a sheepish smile breaking out on his thin lips which seemed to say, "I'm sorry to have caused so much trouble."

He raised the spoonful of soup to his mouth, eyes lowered with embarrassment, thinking, *Adrastia will never let me forget this.*

"No!" screamed Hathor. "Look!"

Old Odysseus lowered his spoon, the soup still untasted, and glanced up in time to see Rophos crumple and fall face down on the floor.

Chapter Four

AFTER A SLEEPLESS NIGHT, Odysseus Memnon arose before dawn and wandered alone through the silent mansion, standing at last on a balcony overlooking the garden, head lowered, fingers clasped behind his back. There were flocks of birds in the brightening sky, wheeling and crying, but their song seemed only to emphasize the profound silence that had settled over the flower gardens, the statues, the high spike-topped walls that surrounded the estate.

"Rophos is dead," he murmured.

Shivering, he pulled his gray wool cloak tight around his fleshless bones, frowning with resentment at the morning chill. In an hour or two it would be the heat he would complain of—for the old, the temperature is never right.

The breeze stirred, bringing to his nostrils the heavy scent of blossoms, but he did not smile. The thought of flowers was too closely linked to the thought of funerals, of his own shriveled mummy smeared with plaster and decked with bright petals of many colors.

He sighed, then whispered again, "Rophos is dead." After a moment he added, "But I'm the one they were after." And who were "they"?

His own family.

His wife, his brother, his son, his daughter.

If any stranger had entered the grounds, certainly the dogs would have set up a howl; as for the slaves—they had no motive. He was the kindest master in all Alexandria; his business associates were shocked at his laxness, but Odysseus knew what life was like at the bottom, knew that he himself might have ended up someone's property had he been sold to pay his debts. That was something Demetrius, in particular, preferred to forget.

There was a special horror to murder when it was between members of the same family. Murder within the family! That was the shadow that darkened so many noble names. Herod. Cleopatra. Nero. And Memnon. Odysseus remembered, suddenly, his father's dying eyes. But that was different. That was self-defense.

Murder—or attempted murder—within the family was worse than a horror. It could be a scandal. And a scandal was bad for business. A scandal dried up credit, the lifeblood of business.

Elbows on the railing, he nodded slowly. It would be better not to inform the authorities about Rophos' death. If something happened to one of his slaves, it was nobody's business but his own. Not one word of the matter must pass outside the walls of the Memnon estate!

A kind of black ecstasy came over him, a perverse delight in the prospect of his own destruction. Was this how those criminals felt? Was this the way of those men who shouted out obscene jokes from the cart on the way to their own crucifixion?

He would do nothing.

He would wait, passively, and let them kill him. If they, after all he'd done for them, still wanted him dead, it was better to leave this world as quietly as possible—this world where there was neither gratitude nor justice. Socrates, the wisest of men, had quietly waited for his enemies to kill him, had even, with his own hands, knowingly lifted the cup of poison to his lips.

And Socrates, thought Odysseus, *had many loving friends in the world. I have none. Does a true gentleman continue to intrude on a party when he learns he is not wanted?*

Or perhaps, perhaps he'd do more than wait. Perhaps he'd save them the trouble of killing him. Perhaps he'd become his own murderer!

A vast weariness had crept over him. It seemed now that the Christian's Heaven and the Egyptian's Western Land were equally worthless. The best, after all, would simply be to sleep and never wake. He closed his eyes.

He thought, *Did they all want me dead? Or just one of them?* What did it matter?

Someone was crying. Someone was weeping softly. He opened his eyes, startled, and glanced around.

A brilliant sliver of sun had appeared on the horizon and he blinked, grimaced and raised his hand to shield his eyes from the glare. The long shadows in the garden were hiding something, someone. Squinting, he could make out a small, bent over figure down near the palm grove. Who was it?

The weeping continued, low and anguished.

The figure emerged from the shadows, still bent over, walking with a slow, unsteady step.

"Sabella!" said Odysseus, astonished.

She heard him and looked up, wide-eyed, frightened.

"Sabella," he called. "What's wrong?" She did not answer, only stared up at him in panic for a moment, then turned and fled toward the slaves' quarters as fast as her spindly little legs could carry her.

Odysseus chuckled indulgently, then laughed out loud. She was his favorite among the slaves. If no one else loved him, at least she did, and now she must be weeping, he thought, because she'd miss him when he sold her to a new master.

This thought broke the spell of his depression; his dry, wrinkled face broke into a cunning smile as, his mood of passive fatalism forgotten, he began laying plans.

■ ■ ■

"Don't eat that!" cried out Hathor in alarm.

"And why not, my dear?" Odysseus paused, the spoon of steaming porridge halfway to his lips.

"It might be poisoned. Let one of the slaves taste it for you."

Smiling, he closed his lips on the porridge, chewed a bit, then swallowed.

Adrastia, reclining next to him on the couch, muttered, "You old fool."

"Fool?" he said. "You call me a fool?"

"An old fool," she repeated, more loudly.

A rustle passed around the breakfast table as the Memnons exchanged nervous glances.

Setting down his spoon, he looked at them all with condescension, almost contempt. "Eat up! Can't you see I'm still alive?"

None of them so much as touched a spoon.

"Come on! The porridge is getting cold!" He took another spoonful—chewed, swallowed.

"You were taking an awful risk," whispered Hathor.

"Not at all, my dear. I know the rascal who's after me expects me to expect poison, so poison is the one thing I'm no longer worried about. Next time, it'll be something else—a knife, a sword—who knows?" He looked around at them again, eyes narrowing. "But whoever you are, you won't find me an easy victim. I, too, know how to do the unexpected." He took another bite, took his time chewing it. They waited expectantly, still not eating.

"What do you mean by that?" It was Demetrius who spoke.

"As of now, you are all my prisoners. The guards have my orders. They will kill anyone who tries to leave this estate without my permission." He smiled at them blandly, thinking, *All those round eyes. They look like a lot of fresh-caught mackerel . . . and I'm the fisherman!*

After a moment of stunned silence, they all began protesting at once, while Odysseus leaned back and unconcernedly licked his fingers, enjoying a few stray bits of cereal that had escaped the spoon. He knew without looking that his men were quietly standing at the doors, swords drawn.

Demetrius had jumped to his feet and was shouting, "I have business to attend to on the docks. You can't . . ."

Tall Serapion was leaning forward, saying in a serious tone, "You must allow me, if nothing else, to keep my appointment with Dionysius, the head of the library in the Holy Temple of Osiris-Serapis. Such appointments are not easy to come by, and if he's offended . . ."

Hathor, seated next to her brother, was pleading. "Please, Father. I have shopping to do in the Agora-Diplostoon marketplace. I promised my girlfriends and . . ."

Adrastia drew herself up and glared down at him. "And I, I'll have you know, have an appointment at the beautician's!"

Odysseus lifted his hand for silence and for once was instantly obeyed.

He raised himself to a sitting position with a faint wheeze of effort, taking his time, as if unaware that all the fisheyes were upon him. He coughed, spat into his napkin and examined the phlegm with frowning interest, then finally said, "Too bad." His voice was cold, emotionless, but slightly husky. "I am staging a gladiatorial spectacle here for your pleasure, featuring myself, a tired old man with a few tricks left up his sleeve, against a clever and unknown murderer—a fight to the death! Nothing else you might have had planned could be half so interesting."

His small-boned green-robed body was erect now as he sat there, swaying slightly, looking at them exactly as a hooded cobra looks at its prey.

■ ■ ■

Odysseus Memnon had convened a kind of court there in his dining room, appointing himself judge, jury and prosecutor all in one.

And perhaps executioner as well, thought Hathor as she stood in the walled-in garden at the center of the great house, watching the gulls high above her and waiting for her father's next command. The morning heat had just begun but already she was sweating.

He had begun by questioning the slaves—the eunuch Wakar, little Sabella, the guards, the cooks, even the three terrified hunchbacked dwarfs—but as nearly as Hathor could make out from their excited whispers when they left his "courtroom," he had thus far been able to establish only one important fact: Three members of the Memnon family had been in the kitchen briefly before the fatal meal.

They had tasted the soup and fussed over the spices to be put into it, so any one of the three could easily have dropped in the poison.

The three were Demetrius . . .

Serapion . . .

And she herself . . . Hathor!

Demetrius stepped up to her, breaking into her gloomy reverie with his harsh, angry, old man's voice. "Why doesn't he torture them?"

"What's that?" She was dazed, unable to focus her mind on what he was saying.

"I said, I don't understand why he doesn't torture the slaves. Everyone knows a slave only tells the truth when he's in mortal agony. One of them is bound to confess."

"He doesn't suspect the slaves," she told him softly. "He's not questioning them as if he thought one of them did it. He's asking them about us. Can't you hear what they're saying? He's asking them about us."

Demetrius took a step backward. "He suspects *us*?"

She nodded.

"By the gods," he whispered. He thrust a narrow forefinger into his mouth and gummed it nervously. Since breakfast Hathor had known Odysseus was certain the poisoner was a member of the family. He'd almost said as much, but apparently only now had Demetrius fully realized that he himself was a suspect.

He was shuffling away from her, finger still in his mouth, when Serapion approached her and whispered something to her too softly for Demetrius to overhear.

Wakar appeared at the doorway, blinking in the sudden sunlight. Shielding his eyes, he called, "Hathor! The Master wants to speak to you next." He beckoned to her, his face expressionless.

She walked slowly toward him, leaving Serapion, arms folded, looking after her.

Adrastia gave her a reassuring pat on the arm as she passed, but Hathor impatiently jerked her arm away. Demetrius, his voice unnaturally loud in the silent courtyard, muttered, "Damn lot of trouble to make over the death of a dirty slave!"

As she passed from the sunlit exterior to the dim interior, Hathor stumbled, then felt Wakar's firm hand on her elbow, guiding her. He'd always been there, she realized. He'd always been there, since she was a little girl, quietly guiding and protecting her. Perhaps Wakar, who could have no children of his own, had, without saying anything, adopted her, made himself the father that her real father, Odysseus, was almost always too busy to be. There were some things she could never bring herself to tell Odysseus, but she had told them to her faithful eunuch father Wakar, without thinking twice.

There was one thing, however, she dared not tell even Wakar! He might understand, but if he didn't . . . she couldn't bear to think of that!

"Here she is, Master," said Wakar.

Odysseus looked up when she entered the room, but did not smile. "Leave us, Wakar," he said, his forehead deeply furrowed.

As the slave bowed out, the old man gestured toward the couch on his right. Hathor slowly crossed the marble floor and seated herself there, her eyes lowered, unable to meet his gaze. He leaned forward, elbows on the table, and searched her face with his glittering, black, animal-like eyes.

"Look at me, girl," he commanded.

She glanced at him an instant, then looked down again. *He thinks he can read my thoughts in my eyes*, she realized. And how did she know he couldn't?

"Look at me," he repeated. "Is there something you want to tell me?"

Yes! She wanted to tell him everything, to confess everything. She had not been raised to tell lies, to keep secrets. It was too much of a burden, too much of a weight on her. *It isn't fair*, she thought. *The gods ask too much of me!* But she did not speak.

"I know there's something," he said gently. "I can tell. Don't be afraid, my dear. If it was you who tried to kill me, I won't punish you. The others, yes, but not you. You can go to Rome and live with your mother. Would you like that?"

Her real mother, Octavia, not that damned Adrastia! Yes, she would like to go. It would be strange to see her mother again, after so long, but she'd also see Rome. Everyone should see Rome at least once. But still she did not answer.

"I'm waiting," he prompted. His voice was not so gentle now.

"Will you . . . do something for me?"

"Perhaps. Ask and see."

"Give up Christianity."

She looked at him at last. His face was clouded, uncertain. "Why?" he asked, gentle again.

"You believe someone in your own family has tried to kill you. Isn't that right? How can there be any good in a religion that sets members of the same family at each other's throats, brother against brother, wife against husband, son against father?"

"And daughter against father?"

She could not answer.

He slowly shook his head, sighing. "Don't you know me yet? Don't you know me well enough to know that once I decide to do something, I do it, no matter what anyone says? I'm too old to change, too old to learn to be soft and easy, like a woman. Don't you know that yet?" Then, after another sigh, he added slyly, "But if I did give up Christianity, would you let me live?"

She was horrified. "But I'm not the one who tried to kill you!"

"You were in the kitchen."

"Yes, that's right. I was there." She was on the verge of tears. The gods were asking too much of her. They always asked too much! "But I had nothing to do with any poison. You know I often go into the kitchen to see that everything is running smoothly. Since that bitch Adrastia takes no interest in the practical side of running this great house, and you're so busy, and Serapion is so . . . spiritual, I have to look after things. You know that without me, the slaves would do nothing."

"Your brother then. Is Serapion our poisoner?"

"No! No! Not Serapion!"

"You love your brother, don't you?"

There was a painful pause, then she answered stiffly, "Of course. It's my duty to love him."

"*My* brother then. Was it good old Demetrius?"

Again she could not answer. It was unthinkably horrible that someone would try to murder his own brother, but there seemed to be no other choice. She began to weep softly.

A moment later she felt a hand on hers, a hand with long bony fingers and dry rough skin, like third-rate papyrus. Her father's voice, when it came, was barely audible. "You've told the truth, and I know it."

She looked up, met his dark and worried gaze.

"I can tell when someone lies to me. I can see it in their face," he said. "You've told me the truth, all the truth you know. Come, sit here beside me. Help me question the others." He patted a place next to him on his couch. "Help me *judg*e the others."

Wordlessly, she nodded her acceptance.

■ ■ ■

"Serapion," announced Wakar.

"You may go, Wakar," said Odysseus.

"Yes, sir." He departed with a low bow.

Serapion stood a moment in the doorway, his face in shadow, but his stance, feet set apart, thumbs hooked into his belt, was as eloquent as any facial expression. He was, thought Hathor, so sure of himself, so proud and defiant. With a nod for his father and a smile for his sister, he stepped into the room.

The old man leaned forward. "I know what you're going to say."

Serapion was amused. "Then why bother to talk to me?"

"You're going to join your sister in trying to blame all this on my religion."

Serapion shrugged. "The ancient gods cannot be pleased by what you're doing."

"The ancient gods are dead!"

Serapion raised an eyebrow. "Oh? They're sleeping perhaps, but not dead, or perhaps . . . perhaps they do not choose to be seen by human eyes. Who knows? They may at this moment be walking among us invisible, searching for traitors and blasphemers." Hathor realized her brother was deliberately baiting Odysseus, trying to goad the old man's famous temper. It was a foolish thing to do, under the circumstances, but Hathor could not help but admire Serapion's courage.

"Superstition!" said Odysseus.

Serapion did not reply, only smiled his faint superior smile.

Odysseus thumped the table with a bony fist. "You smile? And do you still smile when I tell you that, even if your damn gods do kill me, you won't get one drachma of my money? If I died now, it would all go to my brother and my wife, and as soon as I can change my will, everything—everything!—goes to the Christians. Do you understand?"

"I understand."

"Don't you care?"

"Not in the least."

"You're a strange one, Serapion. I've never been able to figure you out."

Serapion turned to Hathor. "Am I so hard to figure out?" He did not wait for her answer, but went on. "Actually I'm a simple man, a simpler man than you, perhaps more like your father and your father's father than you are. I follow the old gods that they followed, love the sea that they loved. You've turned your back on your roots in this land, in its history, in its age-old wisdom. I have embraced my roots, returned to this land. Many families follow the same pattern; the father rebels and the son returns to the old ways. If and when I have a son, he may well be a man like you, a lover of new things, and the little war between you and me will be fought all over again between him and me."

"Philosophy!" Odysseus pronounced the word as if it were an obscenity. "We were talking about money, Serapion!"

"Money is not a subject that holds much interest for me. When you bring it up, I'll admit my interest wanders."

"Where would you be without it? Answer me that!"

"I'll soon find out, won't I?" Serapion's smile broadened into a grin. "It was an adventure for you to become rich. I was born rich, so that's no adventure for me. For me it will be an adventure to become poor, to see if I can live like a philosopher on bread, water and words. Money? Possessions? To you, in spite of your new-found religious pretensions, money and possessions are the only reality. To me, they're illusions, all illusions. Fame is an illusion too, and security. There is no security for mortals! Why, even death is an illusion. All wise men tell us that. The only value there is in our short life here on earth is the effect it has on our other lives in future incarnations, either here or in some realm beyond death. Don't your precious Christians know that?"

A glance of sudden understanding passed between father and son, and Hathor realized that, in spite of everything, the two had a strange hidden affection and respect for each other.

The old man nodded thoughtfully. "There is another life. You're right. But Serapion, my boy, it seems I'm only now beginning to understand what that implies."

■ ■ ■

As Serapion was leaving, old Demetrius pushed past him in the doorway, too impatient to wait for Wakar to announce him.

"Odysseus! You must give up this madness!"

He began pacing nervously in front of Odysseus and Hathor, gesturing wildly as he spoke. Hathor was struck by the difference between the two brothers: Odysseus so forceful and decisive, Demetrius so uncertain and harassed. Yet they looked so much alike physically, they might have been twins.

"What madness?" Odysseus asked.

"Why, this Christianity business, of course. Give it up, man! Give it up! There's nothing in it but ruin, ruin for us all."

"I can't give it up now. People would say I'd backed down because I was afraid."

"A donation then. Give these fanatics some kind of modest donation. I know priests. They'll be satisfied with that, more than satisfied. Everyone will be happy!" He was wringing his hands.

"A Memnon does not do things halfway, Demetrius. You're a Memnon. You should know that."

Demetrius caught the sinister undertone in his brother's voice. "What are you saying? Are you saying I was the one who tried to kill you?"

"Were you?"

"Gods help us, no! How could you even think such a thing? I? I who have spent my life protecting your interests? One of the slaves must have done it. Since the rebellion of Spartacus, no man's life has been safe. A slave did it, I tell you. Torture them. You'll see. One of them will confess!"

"I'm sure one of them would, guilty or not, but this time it will not do simply to find some sort of sacrificial victim to punish. If I don't get the right man, he'll get me!"

"But . . . but I've done nothing yet," blurted out Demetrius.

Hathor leaped to her feet, crying, "Yet? Yet? What do you mean by that?"

Miserable Demetrius was unable to answer, even to speak. Hathor pointed a quivering finger at him and screamed. "You! You did it! You did it! I can see it in your face!" Actually, her vision was blurred by tears, but the man's cringing, pleading body seemed to her to cry out his guilt from every pore.

Odysseus laid a restraining hand on her arm. "Proof, dear," he murmured. "We must have proof."

Turning, she could see that in spite of his words, her father was clearly pleased by her show of emotion.

■ ■ ■

Wakar led out Demetrius, who was still desperately protesting his innocence, and led in Adrastia. Hathor greeted her with, "It was Demetrius, Mother. He almost the same as admitted it!"

"Hush now, Hathor," Odysseus said.

"I'm not surprised," Adrastia commented dryly. She did not remain standing but, without waiting for an invitation, gathered her skirts and seated herself on a couch to the left of Hathor. Hathor was now between her stepmother and her father, forcing old Odysseus to lean forward to talk around her. *It was an awkward arrangement for an interrogation; doubtless that was*, Hathor thought, *why Adrastia had chosen it.*

"And I can't blame the poor man," went on Adrastia, with an airy wave of her delicate hand. "It was, after all, the only way to prevent a financial—and social—disaster to the whole family, and," she added mysteriously, "a disaster also to certain parties outside the family, powerful parties, parties with the power, perhaps, to decide the future of the Empire. I can speak freely and frankly since, of the Memnon clan, only I was nowhere near the kitchen and thus am, like Caesar's wife, above suspicion." She reached across Hathor to touch his hand, and repeated emphatically, "Above suspicion."

"All the same . . ." he began.

"So you must listen to me," she interrupted firmly. "You must listen to me when I warn you to give up your insane religious fancies and join me in enjoying what little time—what little time I say—you have left of this life, or I'll feel no sympathy whatever for you when your actions inevitably bring about your doom. It's like a Greek play," she ended pompously. "Your defiance of your natural duties tempts the vengeance of the gods."

"You are above suspicion?" Odysseus said softly.

"Of course. I was with you all that afternoon. It was the others who were in a position to meddle with the soup."

"To me it seems strange," Odysseus told her, "that you were the only one who took the precaution of establishing that you were elsewhere. I think, if I were going to poison someone, I too would make sure I was seen as far away from the soup as possible."

Adrastia was shocked, but not speechless.

"Very well, you old fool! If I poisoned the soup, how did I do it? Can you answer me that?"

■ ■ ■

Wakar lit, one by one, the lamps in the elaborate petrolabrum, then pulled, hand over hand, the chain that raised the lamps to the ceiling. The fading red glow of the setting sun that filtered in from the courtyard was replaced by the cheery yellow light of the lamps, and as the petrolabrum swung, Wakar's shadow grew alternately longer and shorter, longer and shorter. He stood, looking up with satisfaction, making sure none of the lamps had gone out on him.

Odysseus, Hathor by his side, stood in the dining room doorway, watching his slave with a moody frown. He raised his hand and called, "Wakar?"

"Yes, Master."

"Where is everyone?"

"They've gone to their rooms, Master." Wakar's face looked curiously sinister, lit from below by the lighter lamp he held in his hands. Odysseus stared at him until he dropped his gaze. Such an opaque expression the eunuch had! It seemed so meek, so harmless, so loyal, but who knew what lay behind it? *I wonder, my friend,* thought Odysseus. *Is Demetrius right? Are you, Wakar, the one who wants to kill me?*

The slave was waiting expectantly.

"Good night, Wakar," sighed Odysseus.

"Good night, Master."

Wakar, walking with a soft, quick step, headed for the kitchen.

When he had gone, Odysseus said, "It's getting cold in here, isn't it, Hathor?"

"I hadn't noticed."

Odysseus shivered. "It cools off so fast when the sun goes down. Could you fetch me my green robe?"

"Of course, Father." She hastened to do his bidding.

He stood alone in the great hall, listening to her sandals slapping the marble floors in the distance.

No, Wakar wasn't the attempted killer. Odysseus knew who it was, and why. He had no real proof, but he was certain now, certain in his own mind.

He sighed, and rubbed his goose-pimpled old arms.

Hathor returned with the green robe and helped him on with it. He looked at her. He said gently, "Sometimes you look so much like your mother."

"My *real* mother, you mean." Her normally soft voice had a sudden hardness to it.

"Yes, Hathor. Of course." He hesitated, then quickly, almost shyly, kissed her on the forehead. "Good night, Hathor."

"Good night." She looked down at her feet, a little embarrassed.

Odysseus turned away from her and slowly plodded alone up the long marble staircase to the second floor. He was dressed in expensive green silk robes and tunic, and decked with jewels and rings, but his gaunt face was the face of a coarse shipwright's son grown old in a world of hard work and constant struggle. Once in his room, he closed his door but did not lock it.

I won't shut you out, my dear killer, he thought.

He lit gold and silver oil lamps from the lighter lamp in the wall niche, watched them send out tenuous streamers of acrid black smoke, watched his shadow move over his vast, many-pillowed bed draped in green silk.

He sat down on the edge of the bed, then reached down to pick up his knife, a beautiful jeweled weapon he always kept by his bedside. He drew it from its sheath, watching how the rubies and diamonds set in its handle caught the flickering lamp light.

Behind him the early evening wind rustled the richly-embroidered floral curtains on the open window, rustled one of two papyrus scrolls that lay on his bed table. He half-turned, looked fondly at the scroll, read the title, "The Gospel according to Mark."

With a cautious fingertip he tested the point of his lovely dagger. Ah, it was sharp, so sharp! So curved, so polished, so perfect!

His eyes moved once again to the door. He smiled.

A fair fight! That's all he'd ever asked of life, and that's all he asked now.

There was a soft rustle behind him. Just the curtains or perhaps . . . He half-turned to look.

A hooded figure was framed in the window, silhouetted black against the last fading afterglow in the sky. Instantly Odysseus understood. *So*, he thought, *you climbed up the vines on the outside of the house to attack me from behind!*

The old man turned for his knife.

A javelin hurtled through the air to bury itself in the old man's back.

He grunted, fell forward off the bed onto his knees on the marble floor, tried to rise, then went down flat on his face as the jeweled knife clattered uselessly on the marble floor.

The killer stepped toward him.

Odysseus twisted, looked up, recognized in the flickering lamp light a familiar face. The old man forced an agonized grin.

His last words were a strangled whisper: "I knew . . . I knew it was you."

■ ■ ■

Odysseus died in the autumn of 67 A.D.; in the spring of the following year, on the morning of March third . . .

■ ■ ■

With a crash and a hiss the massive, slightly rusted bull's-head ram, like the brass-knuckled fist of a boxer, shattered the crest of a wave, then arose dripping into the gray dawn light only to crash into another wave with still greater impact. A gale was rising and with it the sea; the water that only a half-hour ago had been smooth and glistening and flat was now pleated with vast moving hills of gray water.

Optio Mannus, cape streaming in the wind, stumbled across the heaving deck and, leaning over an open hatchway, shouted down, "Ship the oars! Ship the oars, I say!"

"With pleasure!" came back a gruff anonymous voice from below. There was scattered laughter, even a little applause.

No discipline, thought Mannus, frowning. The rowers were far from being combat-ready, if they ever would be.

He listened to the clatter of wood against wood as the oars, like the legs of a frightened turtle, were dragged into the hull of the ship. Straightening, he cupped his hands around his mouth to call out, "Raise the sail! Quick now, you cockroaches!"

Still frowning, he watched the broad, square, dull-orange sail go up. The crew, it was true, had been up all night and were tired, but that was no excuse for such almost defiant slowness.

There was a sudden mocking laugh behind him, so close he was startled. Almost automatically his hand leaped to the pommel of his shortsword as he turned to face . . . Daphnis the Clerk.

"Go ahead and kill me now, handsome," said Librarius Daphnis gleefully. "You'll soon drown us all anyway."

Disgustedly, Mannus said, "Go back to bed. I've got work to do."

"You're so nervous. What's wrong? Are we lost?"

"Don't be absurd. We should sight the Alexandrian lighthouse within the hour."

"Is that so? Would you care to make a little wager? Say, thirty silver dinari?"

"I've had enough of your little wagers! And anyway . . ." He broke off and squinted, leaning forward tensely. "By the gods, there she is!" He pointed triumphantly. Ahead of them, rising from the pale mist that obscured the horizon, a whiteness gleamed in the first rays of the still-invisible sun. The thing was only a dot, too distant for him to see in any detail, but it was unquestionably the great lighthouse of the Ptolemies on Pharos Island, tallest building in the world.

"What do you think of that, eh?" Optio Mannus said triumphantly. "If I'd made that bet with you I would, for once, have won."

The hawk-faced clerk was unruffled. "But since you didn't, you lost."

"Damn you!" Mannus cried in frustration, giving the mincing Librarius an angry shove, but when Daphnis shoved back, he ignored it. He had no more time to waste on bets and horseplay. The moment had come to go to the afterdeck cabin and awaken his commanding officer, Centurion Gaius Hesperian.

END OF BOOK ONE

Book Two

Chapter One

THE MORNING SUN STREAMED IN HATHOR'S WINDOW; the wind played with her shoulder-length light brown hair. Humming softly to herself, she slipped a loose-fitting peach-colored tunic on over her head and paused to admire her reflection in a polished-silver mirror.

"Sabella!" she called.

The skinny little slave girl hurried in from the next room.

"Yes, Mistress?"

"What do you think of it?" She pirouetted.

"Oh, that's just fine, Miss. Just fine. Very nice dress."

"But is it shocking?"

"Shocking, Miss?"

"Yes, Sabella dear. You know how much I'd love to shock those staid old philosophers when I get to Athens." The two enjoyed a conspiratorial giggle together, but as Hathor turned away, Sabella's face clouded. "You got to go?" demanded the black girl sullenly.

"No, no, of course not. I *want* to!"

In two days, they both knew, all Alexandria would turn out for the Festival of the Ship of Isis, and after that, when the port of Alexandria, now sealed for the winter storms, would be officially opened, there would be nothing to prevent Hathor from sailing away on the first high tide.

"Don't be sad, Sabella." Hathor patted the slave's kinky hair. "I can't stand to have others sad when I'm so happy."

"Yes, Hathor."

Hathor slipped off the peach-colored tunic and tossed it in her chest, which lay open on the bed. Then, slender and naked, she pranced over to where Sabella had laid out a great pile of clothing, almost Hathor's entire wardrobe. *Yes*, she thought. *I'll take the peach one, and the white linen one with the flowery ribbon border, and this one, and this.*

"Mama Adrastia," said Sabella. Hathor turned to see her stepmother entering.

Hathor loved everyone today, even Adrastia. "Mother, why don't you come too?" she asked her lightheartedly.

"You know why," Adrastia answered wryly. "Demetrius and I have business to attend to up the Nile." The death of her husband had long since ceased to trouble her (if it ever had), but there was a new seriousness about her, a new air of responsibility that was quite impressive in one so young. Adrastia sucked thoughtfully on a strand of her long black hair, and with a bejeweled slender white hand toyed with the hem of her richly-embroidered pale blue gown. It was an emblem of her new seriousness that she wore her hair long and straight, not piled up in a tower on her head as was her former habit. This in spite of the fact that such tall, elaborate hairdos were now in fashion. After a pensive moment, Adrastia continued. "We may even go on to India if political conditions within the Empire become too unsettled. We have extensive holdings in India, you know."

"Really?" Hathor had not known this, but it was just one more surprise among many that had, one by one, come to the surface since the death of Odysseus Memnon. Her father had been a man with many secrets.

"There's revolution in the air here, my dear," Adrastia said. "Revolution has always been bad for the health of the rich. You would be wise to come with me."

"I'll be all right," Hathor said gaily. "My brother will protect me. He's not only a fine sailor, but well on the way to becoming a priest as well, so I'll be safe from all dangers, natural or supernatural."

Serapion, she knew, would be the captain of the ship that took her to Greece, and he had chosen no slow and clumsy cargo ship, but a swift fighting bireme, a rammer. The war in Judea continued, and Serapion was taking no chances.

Hathor slipped on another dress. "There's only one thing that worries me, Mother."

"Oh?"

"The authorities . . . they may not be finished with us."

Adrastia snorted contemptuously. "That so-called investigation has been dead for months. What did they do, eh? Tortured the slaves, asked a few stupid questions, ran around like fools. We've nothing to show for it but poor Wakar's limp."

"Poor Wakar," Hathor repeated sadly. The eunuch Wakar had been the worst tortured. The soldiers had had a half-hearted hope of a confession, or at least some additional information from him. Wakar had said nothing, and now would probably limp for the rest of his life.

"Besides," Adrastia said, "they dare not meddle too much in the affairs of a family as wealthy and powerful as we Memnons. The Praefectus of Egypt, Tiberius Julius Alexander, was a personal friend of your father's, and everyone knows it."

"So the case is closed?"

"Completely closed, dear. I'm certain of it."

Hathor was now wearing a white silk gown that hung sheer to her ankles. She slipped on a necklace with a pendant in the shape of a golden dung beetle and struck a pose, hands on hips, pelvis thrust forward. "How do I look now?"

"Oh pretty," Sabella cried, clapping her hands.

"Delightfully obscene," said Adrastia.

Hathor heard Wakar coming down the hall. His step was now rendered unmistakable by the tortures he had undergone, a pitiful step, scrape, step, scrape. It hurt Hathor to hear it. But now Wakar was hurrying, almost running. What could be wrong? It would have to be something deadly serious to make poor Wakar run.

All eyes turned toward him as he appeared in the doorway, panting and flushed, and leaned against the doorjamb, trying to catch his breath.

"What is it, Wakar?" cried Adrastia. "Speak, man!"

Wakar's words came out between agonized gasping breaths. "There are soldiers . . . at the gates. They demand . . . to question us . . . about the death . . . of the Master!"

Stunned, Hathor followed Wakar to the head of the great marble staircase, Adrastia beside her, Sabella trailing along behind, eyes round with fear. "After all this time," Adrastia muttered indignantly. "It's an insult!"

Hathor looked down the stairs at the chaos below.

The slaves were running about like frightened chickens, certain they were going to be tortured; and there was gaunt little old Demetrius shouting and cursing, trying to calm them, but only adding to their panic. Serapion stood to one side, pale and withdrawn.

Adrastia descended the stairs two or three steps at a time, and ran over to confer with Demetrius in excited whispers. The others followed more slowly behind her. As Wakar reached the foot of the stairs, Demetrius turned to him and commanded peevishly, "Let them in, you idiot! If we don't let them in right away, it will make them all the more suspicious."

Wakar stumped painfully off to obey.

Hathor heard the squeak of hinges as the heavy front door swung open, then the measured tramp of marching feet. As the slaves stepped back to make way for them, a squad of eight Roman soldiers entered the echoing hall and snapped to attention. By their black capes and tunics, and by their huge oval bronze-ornamented black shields, Hathor recognized them as members of Nero's personal guard, the dreaded Praetorians. This was obviously no routine investigation!

The Praetorians had formed two lines of four troops each and now, turning so the two lines were face to face, took three measured paces backward so that a passage was formed. One of the soldiers, speaking Greek with a heavy Latin accent, shouted, "Announcing Centurion Gaius Hesperian, personal agent of our lord and savior, the god Nero Claudius Caesar Drusus Germanicus! You will all please remain standing!" He repeated this announcement in Latin.

Hathor heard Adrastia whisper to Demetrius, "Tell me quick. What is the proper way to address a Praetorian centurion?"

Demetrius hesitated, then advised her uncertainly, "Call him Caesar. After all, he *is* Caesar's personal representative."

In the terrified hush that now fell over the room, Hathor could hear the footsteps of one man in the outer hall.

The man entered, paused a moment to glance sharply around, then strode to the center of the floor. As one man the soldiers thumped their breastplates and gave him a stiff-arm salute, shouting, "Ave Caesar!"

He answered their salute with no more than a faint nod, leaving no doubt in Hathor's mind that he was the man in command.

Unlike his troops, Centurion Gaius Hesperian carried no shield, wore no helmet or armor. He was clad simply but elegantly in a short red tunic, sandy brown cloak and open-toed leather boots, and was armed with a shortsword slung from a shoulder strap and a dagger on his belt. He might almost have been a wealthy civilian except for the swagger stick of twisted vine he held in his right hand, the symbol of his authority. He was clean-shaven (most Romans were), tall, lean and athletic, but his hair was iron-gray and receding, and there were lines of age and responsibility in his face. His thick bushy eyebrows were iron-gray also and the eyes themselves were a cold blue-gray, piercing, but with just a hint of playful irony.

He stood a moment, perfectly at ease, considering how to begin. When finally he spoke, it was in flawless Alexandrian Greek, and his voice was deep and strong, a voice accustomed to giving commands. "Odysseus Memnon was an important man, known and honored in the highest circles in Rome. You are honored too, because you are his family."

He paused, his eyes moving slowly from face to face. "It is to express his high regard for you all that Nero Caesar has sent me, his personal agent, all the way from Rome to seek out the monster who has murdered Odysseus Memnon, robbing you of a loving father and husband, and Caesar of a faithful Roman subject."

His eye lit on a group of cowering slaves and he smiled faintly. "Do not be afraid, any of you. There will be no torture, only a few polite questions. All I want is simple truth." He looked Hathor straight in the eye. "I'm sure," he continued mildly, "that is what we all want . . . isn't it?"

■ ■ ■

The soldier stepped out into the sunlight and took up a position next to the Doric column on one side of the front entrance of the Memnon mansion. He exchanged salutes with the two men who stood there waiting, then said crisply, "Hesperian wants you two inside."

Optio Mannus, Hesperian's second-in-command, felt a poke in his ribs and turned angrily to face his companion, the clerk Librarius Daphnis, who said, "Hesperian had to march in there without us, didn't he?"

"It makes a better impression if an officer enters alone. If he has a lot of flunkies with him it looks like he can't make his own decisions," said Mannus.

"How theatrical! Is he a soldier or an actor?"

As they passed through the doorway Mannus said, "I've never known an effective officer who wasn't both."

Daphnis laughed disdainfully. "I knew you'd say something like that."

They came out of the entrance into the great hall and saw Hesperian at the opposite end of the room, beyond the foot of the marble staircase, at the entrance to the peristyle, an enclosed garden in the center of the house surrounded on all sides by a two-story colonnade, but open to the morning sky. He was standing at ease, legs apart, arms folded on his chest, chatting with the young girl in the long white silk gown who, Mannus was later to learn, was Hathor, daughter of the murdered man.

Mannus and Daphnis came to attention, thumped their breastplates and, right arms extended, called out, "Ave Caesar!"

Hesperian turned to them with a nod. "Ave Caesar."

"Isn't this a beautiful garden?" He gestured through the doorway. "If this lovely young lady grants us permission," he touched Hathor on the forearm, "we can use the garden to discuss the case."

Hathor nodded, blushing.

The three men walked out among the carefully tended flowerbeds and Hesperian selected a circle of stone benches some distance from the entrance. "This will do," he said.

Daphnis seated himself on one of the benches and, from a sack tied to his belt, produced the tools of his trade: A scroll of papyrus, a reed pen, a block of dry ink, and a vial of water. He knew without being told that he would soon be required to record the testimony of the witnesses and suspects. He wet the ink block, touched the pen to it, drew an experimental line on the palm of his left hand and, satisfied, quickly rubbed it out against his other palm. "We won't have much time, sir. The Festival is the day after tomorrow and then . . ."

Hesperian said quietly: "Two days should be enough." He seated himself on the bench next to Daphnis.

Daphnis and Mannus exchanged glances; neither had forgotten their bet.

"Let's begin by having a look at the murder weapon," Hesperian said.

"I don't see how we can get hold of it without contacting the local authorities, sir," Mannus said. "You gave orders that you did not wish the local authorities to know we were here."

Hesperian nodded, fingering his chin thoughtfully. "I see, I see, but according to the preliminary hearing it was a standard issue Roman army pilum. Isn't that right?" The pilum was a javelin or throwing spear. Standing taller than a man, it had a wooden shaft and a long iron point. Only the tip of the point was tempered; the rest of the point was left untempered and relatively soft so that if it lodged in an enemy shield it would bend and be difficult to remove.

Mannus was carrying a scroll containing the transcript of the hearing, but he had read it over so often he almost knew it by heart. "Yes, sir. It was a pilum, sir."

"Our own men here must be carrying pilums almost identical to it," Hesperian said. "Go fetch one for me, will you, Mannus?"

Mannus hurried off and quickly returned with a pilum borrowed from one of the Praetorians. He handed it to Hesperian, who hefted it with an experienced hand. "Daphnis here thinks the weapon indicates our criminal might be a Roman soldier," Hesperian said, looking up at Mannus from under his shaggy gray eyebrows. "What do you think?"

"Sounds possible," Mannus said, straightening.

Hesperian shook his head. "Not to me. Why would a soldier use such an incriminating weapon?"

"He might," Daphnis said stubbornly. "It is impossible to underestimate the intelligence of the average army recruit."

"I say this thing could have been thrown by anyone," Mannus said. "Anyone could buy one. Did you notice as we came through the marketplace? There's all sorts of Roman military equipment for sale in Alexandria from those ghoulish battlefield scavengers who trade in souvenirs from the war in Judea."

"You're right when you say anyone could buy one," Hesperian answered, laying the spear aside. "But could anyone throw one? I wonder."

"What do you mean, sir?" Mannus said.

"Can you remember what happened the first time you picked up one of these things?" He indicated the pilum.

"Why . . . yes, sir, I can."

"Tell me, Mannus."

Mannus was embarrassed. "The point hit the ground, sir. I grabbed it too far back on the shaft."

"Don't let it bother you. Everyone does the same thing the first time they pick it up. It takes time to learn how to pick up a pilum, let alone how to use it." The centurion gave Mannus a reassuring pat on the arm. "Now, bring the slaves to me, one at a time. I saw a little black girl out there. She can be first. If she told any lies to the first investigators, she will have forgotten them by now."

■ ■ ■

Hesperian raised his hand for silence and Sabella momentarily ceased her babbling. She had been so relieved when she learned that she was indeed not going to be tortured that she had begun pouring out everything she knew about the Memnons in a wild disjointed torrent. "Wait a minute, child. Give my clerk a chance to catch up." Daphnis was writing frantically.

"What do you make of it?" Hesperian said to Mannus.

"It seems we were right about the suspects leaving Alexandria, sir. It's so odd, don't you think? I mean this girl Hathor going to Greece with her brother at just this time?"

Hesperian frowned. "Don't forget that Greece is a part of the Roman Empire. If I wanted to disappear, I don't think I'd go there. I'd go east, to India, as Adrastia and Demetrius were planning to do. In fact, once beyond the bounds of the Roman Empire,. what would prevent them from changing course and, steering around the war zone in Judea, ending up at the court of Nero's unfriendly friend, King Vologases of Parthia?"

"You may have something there," Mannus said.

Hesperian returned his attention to the slave. "And you say you saw Hathor in the Egyptian Quarter, dressed as a native?"

"Oh yes. Oh yes, sir. Anyway I think it was her."

Hesperian said little, only guiding her with an occasional question, mainly listening and thinking. Mannus had seen him operate like this before, feeling his way along until something seemed odd or suspicious. The centurion was so casual he seemed almost to be chatting, but it was quickly established that Sabella could account for her whereabouts at the time of old Odysseus Memnon's death. She had been in the kitchen with Hathor.

"You're sure of that, girl?"

"Oh yes, sir; yes, sir. Ask Hathor!"

"I will."

"And the other time, when Rophos died, I was helping with the serving, but I didn't have nothing to do with the soup. I was standing in the doorway when he fell."

"Tell me about that."

"Nothing to tell. Rophos swayed a little, Hathor saw him swaying and yelled out a warning to her father. Old man Memnon, see, was just about to taste the soup, but when she yelled, he didn't. Then poor Rophos, he went down flop on the floor. It was awful!" She threw up her arms.

"Let's get back to Memnon," muttered Daphnis, looking up from his scroll. "He's the important one."

"They were both killed by the same person," Mannus said impatiently.

"Are you sure?" Hesperian demanded. "Perhaps, since we have two murders, we also have two murderers." He raised an eyebrow.

Mannus and Daphnis considered this suggestion uncomfortably. Yes, it was possible.

"My scribe," Hesperian told the girl, "wants to talk about the night of Memnon's death. You're not very heavy, are you?"

"No, sir."

"In fact you must be the lightest person in this household."

"Except for the dwarfs, sir."

"The dwarfs. Yes." He paused, lost in thought for a moment, then said, "Do you think that if you tried to climb the vines on the outside of the house, they would hold your weight?"

"I don't know. Maybe so. I never tried."

"They're pretty thick, sir," Mannus put in. "Daphnis and I had a look at them as we were coming in. I'm sure they'd hold her weight."

"Would you hand me that spear?" Hesperian gestured toward the pilum that now lay at his feet on the multicolored bright mosaic walkway.

"Who, me?" Sabella said, bewildered.

"Yes."

She leaned over quickly and picked it up. Mannus saw that she'd grasped it too far back on the shaft and so was not surprised when the point dropped and struck the walkway with a clank. It seemed obvious that Sabella had never touched such a weapon before.

"That's fine," Hesperian said soothingly. "You can put it down now."

The pilum fell to the walkway with a clatter and Sabella stood looking down at it, round-eyed.

"Sabella," Hesperian continued. "You were present when Odysseus announced his impending conversion to Christianity, weren't you?"

"Yes, sir."

"You heard him say he planned to give all he owned to the Christians."

Mannus realized that Hesperian was now going over the findings of the earlier investigation, making sure of the correctness of every statement made in it. Thus far he had not found out anything much beyond what the others had already uncovered.

"Yes, sir. All he owned. And me he was going to sell!" This last was spoken in a tone of hurt indignation.

Mannus saw the centurion lean forward, suddenly interested. "You didn't want to be sold?" Hesperian asked softly.

"No sir! My Master and Mistress, they was good to me, like as if they was my own mama and papa. I'd of done anything to stay with them."

"Including murder?" Hesperian inquired mildly.

Sabella burst out in a flood of terrified protest: "It wasn't me, sir! Not me! I didn't do nothing! It wasn't me wanted the old man dead. No, sir! No, sir! It's Serapion who wanted the Master dead!"

"Serapion?" This was something new, something the previous investigation had missed.

"That's right, sir! Serapion, he told me he'd rather see his daddy dead than a Christian!"

■ ■ ■

"Demetrius Memnon," announced Wakar, then stepped back to admit Odysseus Memnon's brother. The old man entered the garden already talking, waving his bony arms and protesting his innocence. "I was with Adrastia in her room that night! There were serving maids in the room the whole time! Torture them! They'll tell you."

He reached the bench where Hesperian sat and stopped, wringing his hands. "Torture them," he repeated weakly.

Hesperian waved this suggestion aside. "Demetrius, don't you know that I've given my word not to use torture, and a Roman officer keeps his word, even to slaves?"

Demetrius spied the scroll in Mannus' hand. "Isn't that the transcript of the previous investigation?"

Hesperian nodded. "That's right."

"Then you know from that I'm telling the truth," the old man cried triumphantly. "My story and Adrastia's and the serving maids . . . they all agreed."

Hesperian asked, "You and Adrastia, as things stood, would be the ones to get the Memnon fortune, isn't that right?"

"Why yes, but . . ."

Hesperian raised his hand for silence. "And you have in fact now gained effective control over all that Odysseus had?"

"Yes . . ."

"Then we must consider the possibility that you and Adrastia and the servants are all lying to protect each other and the inheritance. The servants gain a home where they are treated, it would seem, with an unusual laxity. Adrastia retains her wealth and position and you, you gain most of all. The control of the Memnon financial empire rests in your hands and your hands alone. If motive were the only consideration, I wouldn't consider the others as suspects for one moment," he said, studying Demetrius with a calculating eye. "No, I wouldn't consider them for a minute. *Only you!*"

Demetrius was flustered, but still game. "Someone from outside..." he began weakly.

"The dogs rule that out," Hesperian said with amusement. "I noticed that when I arrived they had to be forcibly restrained from attacking my men, but," he added with a faint, mocking smile, "there may be an outside *influence* at work."

Demetrius blinked rapidly.

"There are those who say," continued the centurion, head cocked slightly to one side, "that you and your late brother traded outside the normal officially approved routes, that you traded, in fact, with nations who were enemies of Rome."

"Lies!" cried Demetrius in sudden panic.

"I think not," Hesperian said calmly.

"Do I look like a traitor?" Demetrius demanded, turning to Mannus who stood nearby, arms folded. Mannus shrugged, as if to say he had no idea. He thought, however, that the old Greek-Egyptian did indeed look guilty of something.

"How can you say that?" Demetrius asked Hesperian pleadingly.

"My instincts guide me," Hesperian explained. "You see, my friend, I have trained myself all my life in the art of criminal investigation. My usefulness to Rome and perhaps... yes, perhaps even my pride in myself as a man, is dependent on my success in tracking down the guilty." He had become suddenly confidential, as if speaking to an old friend.

Demetrius was thrown off balance by the change in tone. "What if you... what if you fail?" he blurted.

Hesperian stood up and drew his shortsword. Thoughtfully examining its good Spanish blade, he said, "Then I will know I have become an old man, and neither I nor my emperor has any use for the old. I once saw an old man, Demetrius, and this old man was a poet and teller of tales... very good at his trade. He slit his wrists at a dinner party and slowly bled to death, cynical jokes and sly obscenities on his lips to the last. We did not know he was dying. We did not even know he'd cut himself. And we did not know it when he was dead. We thought he was only sleeping, you see, or that he'd had perhaps too much wine." Hesperian sighed. "He was a brave and wise man, an inspiring example." He touched the shuddering Demetrius on the cheek with the sword point. "Wouldn't you like to die like that, old man?"

Demetrius recoiled, his hand raised to protect his cheek. "I don't want to die at all!"

"But you will." Hesperian sheathed the shortsword. "We all do. Our only choice in the matter is to die well or badly."

"Please, sir..." Demetrius was almost on the verge of tears. Daphnis glanced up from his work, amused. Mannus thought, *Daphnis loves nothing better than to see other men suffer.*

"Pick up the spear," commanded Hesperian, his tone suddenly harsh, almost angry.

"What?"

"The spear! Pick it up!"

Without thinking, Demetrius obeyed, stooping and gripping the shaft exactly at the center of gravity, which was much further forward than one might expect to look at it.

"You handle it well," commented the centurion.

"Thank you," answered Demetrius, hefting the pilum proudly and flashing a smile that slowly faded as full realization of the meaning of this remark dawned on him. He threw the spear down as if it were a snake and cried, "No! Not me! Serapion!"

"Serapion?"

"Serapion handles the pilum a thousand times better than I. Once at sea we were attacked by pirates . . . you should have seen him! Five pilums! Five seconds! Five dead pirates!" He clutched Hesperian's muscular arm. "Serapion has weapons, lots of weapons. Old Roman uniforms and armor. Spears. Swords. Knives. Everything! He collects them!"

"Are you trying to tell me Serapion is the murderer?" Hesperian gently removed the withered claw from his arm.

Demetrius stepped back, shaking his head dazedly. "He's so strange. Only the gods know what a man like that might do!"

Hesperian turned to Mannus. "Take this man out and bring in the wife—what's her name?—Adrastia."

"Yes, sir!"

Demetrius had to be led out by the elbow, shuffling like a drunken man.

■ ■ ■

Gaius Hesperian tendered the polite condolences customarily due a grieving widow, bowing, speaking gently.

Adrastia stood before him, listening with a frown, most impressive in her elaborately embroidered pale blue gown; her long white fingers, rings glittering in the sun, lightly touched her throat as a curious expression of annoyed impatience gradually appeared on her face.

His little speech proving too long for her, she gave a toss of her head that set her long black hair flying, then cut in: "I don't know who killed the old fool—certainly nobody can say I did it—but if you ever catch him, I want you to thank him for me . . . for all of us!"

Daphnis looked up in surprise.

Hesperian raised an eyebrow. "*Thank* him?"

"Of course, " she said firmly. "If he hadn't died when he did, he'd have brought ruin on us all. Whoever may have thrown that spear, it's the Christians who are at fault here. It's the Christians who seduced him with false promises of immortality into taking a position that—well—forced us all to consider the man who had once been, as you put it, a loving husband and father . . . forced us all to consider him our enemy, a menace to our whole way of life. I'm young, centurion, but I've noticed one thing. When a man speaks of rising to the level of a god, it's always a prelude to his descending lower than a beast."

Daphnis laughed, but Hesperian silenced him with a glare. Optio Mannus reflected that this woman, with her artful tongue, would not have been out of place back in Rome, at the court of Nero.

"Not all criminals, sir," she went on, "steal at knife-point or attack people in the streets. The more successful ones steal with words. With words they make off with not only a man's money, but with his mind as well. His mind, sir! They leave their victim a raving madman who throws his cloak and tunic to beggars and runs naked through the streets, screaming that the end of the world is at hand!"

Even sober Mannus was unable to suppress a smile at the sight of this determined young lady waving her finger under the centurion's nose.

Hesperian nodded. "I know, I know. There are Christians in Rome too. Not long ago they started a fire, so I'm told, that burned down a large part of the city. I was away from Rome at the time, but that's the official story."

"You see?" she cried. "Of all the disgusting and disreputable cults hatched from the perverted Jew mind, this is the worst! How can Nero allow it to continue?"

"Nero is a merciful emperor," Daphnis said, straight-faced.

"Of course," she said, turning to the handsome clerk. "But must his mercy extend only to criminals and madmen? What about respectable citizens? Are they to be left unprotected against these wolves who come to take advantage of an old man's failing mind to strip him of everything he owns?" She faced Hesperian again. "If it weren't for that dear sweet killer, you know where I'd be? I'd be in the streets, begging for my supper and sleeping under bridges with the filthy Jewish war refugees!"

Optio Mannus thought it much more likely she'd be in some high-class whorehouse, but he kept his thoughts to himself.

"Madame Adrastia," Hesperian said, trying to cut off her tirade.

"The Christians! The Christians are to blame!" she shouted.

"Silence!" commanded the centurion, then, more softly, added,

"Could you pick up that spear for me, please?"

She looked down at it for a moment with infinite distaste, then bent over and gingerly lifted it a couple of feet off the walkway. Thunk! The point fell and bounced.

"Ugh! Ugly thing," she said with a shudder, and dropped it. She wiped her delicate white hands on her robe.

Daphnis grinned openly.

"Please, my dear," said Hesperian. "I have a few questions about your husband's death."

"Of course," she answered.

Her version of the story agreed in every detail with those of the others, and when she went on to describe the death of Rophos, that story too agreed with the story told by the others. The agreement was, if anything, almost too perfect. "And I never went near the kitchen that day," she finished. "That's more than can be said for Serapion."

"And during the murder of your husband? Where was Serapion then?" Hesperian asked.

She shrugged. "I don't know."

"You didn't see him?"

"How could I? I was in my room with Demetrius and the maids."

"How neatly it all seems to fit together."

"Odd that you should say that. The man who questioned me in the previous investigation used almost exactly the same words." There was a certain smugness in her voice, as if she was daring Hesperian to find some flaw in her story. "But if there's anything else I can tell you . . ."

"No, my dear," Hesperian said thoughtfully. "You've already been more helpful than you probably realize. You can go now, but as you leave, tell them to send in Serapion."

As she strode away, her pert little bottom had a defiant, almost triumphant swing to it.

■ ■ ■

Serapion refused to be led into the garden, but marched proudly in, head high, a few steps ahead of stolid, plodding Mannus. The young aristocrat stopped before the now-seated Hesperian almost like a soldier at attention and Hesperian, looking up at him, blinked in the sun. The sun was higher now, above the red tile roof of the villa.

Hesperian shaded his eyes with his hand, took a deep breath and began: "Your honesty can save everyone much anxiety and uncertainty, my friend. Whatever you've done, you're not ashamed of it, are you?"

"Certainly not."

"Then tell me the truth. You killed them, didn't you?"

Serapion didn't answer.

Hesperian sighed and went on. "Accept the gratitude of your entire family. Accept my admiration too, because, while I can't approve the breaking of the law, I can admire a gentleman too proud to lie. You killed old Odysseus, didn't you?"

"No."

Hesperian frowned, and slapped his swagger stick against the palm of his hand. "Then I presume you can prove that at the time of the murder you were somewhere else. Everyone else seems able to."

"No." Serapion's triangular face reddened slightly.

"Where were you then?"

"In my room, alone."

"You expect me to believe that?"

"Believe what you like. It's the truth."

"And the previous investigator accepted that story?"

"Of course. He knew I was a gentleman."

There was a note of falseness in Serapion's voice. Mannus could hear it plainly.

"At least he knew you were a man of wealth," Hesperian said coldly.

"Do you want money too?" demanded the young man with contempt.

"Did you give money to the previous investigator?"

"It was an experiment. I wanted to find out if Roman officials are really as corrupt as everyone says they are."

Mannus grinned openly at Daphnis, who smiled feebly and lowered his eyes to the scroll he was working on. It seemed to Mannus that Hesperian had once again triumphed, and that Daphnis had as good as lost the bet already. Mannus could almost taste the wine . . . nothing but the finest Falernian. And let it be a red wine, but not too heavy.

Hesperian ignored the insulting implications of Serapion's remark. "Sabella claims you said you'd rather see your father dead than a Christian."

"I don't deny it."

Point by point, Hesperian ran down the list of incriminating evidence that had so quickly piled up against the young Memnon. Serapion denied nothing, made no effort to defend himself, except that several times he repeated, in the tone of a parent explaining something to a retarded child, "But I didn't kill anyone."

Finally he added impatiently, "And they tell me, Roman, that you're testing people's skill with the pilum." Serapion bent over and picked up the weapon with the hand of an expert. He pointed to a wooden ram-headed sphinx at the far end of the garden. "I can spear that sphinx right between the eyes. Watch!"

He raised the pilum to eye level, holding it perfectly balanced, stepped back, and extended his left hand. His form was perfect, worthy of an Olympic athlete.

With a grunt, Serapion hurled the pilum. It hissed faintly as it flew, and there was a resounding, solid thunk as it lodged in the ram's head . . . right between the eyes. Serapion gave a little laugh, half pride and half nervous exhilaration.

Hesperian looked up at him, trying to appear unimpressed. "My friend, don't you realize you might as well have driven that point between your own eyes? That throw may well kill you."

"Kill me? Only my body, Centurion."

Serapion turned on his heel and strode out and, though he had not been given permission to leave or even asked for it, no one made a move to stop him. Optio Mannus said softly to Hesperian, "I think we have our man, sir, and it's not yet noon!"

Centurion Gaius Hesperian glanced up at the sun but did not reply.

■ ■ ■

"Let me go, damn you!" shouted Hathor, struggling in the grip of the guard who was dragging her into the garden.

He held her firmly but somewhat awkwardly as he thumped his chest and gave Hesperian a stiff-arm salute. "Ave Caesar!"

"Ave Caesar," replied the centurion. "Now what's the trouble with her?"

"She was eavesdropping on you, sir."

"Why didn't you stop her?" Hesperian demanded. Then, when the soldier did not answer, he went on. "You're allowing them to come and go as they please. They're talking to each other, comparing notes, listening in on us here. By the gods, soldier, I expect some semblance of discipline!"

"I . . . I didn't know the Memnons were prisoners," the poor soldier stammered.

There was a tense pause, then Hesperian sighed and said more agreeably, "And so they're not . . . except, of course, that they can't leave."

The soldier saluted and departed.

Hathor stood before the Romans, a defiant tilt to her chin, and without waiting for Hesperian to begin questioning her, announced: "My brother is lying."

Hesperian raised a bushy eyebrow.

"He was not alone in his room, as he claimed," Hathor said. The faintest of breezes stirred in the garden, but it was enough to press the sheer white gown against her body. Mannus licked his dry lips and, almost embarrassed, looked away.

"Someone was with him?" Hesperian prompted.

"I was with him!" Hathor said with a toss of the head.

"Really? Then why didn't he tell us that?"

"He was protecting me."

"From what?"

"I have . . . a lover." She lowered her gaze and began toying with her gown, near the waist.

"Go on, my dear."

"No one must know, you see. And Serapion was . . . was bringing me a message."

"From your lover?"

"From my . . . lover." She seemed to find it difficult to use the word "lover," as if it made ugly something that was not ugly to her.

"And you expect us to believe that your brother would risk his life to protect your secret?"

"Of course he would!" Once again she was proud and defiant. "But I can't let him!"

"Such nobility," muttered the cynical Daphnis.

"All right then," Hesperian said, sitting back with an air that seemed to say that at last he was getting somewhere, "Tell me the name of this lover of yours."

"I won't! I don't have to."

"Oh, but you do."

"I won't tell, and Serapion won't either. He knows how to keep a secret, and so do I. We'd rather risk being tried as murderers than tell." She looked so fierce that Hesperian almost burst out laughing.

"Then I must assume that it is you who are lying."

"Me? Why?"

"Your slave Sabella testified to being with you—in the kitchen—at the time of your father's death."

"I wasn't in the kitchen. I was in my brother's room."

"Then why did the slave girl tell us you were in the kitchen?"

"She's trying to protect me too."

Hesperian turned to Mannus. "Did you hear that? This whole family—slaves and all—are right out of some myth of the virtues of Republican Rome."

"Yes, sir," said Mannus.

"The greater the seeming virtue, the greater the hidden corruption," Daphnis put in suavely. It was a saying he'd picked up in Nero's court, where Mannus had heard it quoted so many times he was sick of it.

Hesperian returned to the interrogation. "Hathor, my dear, don't you realize that if Sabella was lying and Serapion does not support your story, then you yourself must come under grave suspicion? Don't you realize that?"

"But . . . I couldn't have done it!"

"Why not, young lady?"

"Because I loved him. I loved the old man! I could never kill him, not for anything."

Daphnis looked up from his writing and stared at her with open disbelief, but Mannus, studying the centurion's face, saw that Hesperian had taken a liking to the young creature. *You old fool*, Mannus thought, but said nothing. Mannus knew about Hesperian's weakness for such females, but had never seen it stand in the way of duty . . . not until now.

"I see, I see," the centurion said. "Well, you may go now." He dismissed her with a vague wave of his hand.

Mannus, worried, said, "Aren't you going to give her the pilum test, sir?"

"No, no, the pilum's stuck in that statue over there."

"But, sir, I could run and get you a fresh one."

"Never mind, Mannus. Look at her." He gestured toward the white-gowned figure now walking without haste toward the exit from the garden. "Could a delicate young lady like that have the strength or skill to hurl such a weapon?"

Mannus sighed. "So you believe her?" He was frankly disappointed. "Then I guess that clears Serapion. I could have sworn he was our man."

Hesperian was still watching Hathor disappear into the house and seemed not to have heard.

"Sir, I said that I guess that clears Serapion," said Mannus gruffly.

"Oh? What's that you say?" Hesperian looked around blankly.

Daphnis laid down his reed pen on the bench and said disgustedly, "You shouldn't have been so sure Hathor was unskilled with the pilum. According to the records of the original inquest, this girl was brought up as a boy. She's as skillful with the pilum as any Roman soldier."

Hesperian was surprised and, it seemed to Mannus, dismayed. Musing, the centurion said: "Was she with Serapion, or was she with Sabella after all? Perhaps she was actually with neither!"

Daphnis turned to Mannus. "You thought Serapion was our man? Wouldn't it be charming if all the time we were looking for a man, the killer was really . . ." His lip curled with distaste ". . . *a woman!*"

Chapter Two

THANKS TO THE MASSIVE STONE from which it was built, the Memnon mansion provided, in its inner rooms, a cool shelter from the stifling noonday heat. In one of these dim windowless rooms, a small auxiliary dining room whose walls were decorated with a mosaic mural of Osiris and Mother Isis enthroned in the Land of the Dead, the Memnons gathered for a spiritless lunch.

"No desert?" inquired a concerned Wakar, leaning over the couch where Hathor, together with a gloomy Serapion, reclined.

"No. No, thank you," Hathor replied, nervously toying with the golden dung beetle pendant on her heavy necklace. She had been sweating, and the damp white silk of her gown clung to her flesh.

"And you, Master Serapion?" the eunuch asked.

"I'm not hungry," Serapion said, almost angrily.

The slave offered his basket of assorted fruits to Adrastia, then to Demetrius, but no one showed the slightest interest, in spite of the fact that they had eaten almost nothing during the other courses of the meal.

"Here, gimp!" the Roman guard standing near the door called out. "There's one man in this room who still has the belly the gods blessed him with."

Wakar limped over and stood submissively while the soldier picked through the fruit, selecting the most attractive to stuff between his broken teeth. With his mouth full, the soldier went on, "Good conscience, good appetite. That's what they say." He chuckled, juice dripping from the point of his bristly chin.

Serapion looked across at the Praetorian with unconcealed disgust, but the other Memnons totally ignored their unwelcome guest.

Wakar turned to leave.

"Hey, gimp!" snapped the Roman. "Did I tell you you could go?"

Wakar stopped, his face in a frozen smile.

"That's it, gimp. I'll take one more bunch of dates to keep me going." He helped himself. "*Now* you can go."

Wakar bowed and departed.

Hathor was furious, but she made no outward sign. How dare this swinish Roman bully her slave, the slave who was almost a father to her? She had an impulse to leap to her feet and protest, perhaps even to report the guard to Hesperian. Old Hesperian liked her and might listen to her, might even have the soldier flogged. That would be satisfying! At some other time that is exactly what she would have done, but now she found her usual moral resolution wavering. Was it that remark the soldier had made about good conscience? How much did he know? How much had Hesperian guessed and told this guard in those brief whispered conferences before lunch? There must be something. Why else would this simple soldier grow so bold? How else would he dare?

She could not restrain herself from taking a quick glance at the guard. He had obviously been gazing at her body, and now, when she locked eyes with him, it was she who looked away first. The game of glances . . . she'd played it many times, but usually she'd won. This was humiliating.

She'd heard a saying: "To be brave, you must first be without secrets."

Without secrets! Would she ever again be able to enjoy the luxury of being without secrets?

Speaking loudly, as if to make sure the Roman overheard her, Adrastia burst out, "I believe I have the answer."

"Oh?" Demetrius turned toward her politely.

"It doesn't have to be one of us that did these dreadful things." Adrastia, as she spoke, was watching the guard from the corner of her eye.

"Who then?" Demetrius asked.

"Octavia! Octavia, Odysseus' first wife." Adrastia looked around at them in triumph.

"How can you say such a thing?" Hathor demanded.

"Please Hathor, spare us your misplaced loyalty. Think how she must have hated the old man for divorcing her and exiling her to Rome. Think how she must have longed for revenge! By Isis, I would have wanted revenge if he'd done the same to me."

"She's not like you," Hathor said, with venom.

"She's not petty," added Serapion.

Even Demetrius spoke up. "She's a good woman." He nodded slowly to himself, like a judge satisfied with his verdict.

"What's this?" cried Adrastia, as if appealing to the gods Osiris and Isis enthroned in the mural on the wall. "Are they all against me? I call the gods to witness . . . if she had been so very good, why did the old boy kick her out of his bed and pull me in? Can you answer me that?"

Serapion, forefinger to lips, said in a low voice, "Please, Mother. Must you babble everything you know?" He nodded meaningfully in the direction of the Roman guard, who now had his back to them, eating the last of his dates and seemingly paying no attention to them.

"Me? Babble?" She shook her finger in Hathor's general direction. "You want to see a big mouth? There! Your sister! Have you seen how she talks to that vile ape, Hesperian? I'm sure that, thanks to her, we haven't one family secret left!"

Wakar had entered the room, bowed slightly to the guard's back, and come shuffling up to the table to clear away the dirty dishes and uneaten food.

"That's unfair," Demetrius said. "You don't know . . ."

"I'm never unfair!" Adrastia howled. "She's the one who's been babbling! I know she has!"

Adrastia's outbursts had a calming effect on Demetrius, making him feel that, as her elder, he ought to calm her somehow, make her behave. He leaned forward and laid a bony hand on her wrist. "There, there, my dear. We all know that if there's a babbler around here, it's your little friend Sabella."

"Sabella?" Adrastia stared at him blankly.

Hathor sat up suddenly. "Sabella?" she echoed, looking around with quick anxious eyes. "Where is that girl? I haven't seen her since before lunch . . . and she usually hangs around at mealtime, hoping to get her little paws on some scraps. Where is she?"

Demetrius shrugged. "Who cares?"

"I haven't seen her," Serapion said.

Hathor caught hold of Wakar's arm. "Wakar Tell me! Where's Sabella?"

He said gently, "She went somewhere with Centurion Hesperian."

There was a moment of stunned silence, then Demetrius said, puzzled, "I wonder where?"

Hathor's voice was an anguished whisper. "I think I know."

■　■　■

The little Egyptian landlord held the small, dull greenish-bronze portrait bust in his fat hands, examining it carefully.

"Are you sure it's a good likeness?" he asked.

"A very good likeness," Hesperian answered. He had found the head in Odysseus' bedroom and instantly realized that it might prove useful. It was not in the flattering Greek style that made everyone look like a god or goddess, but rather was in the realistic Roman style that delighted in showing every pore and wart. It could not have looked more like Hathor if it had been her real head turned to bronze, and if it was beautiful it was only because the subject was beautiful.

"She has light brown hair," Mannus prompted. "You're sure you haven't seen her?"

"Never!" The fat little man returned the portrait bust to Mannus with impatience.

Daphnis grasped Sabella by her skinny wrist and snarled, "If you're lying, slave . . ."

"No! No!" she squealed, trying to wriggle free. "I saw her! I saw her!"

Hesperian laid a restraining hand on Daphnis' shoulder, then turned to thank the landlord for his help.

"It was nothing," the fat man said with a bow. "I am always ready to show my friendship for the senate and people of Rome."

The group—Hesperian, Mannus, Daphnis and Sabella—mumbled their farewells to the landlord and stepped out of the dark doorway into the hot light of early afternoon. Like most of the streets here in Rhakotis, the Egyptian quarter of Alexandria, the street in which they stood was narrow, dirty, and crowded. As a donkey loaded with dried peat clopped past, they were forced to press themselves against a wall to let it by.

"You're too impatient," said Hesperian to Daphnis as they continued on their way.

"Too impatient, sir?" Daphnis replied defensively. "We've shown that head to almost all the landlords and innkeepers in the neighborhood and not one . . ."

"There's a difference between almost all and all," Hesperian said with a faint smile.

"There's another inn up ahead," said Mannus, pointing. Mannus had felt sure Hesperian would find what he was looking for, so he was pleased but not surprised when the old woman who kept this next inn recognized the bust instantly. The woman, whose name was Hecate, was delighted to volunteer not only what she knew, but also what she only suspected.

"She called herself Octavia," Hecate cackled, looking up at Hesperian from the doorstep where she sat. "Yes, I know her all right. She lives right here in this building." She gestured with a gnarled hand toward a narrow passage leading back into the building. At the end of the passage, dimly visible in the gloom, was a crude ladder leading to the second floor.

The old woman lowered her voice. "I knew she was no common street girl. She tried to talk like one, but she didn't fool old Hecate. Her Greek was too good, and when I tried to speak to her in Egyptian, like people talk around here, she didn't understand hardly a word. I knew then, sir, that she was some rich aristocratic Macedonian-Greek lady living under a false name, probably so her highborn family and friends wouldn't know she was the whore of a common Roman soldier." She favored them with a grotesque wink.

"Did you ever speak to this soldier?" Hesperian asked.

"No, sir. It was always the woman who gave me the rent money. The soldier always stood back in the shadows, like he didn't want me to see his face."

Hesperian leaned forward. "Was he wearing his uniform?"

"When he was wearing anything at all," crowed the crone.

"Can you tell me anything about the uniform?"

"It was the same as yours, sir. All Roman uniforms are alike, aren't they?"

Hesperian frowned, frustrated. "The color . . . was it red? Black? Blue?"

"I don't remember. Never did see him in a good strong light. He came and went at night, you see. Otherwise he stayed in his room."

"Can we see the room?"

"Of course! Glad to show it to you!" She dragged herself to her feet and led the way down the dim passage and up the ladder. They paused in the second floor hall while she unlocked the door with a large rusty iron key she wore, along with several others, on a cord around her neck.

There was a foul smell in the room. Mannus noticed it the moment they entered, but it took him a while to locate the source of the odor, some decaying fruit in a dish on the floor next to the bed. There were ants on the fruit, millions of them. Mannus shuddered. He could smell the stale sweat in the dirty linen bedsheets, the rancid olive oil in the unlit lamp that stood on a rickety table, and the stench of hot fermenting camel dung that wafted in through the slightly-open shuttered window.

"Disgusting," sniffed Daphnis.

"But understandable," Hesperian added. "Hathor is used to having slaves do all the housework. It's not easy for her to get used to having to do such things for herself."

A pile of rags was in one corner of the room. Hesperian crossed quickly, knelt, and examined them.

"This tunic must be Hathor's," he said, holding up a bit of soiled cloth.

"It seems to be about the right size," said Daphnis. "But how a fine lady like her could bring herself to wear such a thing . . ."

"A woman in love will do anything," Hesperian said. He had picked up another tunic, stood up, and was measuring it against himself. "Our soldier must have been tall." He glanced toward the old woman for confirmation.

"Oh yes, yes, he was a tall one. That's right," she said.

There was a belt there, too—a worn army belt. Hesperian slipped it around his waist.

"Too small for you, sir," Mannus said.

"Our soldier . . . he's thin, isn't he?" Hesperian asked Hecate.

"That's right. Now that you mention it, I remember he's quite a skinny fellow."

"Search the room," commanded Hesperian.

They searched, but found nothing more.

Hesperian turned to the old woman and began, "I want to thank you for . . ." He stopped, squinting at the wall.

"What's wrong?" Mannus asked.

"There's a scratch up there on the wall. You see it?"

"Yes," Mannus answered, puzzled.

Hesperian's eye darted toward the floor. "And there's another on the floor." He measured the distance between the two scratches with his eye. "There was a pilum standing here. It's just the right distance between the scratches!"

"I'm not surprised," Daphnis said airily. "It's obvious what happened. Odysseus found out his daughter was overly fond of Roman soldiers, and she had to kill him to silence him."

Hesperian sighed. "I would not like to think so. She seems such a gentle creature." He turned to Hecate. "Is the soldier here often?"

"Oh yes. Sometimes I saw him slip in every evening for weeks at a time."

"That's strange," muttered Hesperian.

"Strange? Why?" asked Hecate, but Hesperian, deep in thought, was already leaving.

"Post a watch outside the inn," he told Mannus. "But have him dress as a civilian. I want to know immediately if this mysterious soldier appears."

■ ■ ■

It was mid-afternoon in Alexandria; hot, humid, oppressive.

Mannus, on a brown mare, rode ahead, trying as best he could to clear the way for Hesperian, who followed on his black stallion, the portrait bust of Hathor in his lap and Sabella gleefully perched on the saddle in front of him. Daphnis had remained behind to keep an eye on the inn until a suitably unobtrusive soldier could be sent to relieve him.

"Clear the way! Clear the way for a Roman officer!" Mannus cried, but out of a combination of sluggishness caused by the heat and a sullen resentment toward all Romans, the Alexandrian citizens seemed very reluctant to obey.

Thus Mannus was quite irritable and morose when they finally came in sight of the gates of the Memnon estate. One of the Praetorians, on foot, could be seen hurrying a pair of fat prisoners along ahead of them. Mannus took no notice, but Hesperian, with a slap of his reins, galloped on ahead and hailed the soldier with a hearty, "Ave Caesar."

"Ave Caesar," the soldier answered, with a stiff-armed salute.

"And what do we have here?" Hesperian was dismounting as he spoke, then reached up to help Sabella down.

The soldier laid a hand on the shoulder of a plump little man in a brown wool tunic. "Let me introduce you, sir, to T. Vindaius Ariovestus, drug dealer and compounder of panaceas." The little man seemed speechless with terror. The soldier turned to an equally fat and equally frightened middle-aged woman. "And this is his wife, Livia."

"Good afternoon, friends of Rome," Hesperian said to the prisoners, then added, "I trust you *are* friends of Rome."

The prisoners said nothing, only stared at him.

He turned to the soldier. "And why, may I ask, have you placed these good people under arrest?"

"They've made two mistakes, sir."

"So?"

"The first was to sell poison to someone who may well be our murderer."

"And the second?"

"The second was to discuss it at a tavern where they were overheard by men willing to talk in return for a few silver drachmas." He gave his moneybag a knowing jingle.

Hesperian's voice grew softer, almost gentle. "Vindaius, I have no wish to harass an honest merchant. If you'll simply tell me to whom you sold that poison, I'm sure I'll have no need to bother you any further."

The little man awkwardly rubbed the sweat from his bald head with his gross forearm. "Mercy, sir. Have mercy."

"Of course. Just answer my question."

"But that's just it. I don't know who it was! It might have been a woman . . ."

"A woman?"

"I couldn't see her face, but we all know poison is a woman's weapon. A man settles his affairs with a tempered blade."

"So you say it was a woman?"

"It might have been," said the miserable little man. "I told you . . . I don't know."

Hesperian stood a moment, vexed, then, "If you saw this poisoner again perhaps . . ."

"Perhaps I might recognize her? It's . . . it's possible."

A faint smile appeared on Hesperian's thin lips.

"Come into the house and we shall see," the centurion said, leading the way.

■ ■ ■

Book Two Chapter Two

The Memnons had remained at table, though the food had long since been cleared away and the conversation had degenerated to dispirited and sporadic trivialities. It was in one of those all-too-frequent embarrassed pauses that Hathor heard the footsteps approaching and glanced up to see the guard at the door snap to attention, thump his breast and give a straight-arm salute.

"Ave Caesar!" he bellowed as Gaius Hesperian entered.

Behind the tall balding Roman came Mannus and a fat middle-aged couple, Alexandrians of a fairly low social class from the cut of their somewhat crude tunics.

Hathor, Serapion, Adrastia, Demetrius; all turned as one to face the newcomers, but Hathor, after a moment, shrank back as if to hide behind her brother Serapion, who continued to stare at Hesperian with a superior smile.

"Good afternoon, honored friends," began Hesperian with a slight inclination of his head. "If I may have a moment . . ."

Blustering old Demetrius, made more-than-usually brave by wine, interrupted. "How long are you going to hold us under house arrest, eh?"

Hesperian, unperturbed, answered, "I assure you that when the port opens the day after tomorrow, you will all be free to go wherever you like except, of course, for those guilty of some serious crime. Until then, where is there to go?"

"Can we depend on that?" demanded Serapion defiantly.

"Absolutely." Hesperian met the tall young Alexandrian's gaze, unimpressed by the Memnon pride. "I'm a sportsman. If I don't bag my prey by then, I'll concede defeat gracefully."

Adrastia protested, "We're not prey! We're human beings, not animals."

The guard at the door laughed and said, "In the arena it's not always easy to tell the difference."

Hesperian silenced him with a frown.

Demetrius drew himself up with drunken dignity. "I fail to see the humor of your underling's little joke." He swayed, blinking. "Perhaps that is because, sir, if you are successful, one or more of us might actually end up wrestling with a tiger or sparring with a gorilla."

The centurion shook his head. "No, no. It is rare for persons of your station in life to end up in the arena or the mines. A single merciful stroke of the sword . . . that's the worst you have to fear, and it might be possible to escape punishment completely if, let us say, the victim turned out to be an enemy of Rome."

Demetrius fell silent, an expression of thoughtful guile on his bony features.

All this time the plump little Alexandrian and his wife had been studying the faces of the four Memnons, their eyes darting from face to face with increasing desperation. Hesperian turned abruptly and, with a gesture toward the four, commanded, "Choose, Vindaius!"

Hathor closed her eyes and tried to imagine Mother Isis bending over her, protecting her. She had her doubts about the gods. She was not like her brother, who almost seemed to take the Immortal Beings for granted, but now she felt suddenly that Isis must be real. She must be real because . . . because poor mortals needed her so much.

After a long painful silence, Vindaius blurted out, "I can't choose! It could have been any one of them, or none."

Hesperian turned to his wife. "And you, Livia?"

"All I saw was a cloaked figure in the distance."

"How did this figure walk? Quickly? Slowly? Like a man? or like a woman?"

"I don't remember," cried Livia in an anguished voice. "It was so long ago."

"Nor do I," wailed her husband, wringing his hands.

"Perhaps if you heard the voice . . ." suggested Hesperian urgently.

"He always spoke in a whisper," the shopkeeper moaned.

Hesperian's broad hands lifted skyward, then fell limply at his sides in a gesture of defeat. "Take them out and let them go, Mannus."

Mannus obeyed, glancing at Hesperian with weary sympathy. When they had departed, Hesperian turned once again to the four Memnons around the low table.

"So, they saw nothing," Serapion remarked.

"Almost nothing," answered the centurion. "But I," he added. "I saw something."

There was an uneasy stir around the table.

Hathor opened her eyes and realized with a start that Hesperian was now looking directly at her.

"Hathor," he said gently. "Could I have a few words with you, my dear, in private?"

She got up from her place on the couch beside Serapion and walked unsteadily across the room, and it seemed to her that the Osiris and Isis who sat in judgement in the mural on the wall might very well be sitting in judgement—of her.

Then she felt Hesperian's powerful fingers on her elbow, guiding her out of the room, down a passageway, out into the bright courtyard garden. There he released his grip and they walked slowly, side by side, along the stone walkways between the flowerbeds, saying nothing.

"I found your room in the Egyptian quarter," Hesperian said at length.

"I thought that's what you were doing, Centurion."

"Call me Gaius, Hathor. It makes me feel young again to have someone like you address me by my first name."

"Gaius." She tried the name on her lips experimentally.

"Yes."

She paused to pick a flower. "All right. If you like, Gaius."

"I do not wish to pry into your private life. I can understand why you might want to keep it a secret if you were living with a common Roman soldier. He *is* a Roman soldier isn't he? Your lover?"

She nodded slowly. "I can't seem to conceal anything from you, Gaius. But please don't tell the family."

"Why should I tell them a lie?"

"What's that?" She faced him abruptly.

"It's a lie, Hathor. Your lover is not a Roman soldier. He dresses like a Roman soldier, but no Roman soldier could spend so much time away from camp. Every night for weeks at a time . . . it isn't possible. You could fool the neighbors in Rhakotis, but if you'd seriously wanted to fool a Roman officer you should have met with your love not more than once a week, twice at the most. That I could have believed."

She sighed. "It seems we were not as clever as we thought. You know, that never once occurred to us."

"Cleverness does not become such a charming young lady. Leave cleverness to old men like me and embrace honesty instead, a grace that is much easier for the inexperienced."

"Honesty, Gaius?"

"Tell me your lover's name."

"No. I can't."

"You must. We found certain marks in your little love nest, marks that indicate a pilum was kept there, standing against the wall." He took her hands in his, spoke more softly. "You are an intelligent woman, but love and loyalty may have made you blind to certain unpleasant possibilities."

"Speak plainly, Gaius."

"This lover, this false soldier you are trying to protect . . . he may be the man who murdered your father."

She shook her hands free of his and stepped back from him, and her voice, when she spoke, was full of bitterness. "You are an intelligent man, Gaius, but you don't understand women. Don't you see? That's the very reason I can never, ever tell!"

Chapter Three

AS THE SUN NEARED THE HORIZON the temperature began to drop, slowly at first, then more quickly, and a cooling breeze came in off the Mediterranean.

Hesperian once again held court in the courtyard garden, questioning and re-questioning everyone in the Memnon household, but his questions, even to the loyal Mannus, seemed pointless, stupid, almost absent-minded. Finally, one of the Praetorians arrived from somewhere out in the city and, taking Hesperian to one side, whispered something in the centurion's ear.

A moment later, with renewed energy, Hesperian sent Mannus to fetch Demetrius.

"Ave Caesar," said old Demetrius, as he stumbled into the courtyard and gave a drunken salute. "Ave Caesar," he repeated, swaying and almost falling. It was obvious the man had spent the afternoon drinking unwatered wine.

"Ave Caesar," Hesperian answered, standing up and beckoning. The Roman's voice was deep and calm, and Demetrius seemed pleased to hear it. Moving in an almost-straight line, Demetrius reeled toward the benches in the center of the garden where Hesperian waited.

"Ave Caesar," the old man said a third time as he collapsed on one of the benches.

Hesperian settled himself on a stone bench across from him. At his side sat Daphnis, once again busy taking notes after having returned from a stint of watching the inn, and a little ways away stood Mannus, arms folded on his chest, listening.

The garden was suffused with a sulphurous red glow and Mannus wondered how long it would be before there was no longer enough light for Daphnis to continue working. The smell of supper was on the air. Was that roast pork? Mannus found that his mouth was watering.

"I didn't do it," announced Demetrius firmly.

"What didn't you do?" asked Hesperian.

"Nothing. I didn't do nothing." He glowered at them belligerently.

"Someone did something." Hesperian was sweet reason personified.

"The slaves did everything. The slaves always do everything. That's what I keep telling you, but nobody ever listens to me." He leaned forward and lowered his voice. "A Roman friend of mine—oh, yes, I have Roman friends—he was a kind man, and a moderate man, and a very easy master to his slaves. Yes, he was. He would get up in the middle of a drinking party and, right in front of his slaves, he'd tell everyone a slave was just as good as a Roman citizen. He'd say that, right in front of everybody. I heard him myself. And he'd put his arm around a slave's shoulder and sing songs with the lowborn barbarian right there in front of everybody. By the gods, sir, it made me vomit!" He looked like be was about to vomit. "And you know what happened to that fine Roman gentleman?"

"No, what?"

"In the dead of night his slaves crept into his bedroom and tied him spread-eagle to his bed. Then, one by one, they killed his wife and children while he watched . . . killed them all by slow torture. They used little knives heated over a candle flame, sir. Little knives! One little cut at a time. They killed the Roman gentleman last. And those slaves . . . the next day they tried to pretend it was robbers that got in somehow. Do robbers torture like that? I ask you, do they?"

"No, I suppose not."

"Well, the Roman officer who investigated wasn't fooled. He put the slaves to the torture, and sure enough, two days later there was a full confession. Every slave in the household had been in on it, even the women and children. And it was totally without motive! They didn't even steal anything. Just plain bloodlust."

"And you think something like that happened to your brother."

"Exactly! Exactly! At last someone who understands! Why, my brother Odysseus would still be alive today if he'd followed the wise precaution of executing every slave in his household as soon as Rophos was murdered, rather than wasting time trying to find the murderer."

Daphnis broke in, "It's getting dark. Maybe we'd better have someone bring out a lamp."

"No," Hesperian said, rising to his feet. "That's enough questions for the moment. Let's go in to supper."

Grinning with relief, Demetrius got up and, as he almost lost his balance, Mannus steadied him.

Hesperian pretended not to notice, but as he passed the old man, said casually, "By the way, Demetrius, I've taken the liberty of inviting a guest to dine with us tonight."

"Who?" Demetrius asked, still grinning.

"A business associate of yours, or so I'd gather from the transcript of the first hearings. Simon Baal."

The grin vanished.

■ ■ ■

Mannus, guiding Demetrius into the dining room with a gentle pressure on the elbow, felt the old man shrink back at the sight of Simon Baal.

Simon had his back to them, and was chatting with Adrastia, making polite conversation in a way that gave the impression he did not know her well. Hathor and Serapion were already reclining, sharing a couch at the far end of the table.

"The Jew has a reputation for being clever at business. I find him rather stupid myself," Simon was saying with an expressive gesture of his small bejeweled hand. His long black hair, hanging in braids down his back, bounced and jiggled with every movement; his generous sleeves, richly brocaded in a serpentine design of silver and gold thread, created a breeze in the heavy air strong enough to set the lamp flames dancing. He spoke Greek in the flowery Alexandrian style, with the flavor of a foreign accent.

Hearing footsteps, he turned and smiled up into the face of the approaching Hesperian. "Ave Caesar," said Simon Baal, saluting. "You must be Centurion Hesperian."

Hesperian returned the salute. "Thank you for coming."

"I felt I must." Baal cast a meaningful glance at two of Hesperian's black-cloaked Praetorians who had taken up position near the door.

"Simon!" Demetrius shuffled forward, hand extended. Simon regarded him with unconcealed alarm, and Mannus smiled, almost able to read the dark little man's mind. Here was Demetrius, obviously drunk, perhaps overly talkative. Here was Simon Baal, unexpectedly invited to supper with representatives of Nero's personal guard. No, it did not look healthy, not healthy at all.

The two grasped each other by the wrist for a limp handshake. Simon said, "Demetrius! It's good to see you. Now can you tell me what this is all about?"

Before Demetrius could answer, Hesperian broke in. "Come, let's be comfortable. We can talk as we eat." He guided Demetrius to the couch where Adrastia was already seating herself.

Hesperian's actions were, for once, clear to Mannus. Simon and Demetrius must not be allowed an opportunity to compare notes. Each must be left to wonder what the other may have told Hesperian, and neither must be given any clear idea what Hesperian had found out for himself.

As Hesperian passed close to Mannus, the centurion said in a low, almost inaudible voice, "Did you see their faces? Be prepared to make an arrest, but not, of course, until after dessert." The smile that passed between the two Romans was not lost on Simon and Demetrius, who looked on with scarcely-concealed dismay.

Simon, however was still able to maintain a fairly suave facade, even when Hesperian laid a broad hand on his narrow shoulder and said,

"And you, sir, may share my couch, in the place of honor."

When all were in their places, Simon found that both Hesperian and Adrastia were between him and Demetrius. Mannus, strolling over to join Daphnis and the guards by the door, noted in the lamp light the glisten of sweat on Simon's forehead.

"I win," Mannus told Daphnis. "Hesperian says to be ready to make an arrest." His voice was barely a whisper.

Daphnis frowned.

Hesperian rang a small silver bell.

Sabella came in with a basket of fruit, and the meal began.

As they progressed from one course to another, Adrastia monopolized the conversation with anecdotes about her "darling dwarfs." There was an edge of repressed hysteria to her voice. Hathor and Serapion occasionally answered her in muttered monosyllables. Demetrius and Simon Baal said nothing, ate little, and tried not to look at each other.

"Well, Demetrius," Hesperian said finally, with a frightening gentleness, "it is fortunate that we are not all as silent as you."

"What . . . what do you mean by that?" Demetrius demanded. His voice was so loud that every eye in the room turned to stare at him.

Hesperian did not immediately answer, and when he did his voice was even gentler, more deadly. "Your friend Simon Baal here is famous for his conversational skill."

"No, no . . ." Simon protested. His teeth, exposed in a horrified grin, seemed to glow in the fitful lamp light.

"Such modesty!" The centurion raised a bushy eyebrow. "Why, your fame has spread all the way to Rome. Nero himself once remarked that he'd like to talk to you."

"Nero himself?" Baal did not seem pleased by the honor.

"Nero himself, and what's so surprising in that? You're a traveler. You go everywhere, speak to everyone. What tales you must have swapped in the waterfront taverns of the world! In Spain, for instance."

"Yes," Simon admitted guardedly.

"In India!"

"Yes."

"In Parthia!"

"Well, I . . ."

"You've been to Parthia, of course."

There was a pause, then Demetrius blurted drunkenly, "He goes to Parthia all the time. Now me, I've never been outside of Alexandria, so you see . . ."

"Thank you, Demetrius," Hesperian said.

Baal was glaring openly at the old man.

Hesperian continued. "So, Simon, you go to Parthia and swap tales with Parthians, perhaps with actual agents of the Parthian king. Do you wonder that Nero wants to talk to you? Parthia is Rome's enemy. What seems like idle gossip to you might be valuable information to Nero. He might feel moved to reward you. That is, if you were as willing to talk to us as you are to talk to them."

"Of course. Of course I am!" Simon said hopefully.

"You are *what*? Willing to talk to us or to them?"

"To you! To you!"

"Or to the highest bidder, eh? That's only good business. You pride yourself on being a good businessman, don't you?"

"An *honest* businessman, Centurion."

Daphnis, standing nearby, laughed.

Hesperian smiled. "You must pardon Daphnis. He does not believe there is any such thing as an honest businessman."

Demetrius roused himself to speak again. "What are you saying? Is Simon Baal a spy? A traitor? This man my brother and I accepted in good faith?"

"Shut up!" snapped Simon.

"I can't believe it!" Demetrius reared back so violently he almost fell off his couch. "My friend . . . a traitor!"

"You drunken idiot!" Simon cried in exasperation. "He's tricking you. Can't you see he's tricking you?"

"I have nothing to hide." Demetrius drew himself up in righteous indignation.

"Naturally," Hesperian said soothingly. "It's jealousy, nothing but jealousy, that makes your competitors in Rome say that when they'd almost driven your brother out of the shipping business, it was Parthian money that saved him."

"Yes, that's it. Jealousy. They're jealous." Demetrius was blinking stupidly.

"You men!" Adrastia broke in with a ragged laugh. "Always talking business. We need some entertainment. My dwarfs!"

"Yes, the dwarfs!" agreed Demetrius, swaying.

"My dwarfs, Wakar! Summon my dwarfs!" she repeated, more loudly.

Wakar, who had been carrying a tray of dirty dishes toward the door, paused and glanced questioningly at Hesperian.

"Yes," said Hesperian. "By all means, let us have a little entertainment."

■ ■ ■

"Bravo!" shouted Demetrius.

The dwarf Suchos played a double flute, producing a lively cascade of two-part harmony and counterpoint with an occasional deliberate wrong note thrown in for comic effect. Horus thumped out the rhythm on a broad one-headed drum he held in one hand and struck with the other, at intervals breaking into song in his high, cracked voice. Bubo, who seemed to be the leader of the dwarf trio, did a dance that included an inordinate number of cartwheels and somersaults. In spite of the hump on his back, he was amazingly quick and graceful.

Mannus paid no attention to the "entertainment." His eyes were fixed on the figure of Gaius Hesperian, trying to guess the centurion's next move. Simon, too, was watching Hesperian, but Hesperian seemed to have forgotten all about the questioning as he leaned forward and selected a large polished red apple from the fruit dish on the table in front of him. He leaned back, bit into it, chewed.

No one else was eating.

Suddenly, without warning, Bubo leaped up on the table and, to the horrified amazement of all, flung himself into Hesperian's lap.

Adrastia was on her feet in an instant. "Bubo! How dare you! Oh, this time you've gone too far! I'll have you whipped until you . . ."

"No, no," Hesperian protested. "Don't punish the little fellow. Really, I thought it was quite amusing." The dwarf had already bounded from his lap and scuttled away. "Let the entertainment continue."

"Well, I . . . oh very well," Adrastia reluctantly agreed, settling once again onto her couch. Mannus noted that she seemed relieved at not having to punish Bubo. The double flute, which had been momentarily silent, burst once more into song as Bubo turned handsprings.

Simon Baal, sweating, leaned forward. "You've been making some serious charges against me, Centurion. I demand . . ."

"I've made no charges. It's your friend Demetrius here . . ."

Baal turned on Demetrius. "You! You! You think that by giving evidence against me, you can buy your own freedom. You think a miserable drunk like you can best Simon Baal! Well, that's not the way the world goes! I know things about you . . . and now that the seal of silence is broken . . ."

Hesperian took another bite of the apple.

Demetrius interrupted with a savage, "Barbarian snake! Outlander! I take no more of your insults, your bullying. All the gold in the world wouldn't buy my silence now. I shout it so all can hear. Simon Baal is a spy! Simon Baal is a spy! Simon Baal is a smuggler of money and weapons to Rome's enemies!"

Simon Baal was shouting too. "Demetrius sells secrets to Parthia!

Demetrius transports spies and enemies of Nero on his ships, his ships bought with Parthian gold. Demetrius trades in forged documents!"

Hesperian chewed, swallowed. The others were speechless. Daphnis, tablet in hand, had begun writing rapidly. Mannus strained to hear the frantic voices of the two conspirators as they hurled charges and countercharges. The dwarfs fled from the room.

Hesperian stood up, bowed to the assembled company. "I thank you all for a most instructive evening, but now I must leave you. Pressing affairs . . ."

Demetrius sprang forward and clutched at the Roman's arm. "At least I'm not a murderer!"

Hesperian gently removed the old man's claw-like hand. "True. You have obviously neither the courage nor the physical strength to have done it, but since you could have bought with your life both treason and murder, you missed a bargain by being guilty of only one."

The centurion paused at the door to beckon to Mannus, who followed him out. In the hall, the two men stood a moment as Hesperian unrolled a scrap of crumpled papyrus. "Look at this, Mannus. That dwarf slipped me a note when he was in my lap there."

They strained to read the crude, awkward Greek letters in the dim lamp light.

"He wants you to meet him in the slave's quarters," Mannus said, looking up with a frown. "He says he knows. Knows what, sir?"

"Let's ask him."

Daphnis appeared in the hall, chuckling, and Hesperian called to him. "Come, my faithful scribe. I think we may have more work for you tonight."

The next to enter the hall was Simon Baal, tight-lipped and pale. Then came the guards, with Demetrius. Demetrius was weeping shamelessly.

■ ■ ■

The slaves' quarters were in the rear of the villa, on the other side of the kitchen. They stank of rancid olive oil, smoke, and urine, and were so dimly lit that Hesperian had to walk with care. Daphnis and Mannus followed close behind him.

Hesperian called, "Hello! Is there anyone here?" There was no answer.

"I guess we'll have to wait," Mannus sighed.

"We gave the little monster ample time to get here already," Daphnis said crossly. The scribe had a fastidious nature and obviously found the filth of the slaves' quarters revolting.

There was a rustle in the darkness, then the sound of quick footsteps,

footsteps made by light, bare feet. The Romans glanced hopefully in the direction of the sound and, a moment later, Sabella stumbled into the circle of light surrounding the hall's one oil lamp. She blinked and squinted, as if even this faint glow was too bright for her.

"What you want?" she mumbled.

Hesperian answered, squatting down so his face was level with hers. "We're looking for one of the dwarfs."

"Which one?" Her lower lip jutted out and her eyes narrowed with suspicion.

"I think they call him Bubo," Mannus said.

"Bubo?" She considered this a moment. "I saw Bubo. Yes, I saw him. He ran through here. Looked scared."

"Where did he go?" Hesperian laid a hand on the girl's bare, bony shoulder. She was wearing the same dirty tunic she usually wore; it would appear she even slept in it.

She pointed toward a doorway at the rear of the hall. "He out there somewhere."

"Thank you, Sabella." As he stood up, Hesperian gave her a friendly pat on the head. She ducked away, still sullen and suspicious.

The Romans stepped through the doorway and found themselves under the stars. The trees around them and the building behind them registered as no more than areas of black where the stars were not visible. The moon had not yet risen.

The gardens where they stood were silent, but a slight breeze from the northwest brought to their ears the faint murmur of Alexandria, the city that never sleeps. In spite of the breeze it was a warm night, and humid.

"What do you suppose he was afraid of?" Daphnis said softly.

"Us, more than likely," Hesperian answered. They walked slowly past statues and bushes, feeling their way along.

"There's nothing back here but the stable," Daphnis remarked, sniffing the air with distaste.

"Then that is probably where we will find our shy little friend," Hesperian said.

"Probably," Daphnis agreed gloomily.

Somewhere ahead of them a horse whinnied softly.

Mannus thought, *What a perfect place for an ambush*, and rested his hand on the handle of his shortsword.

When they reached the stable, they found the wide double door in front slightly ajar. "How careless," murmured Hesperian, stepping inside. Mannus and Daphnis followed.

They could hear but not see the horses rustling around in the darkness, snorting and stamping, reacting to the presence of strangers.

"Maybe I should go back to the house and get a lamp," Daphnis suggested nervously.

"No, wait a moment," came the voice of Hesperian. "I thought I heard something."

"Just the horses," Daphnis grunted.

"Wait," the centurion whispered.

Suddenly the silence was broken by the sound of a stifled sneeze. Mannus sprang forward in the direction of the sound and, much to his own surprise, found his fingers closing in on the wriggling, kicking form of a little man. The dwarf was surprisingly strong and almost managed to struggle free, but Mannus hung on grimly, crying, "I've got him! I've got him! Over here, sir!"

It took the combined efforts of all three Romans to drag the gnarled little figure out into the starlight, but once there, he seemed suddenly to give up and slumped dejectedly in their hands.

"Bubo?" Hesperian asked.

"Yes, that is what I'm called." The cracked, high-pitched voice was dejected, tired.

"You passed me a note?"

"Yes."

"Well, here I am. What did you want to tell me?"

"It's too late. I can tell you nothing now."

"Why not?"

"I was seen. When I passed you the note I was seen."

"That doesn't matter. We'll protect you."

The dwarf laughed, and it sounded harsh and bitter, almost like the bark of a rabid dog.

"I know you don't like torture, sir," Daphnis suggested, "but in this case . . ."

The dwarf laughed again. "Torture? There are more fearful things than pain and death. There are those who have power over us not only in our present lives, but after death as well."

"He sounds like a Christian," Daphnis said, puzzled.

"Are you a Christian, Bubo?" Hesperian demanded.

"Not I! Never!"

Mannus glanced toward the house and saw a light moving toward them. "Someone's coming," he warned.

A moment later they could make out the face of the oncoming figure, illuminated by an upraised oil lamp. "Hathor," breathed Hesperian.

The dwarf began struggling with redoubled efforts, muttering incomprehensibly in Egyptian, as the young Hathor strode steadily forward, her face transfigured by a strange and otherworldly smile. With one convulsive effort, Bubo broke free and scrambled away into the darkness.

"Gaius?" Hathor called out softly.

■ ■ ■

Mannus could not help feeling sorry for her.

Hathor had come to expect Hesperian to go easy on her, to treat her with a special kindness and respect, so that now, after the centurion had subjected her to a harrowing cross-examination for several minutes, she was dazed, bewildered and wistful.

"I ask you again, girl," snapped Hesperian. "Why did you come out here?"

"Sabella told me you'd come out here. I thought you might need a lamp."

"Really? Are you sure you didn't come out here to make certain Bubo wouldn't tell me anything?"

"Don't be silly!"

"He was afraid of you. How do you explain that?"

"The dwarf is afraid of everything. He's so small and helpless."

"But particularly afraid of a murderess!"

"Gaius! I thought you were going to be my friend!"

"You told me that at the time your father died, you were with your brother."

"Yes, and it's true!"

"And he was with you, you said, to bring you a message from some lover of yours, some lover you refuse to name."

"That's right."

"You're strong and light. You could have climbed those vines outside your father's window. And you've been trained in the use of arms. You could have thrown that pilum."

"But I didn't!"

"And this lover of yours. He's not really a Roman soldier, as he seems to have pretended to be. There's something shadowy, something unreal about him. You could have bribed that old woman to tell us about him. You could have thrown a bit of cloth in the corner of your room, knowing that someday, if the investigation went far enough, someone like me would find it. How do I know this man exists? How do I know he's not a myth, a phantom killer you created to blame the murder on?"

"He does exist! He does!"

"Then who is he? Don't you see? You must tell me now!"

"I can't!"

"Then you must be . . . wait." Hesperian fell silent, then whispered. "I see it all now." Another pause, then, surprisingly, a soft chuckle.

"See what?" Daphnis demanded impatiently.

Hesperian spoke slowly, looking down at Hathor's lamp lit face with an expression of dawning understanding. "Hathor, Serapion is your lover." It was not a question, but a statement of fact.

Hathor looked down, unable to meet the centurion's gaze, but she said nothing, made no attempt to deny the accusation.

Mannus, in the darkness, whispered, "By the gods!"

Hathor, still holding the lamp, spoke at last, in a faraway voice. "In the eyes of the gods of Egypt, it is no sin for brother and sister to be lovers."

Daphnis said, "Ah, now things are getting clearer."

But Hesperian answered: "Clearer? As I see it, the solution to this puzzle has become not only more difficult, but impossible! In a schedule so crowded with mischief, how could any of these ladies and gentlemen have found time for the murder?"

Chapter Four

As they re-entered the dining room, Mannus noted that all the guests had departed and, except for a bit of broken bread on a plate, all the food had been cleared away.

"Then you're not going to arrest me?" Hathor asked incredulously.

"What for?" Hesperian told her. "Incest? If I started arresting people for incest, I might end by slapping the Emperor himself in irons. Murder? It's more certain than ever that you were with your brother at the time of your father's murder ... in your brother's bed, more than likely."

Hesperian and Hathor seated themselves on the couch at the head of the table. Mannus stationed himself nearby, leaning against the wall. Daphnis had gone to check with the guards.

"But how did you guess?" she asked.

"That Serapion was your lover? Better to ask how I failed to see it instantly. Odysseus had the entire family sealed in here for almost a whole day before he was killed. How then could any message have been brought in from your lover, *if he was outside*? And here inside, who but Serapion, among all these women, old men, dwarfs, children, and eunuchs, was *able* to be your lover? By the gods, if Nero ever hears I'm making blunders like this, he'll have me on a platter with an apple in my mouth!"

Librarius Daphnis appeared in the doorway and saluted. "The Christians are here, sir. Your men brought them in just a few minutes ago."

"Excellent, Daphnis. I'll question them immediately." Daphnis stepped to one side to allow two of the guards to roughly push two plainly-dressed Jews into the room. "They call themselves Annianus, Bishop of Alexandria, and Mark the Apostle," said Daphnis.

"You are Annianus?" Hesperian demanded of the Jew nearest him.

"Yes, that is my Greek name. My Jewish name is Hananiah." Annianus, unlike the Romans, Greeks and Egyptians, wore a beard, a short gray one, neatly trimmed. He was a hawk-nosed, sunburned little old man with a bald head that gleamed in the lamp light, and a toothless smile. He wore a long gray wool tunic and a camel hide cloak and sandals, and into the hem of his tunic was woven the blue thread that identified him as a Jew, a symbol of long standing among the Hebrew people.

Hesperian turned to the other man. "And you are Mark?"

"Yes. John Mark is my name. My Jewish name is Jochanan. I am a traveling scribe by profession." Mark was younger and taller than Annianus, a fine figure of a man. He was clean-shaven but his dark hair hung down to his shoulders, much longer than was the fashion among the better classes. He also wore the blue thread in the hem of his tunic, a grayish linen garment, and his cloak was of brown wool. On a leather thong around his neck hung a wooden cross with a loop on top, the Egyptian hieroglyph for Eternal Life.

"And your profession, Annianus?"

"I'm a maker of boots and sandals," answered the old man.

"I have a few questions I'd like to ask you both."

"With all due respect, sir, I must protest," Annianus said, drawing himself up with dignity. "We are Jews, sir. You must be unfamiliar with the laws of Alexandria; otherwise you would know that here a Jew is tried only by Jews. We demand to be taken before the Ethnarch or some other official of the Jewish Council!"

Hesperian waved aside these objections with a weary gesture. "You're not under arrest, Rabbi. No, indeed not. Rather, say that you're my honored guests. I've heard of your sect in Rome. Of Paul, and Peter. You were Peter's scribe, were you not, John Mark?" Mark nodded. Hesperian continued, smiling. "So I know that you profess to love all men like brothers, even Romans. And that you profess never to tell a lie. Most admirable! And really I should think you'd be glad to face Roman rather than Jewish law. As I understand it—at least this is how it is in Rome and Judea—you Christians are an object of contempt for all the more respectable Jews. Don't they call you *Am-ha-arez*, People of the Dirt, because you fail to follow all the nit-picking rules of Jewish ritual cleanliness?"

Bishop Annianus looked at the centurion with new respect. Few indeed were the Roman officials that took the trouble to learn the differences between the myriad Jewish sects rather than lumping them all together into one category unworthy of serious consideration.

The Apostle Mark, however, still looked at Hesperian with ill-concealed suspicion. "If you plan to torture us, I must warn you our God gives us a courage that may surprise you."

Hesperian sighed. "I've always felt that if I couldn't learn what I wanted to know by the use of my wits alone, I deserved to remain in ignorance." He picked up the bit of broken bread from the plate on the table and bit into it, then continued, speaking with his mouth full. "But somehow I always seem to find out everything anyway, sooner or later."

"If you wish to learn about Our Lord Christ Jesus," Annianus said, "Brother Mark here has written a wonderful scroll containing all the stories told him by the Apostle Peter, who knew our Lord when . . ."

"No, no, I'm familiar with the claims of your sect, Rabbi. But, like most Romans, I'm more interested in men than in gods. A certain man, in this case. Odysseus Memnon."

The Christians glanced uneasily at each other

"Memnon was not a Christian," Mark said.

"I doubt if he had what it takes to become one," Annianus added. "Our path is not an easy one. We hold all our property in common, and this Memnon was a rich man. It is easier for a camel to pass through the eye of a needle than for a rich man to learn to share."

"This rich man," Hesperian said, "might have surprised you."

"Why do you question us now?" asked the Bishop. "That was all long ago. We told all we knew to the Alexandrian authorities then, when the memory was fresh. Consult the testimony we gave then; it's all we know about this man, and little enough it is."

"You did speak to him," prompted Daphnis, who was writing.

"Just once," Mark answered. "He asked me what one must do to become a Christian. I told him, and he left in a great hurry." The Apostle permitted himself a faint smile.

"But was that the only time he came?" persisted Hesperian.

"That's what they testified," Daphnis said.

"Yes, that's right," Mark said.

"No, wait," broke in Annianus. "I didn't remember then, but I have thought about it a great deal since, and I believe he was at our services several other times."

"Several times?" asked Hesperian.

"Many times, " said the Bishop, nodding and frowning. "I heard from some members of the congregation that he'd attended our services often, over a period of perhaps a year, but always stood apart, unwilling to respond to the friendly overtures some of us made to him. Actually, come to think of it, I saw him myself. Yes, now I remember. You saw him too, Mark. I pointed him out to you." The old man had become quite excited.

"Is that right, Mark?" Hesperian inquired.

"Yes. Yes, I believe so." There was an odd expression on the tall Jew's face, as if the man was undecided about something.

Hesperian leaned forward. "When Odysseus came to your services, was he alone?"

"His slaves were with him." Mark was still hesitant.

Annianus broke in. "If we did not tell this before, it was only that we did not want our sect to appear somehow at fault. The Greeks are always looking for some excuse to riot against the Jews, and the Jews . . . they too have no great love for us."

"We wished to avoid trouble," Mark explained. "You understand."

"Of course," Hesperian said softly, " but go on. Besides his slaves, was there anyone with him at your services?"

Reluctantly Mark said, "No, not with him, but there was someone . . . a stranger in a cape . . . who came several times and watched old Memnon from a distance."

Hesperian studied the Apostle's face. "You know, don't you? You know who that stranger was!"

"No, no, sir. I never knew!" He glanced at the Bishop as if for approval.

The Bishop sighed and added, "Nor did I . . . until now."

Hesperian followed the Bishop's gaze.

Annianus was looking directly at Hathor.

■ ■ ■

After the Christians had been dismissed, Hesperian took Hathor by the hand, saying, "Come with me, my dear. It will be cooler out in the garden." Daphnis and Mannus were about to follow, but he stopped them with a glance.

The night air was a little cooler now and the moon, almost full, had arisen, illuminating the courtyard garden with a cold, dead white light, bright but utterly without color. The aroma of nightshade was faint, but unmistakable.

The tall Roman officer and the short, slender Greco-Egyptian girl walked slowly, side by side, saying nothing.

It was Hathor who broke the silence. "You don't trust me anymore, do you, Gaius?" She took his arm.

"No. Why should I?" His voice was without emotion.

"I didn't lie to you about anything important."

"Your relationship with your brother . . . that wasn't important?"

"I couldn't tell you about that. Romans don't have the same morality as we Egyptians. You know all the bad feeling there is in Rome against Berenice bas Agrippa, Princess of the Jews, because she is suspected of doing what I've done. You Romans are a young people, young and naive. In spite of all your frantic efforts to be wicked, you're still shocked by so many things that for centuries we Egyptians have taken for granted. What my brother and I did was nothing that had not been done time and again by our kings and queens, even by our gods. What we did was not wrong by our standards. In an earlier age, before you Romans came to Egypt, we would not have bothered to hide it. Now you Romans have turned morality on its head; it's all right to torture and kill animals for a public spectacle, something we Egyptians will never get used to, but for brother and sister to love each other—the most natural thing in the world—that is a sin, a crime, a scandal."

He was looking at her, but the moon was behind him so she could not see his face. "You think of yourself as an Egyptian?" he said softly.

"Yes. Oh, yes. My father was like you, more Roman than a Roman in his attitudes and beliefs. I'm not like him. My blood is Greek, but it's Egypt, not Rome, that has seeped into my soul. My brother and I, we see everything through the eyes of the ancient gods and goddesses . . . or, better perhaps, we are not ourselves, but are those gods and goddesses looking out through our eyes. My brother is Osiris-Serapis, King of the Dead, and I am his sister and wife, the Great Mother Isis. Many Egyptians feel this way, even poor peasants hardly better than slaves."

"It is easier, I suppose, to live the life of a slave if you believe you are a god."

"Have you never felt, Gaius, that you were a god?"

"Never." His voice was firm. "I am a man, nothing more. Nero thinks like you, and perhaps this man Jesus thought like you. They say he claimed to be a god! Well, I look at such men and am glad, very glad, that I am not whatever it is that they are."

"So, when you die, there will be nothing left?"

"There will be something. There will be Rome."

"I see."

They stood now in the very center of the garden.

Hathor spoke, after a pause, with a wistful tone. "Are you married, Gaius?"

"No."

"Soldiers do marry, don't they?"

"Troops stationed in one place a long time often have wives . . . of a sort. So did I, when I was younger, but at long last I've learned that it's better to be alone. Parting is hard, and it always comes sooner than you expect, sooner, for me, than for most. In the last twenty years I've rarely spent more than a month or two in one city. I'm sent wherever Nero has enemies, and his enemies are everywhere."

"Poor Gaius," she whispered, touching his cheek with her long fingers. He turned away. "I meant no harm," she added defensively.

"You're a lovely woman, Hathor, a charming woman." His voice was heavy, regretful. "But your charm could cloud my judgement if it turns out that it's you who killed old Odysseus." He turned toward her again. "The truth now. Was it you?"

She did not answer, only gazed at him with eyes full of pain.

■ ■ ■

Centurion Gaius Hesperian and Optio Mannus faced each other across the dining room table. Everyone else had gone, and through all the halls of the great mansion scarcely a sound could be heard. Mannus nodded, almost sleeping. Hesperian brooded, elbows resting on the smooth stone of the tabletop, bushy brows knit in a frown of concentration—or was it depression?

Mannus yawned. This was not the first night watch he'd kept with his commanding officer. He knew, by now, just how far he could relax discipline, just how far he could go before Hesperian would give him an abrupt reprimand.

The light was dim; only a few small oil lamps burned fitfully in the tall petrolabra that stood nearby, and the room was full of a dense, almost motionless veil of smoke. It had a bitter smell, this smoke, and made the eyes water, but Mannus ignored it.

"Hathor?" asked Hesperian, his far-away gaze coming to rest on the rugged features of his friend.

"Daphnis has taken her to her room, as you ordered, sir."

"As I ordered? Oh, yes, so I did."

The centurion leaned back on his couch and stared up at the ceiling. Mannus waited expectantly.

"We must have the answer tomorrow," said Hesperian, more to himself than to Mannus.

"Yes sir. One might even say today if, as I suspect, it's already past midnight."

"Always exact, eh, Mannus?"

"You've taught me that, sir."

Hesperian chuckled softly, then inquired: "Tired, Optio?"

"Yes, sir."

"So am I. It's all such a jumble in my mind. I need to think, but I can't. The answer is there, but somehow I can't quite grasp it."

"Perhaps you don't want to, sir."

"Eh? You mean you think it's Hathor?"

"It is, sir. We both know it is."

"But I'm an old fool, eh Mannus? An old fool blinded by his feelings for a young girl?"

"Yes, sir."

"Another officer would have you in irons for that, but . . . but it's only honesty. I need honesty around me. I need a little truth, or at least the memory of truth, or I'll forget how to recognize a lie. One must have some standard of comparison." He closed his eyes, and for an instant Mannus thought he was sleeping, then he went on, "But you're wrong. I know it."

"Can you prove it, sir?"

"No." It was a sigh, almost inaudible.

"I questioned Serapion, sir."

"And?"

"He does not support Hathor's story. According to him, Hathor was not with him at the time of old Memnon's murder, but Serapion also insisted that Hathor must be innocent."

"He would," said Hesperian gloomily.

"So Hathor cannot account for her whereabouts, she can throw the pilum, she could easily climb those vines, and she also could have poisoned the slave easily. She has money for a motive, and the Christians, whom I've heard never lie, say she was spying on her father at their religious services. And did you mark this, sir? That the Christians saw her in a cape . . . perhaps it was hooded? The dealer in poison told us he sold some deadly stuff to someone in a hood, someone who could have been a woman. And she lied to you, sir, about her lover. She was all along concealing her incest from you. She looks pure, I grant you that, sir, but would a pure and honest woman do such things?"

Hesperian sighed. "I know. I know all that."

"Then act, sir! Arrest her!"

"So you can win your bet, Optio? Is a beautiful young lady to pay with her life for your wine?"

Mannus said in a low voice, "If you think I am such a man as that, you should have me transferred. An officer must have a second-in-command he can trust."

The two men looked at each other uncomfortably for a moment, then Hesperian leaned forward and said earnestly, "Back off, Optio. Back off. I do trust you. I trust you with my life. I'm tired, you see. I don't know what I'm saying. Of course I trust you!" Hesperian grasped Mannus's wrist in a comradely handshake.

"If you trust me, sir, then arrest her." Mannus would not give up.

"No, no. I can't." He looked at Mannus with haunted eyes.

"She's guilty!"

"No . . ."

They heard approaching footsteps in the hall and broke off their argument, both men a little ashamed of having given way to their emotions. The footsteps were quick, almost running.

Librarius Daphnis appeared at the door. He was excited, so excited he forgot to salute, and while his handsome, hawk-like face wore an expression of sardonic triumph, his hands fluttered in the dim lamp light like a girl's.

"It's Hathor, sir," Daphnis cried. "She told me to tell you she is ready to confess!"

■ ■ ■

Hathor's footsteps, as she came down the hall, were slow and halting. She stopped, framed in the doorway, her white dress making her seem like a female ghost.

"Come in, my dear," Hesperian commanded gently. "Come over here where I can see your face."

Without meeting his eyes, she advanced into the dim flickering lamp light.

"Gaius..." she began.

"Wait a moment. Daphnis is not ready."

Daphnis had seated himself at the centurion's left and was hurriedly unrolling a fresh papyrus scroll, wetting his ink stick, inking his reed pen.

"Now," Hesperian said, "as you see, Daphnis will be writing down every word you say, so think well before you speak." He studied her intently. "Do you understand?"

She nodded.

"Hathor." Never before had there been such gentleness in his voice. "Tell us, in your own words, how it happened."

She seemed unable to speak, unable even to look at him.

He went on. "I know that whatever you did, you must have had good reason."

She raised her eyes, but there was little hint of the Memnon pride in her pale features.

"Was it the money?" Hesperian prompted.

"No. No, not that."

"What then?"

"We Memnons would have survived somehow, even without my father's money. We have rich and powerful friends, and we know how to manage things. It would have been hard for a while, but we would have managed."

"Then why..."

"The House of Memnon does not stop with members of our family. There are the household servants. There are the merchants, the sailors, the workers... all the hundreds of innocent people who depend on the Memnon enterprises for their living. It was for their sake... for their sake..."

"For their sake you killed him."

"Yes, Gaius."

"But you said you loved your father."

"I did love him, but he was no longer himself. The Christians changed him, made him forget who he was, made him forget his responsibilities, made him believe he could save himself at the expense of the multitudes who depended on him. That's the way it is in this house.

The loads my father and mother and brother slough off, I must shoulder. Don't you see? It was my duty, my duty to everyone, to defend what he had built, even against his own hand."

"Even at the expense of his life?"

"You don't think like an Egyptian, Gaius. I did not kill his soul, only his body. I will meet him again, I'm sure, in some future incarnation, and at that time he'll have the opportunity either to forgive me or to take his revenge."

She was calm now, and very sure of herself. It was Hesperian whose voice shook as he said, "And Rophos? Will you meet him too in some future life?"

"That was an accident. He won't blame me for it."

"Are you getting all this, Daphnis?"

"Yes, sir," the scribe answered.

"Let him write this," Hathor said, once again completely a Memnon, proud, ruthless, cunning. "That I said goodnight to my father at the foot of the great staircase, then, as soon as he was out of sight, I ran out of the house with a pilum from Serapion's weapon collection. That I climbed the vines outside my father's window. That I held the pilum exactly as my father had taught me, and threw it, and killed him. Let him write it, I say!" Her voice, toward the end, had become shrill.

Hesperian gazed at her, but did not speak.

The reed pen scratched a moment longer, then stopped. Daphnis looked up expectantly. Mannus, who had been staring at the girl, turned a puzzled eye on Hesperian. Wasn't this the thing they'd all been waiting for? A full confession . . . with witnesses?

But the centurion went on staring at her, almost as if he did not see her, as if he was looking through her at something only he could see. The great house was so silent they could hear the sound of their own breathing.

"I don't believe you," Hesperian said softly.

■ ■ ■

In the flickering lamp light, through the haze of oily smoke, Hathor gazed into the centurion's shadowed eyes, gazed down at the muscular Roman who reclined on the couch on the other side of the marble-topped table. She knew there were some who could read minds, but she was not one of them. Yet she felt Hesperian's certainty as if it were a cold, heavy object she could hold in her hands. For the space of a few heartbeats she did not answer him, and those few beats were as much an admission of lying as anything she might have said. Then she cried out, "It's true, by Isis!" but the conviction that, a moment before, had filled her voice with power, was gone. It was a small, weak voice now, a liar's voice.

But what she felt, more than anything else, was relief.

No more lies! I was never meant to tell lie, never could do it well.

Hesperian sighed, then said, "It was, in its way, a beautiful tale you've been telling me, a tale that would not have been out of place in some ancient Greek drama. And with all the evidence pointing to you, how could I doubt you? Yet almost from the beginning there was something nagging at my mind, and now this attempt at confession finally brought it to the surface." He smiled ruefully and slowly shook his head. "In fact, if you had not tried to confess, the weight of the evidence might finally have overcome my doubts, but this confession . . . it was too much. I could see you might have motivation for the murder of your father, *but what motivation did you have to confess it?* And when I began to think about motivation it was all suddenly clear. Yes, it seems I made a mistake, and kept on making it . . . a small but crucial mistake. Well, as the philosophers tell us, that's the only way we poor mortals learn. We blunder, correct ourselves, then blunder again, until finally we stumble on the truth."

"I didn't want to lie," she told him. "Particularly to you." *I* wanted to tell you from the very beginning. I wanted to tell you everything. You seemed so strong and kind . . . but you were the Law, and the Law is never kind."

He leaned forward, a little awkwardly, leaning his left elbow on the table, reaching with his right hand for her hand. "I know, Hathor."

"Do you hate me, Gaius?"

"Hate you? On the contrary, even if you'd murdered your father I wouldn't have hated you. I'd have admired you . . . for your motives though I could not, of course, have let you go. Now that I see the truth, I admire you even more. You're a remarkable woman, Hathor. I can't recall I've ever met another like you."

He held her hand.

He's the most powerful man in this city, in his way, but he likes me. I know he does.

Mannus interrupted impatiently, "By the gods, sir, if you know who the murderer is, tell us!"

Daphnis joined in. "Yes, damn you! Tell us! It's beastly to keep us in suspense like this!"

Hesperian faced the two men and said mildly, "Certainly by now you both must know too. I have hidden nothing from you. Every fact revealed to me has also been revealed to you. Come then! Let's have your solution!"

END OF BOOK TWO

Book Three

Chapter One

THE SKY TO THE EAST GREW BRIGHTER, and nearby a cock crowed. The air was cool and still. On all the Memnon estate nothing moved; neither palm tree nor statue, nor flowering bush.

A seagull glided in and settled on the lawn. Just one gull. No more. There were other birds to be heard, singing their salute to the coming day, but only this one white gull was in sight.

The murderer Serapion stood alone at his window and watched the gull.

The murderer Serapion stifled a yawn. He had not slept and his body craved air, but Serapion stifled his yawn because he was too considerate to risk frightening the gull.

The murderer Serapion thought, *Is there no end to it?*

The answer came to him, and he smiled faintly.

One more day.

One more day and it would be over. Tomorrow was the Festival of the Ship of Isis, when all Alexandria would turn out to march in procession down to the sea, carrying the statue of Mother Isis, when there would be feasting and dancing. The bonfire would be lit at the top of the great lighthouse and the port would be opened ... and then Serapion would be free to set sail for the farthest reaches of the Empire and beyond, his sister-wife Hathor at his side. And that blundering fool, the centurion, would have to let him go. Without proof, a Memnon could not be held beyond tomorrow morning, and there was no proof.

You poor idiot, Hesperian.

Serapion smiled.

The gull fluttered from the lawn to a birdbath of pink marble.

Serapion went on smiling.

He thought, *I've been a good son.*

He had not taken his father's life. No, he had saved it! Odysseus died as an Egyptian, as a member of the church of Father Osiris-Serapis and Mother Isis. A man has two spirits, the Ka, spirit of the body, and the Ba, spirit of consciousness. The Ka of Odysseus would now remain with the body of Odysseus, the properly embalmed and ritually prepared mummy, guarding and protecting it. The Ba of Odysseus would now journey safely past all the dangers of the afterlife, journey to Amenti, the Western Land, the Land of the Ancestors, to dwell in union with Osiris-Serapis for a while. Then it would return to earth in a new body, and to a better world; where Christianity had passed and been forgotten and the ancient gods of Egypt, who have endured down the centuries and would continue to endure in ages to come, would have regained their former supremacy.

If Odysseus had lived to become a Christian, he would have died not once, but twice, and from the Second Death there is no returning. Serapis saves only those who believe in him.

Odysseus is in the Western Land, and when he thinks of me, he thanks me.
Serapion wept silently with bitter, triumphant joy, still smiling.

And the slave Rophos?

It must have been the hand of Osiris-Serapis himself that caused the death of the slave. Now Odysseus would have someone with him in the Western Land to wait on him in death as in life. In the days of the Pharaohs a whole household of slaves often accompanied their master into the other world!

I am a good son, and a good priest.

Actually, Serapion was not yet an ordained priest of Osiris-Serapis, but he was a priest in his heart. He knew the slaves believed he was a priest. The dwarfs, in particular, were in awe of him. Even his sister struck terror into them, because they knew he loved her.

If a priest kills, it is not murder. It is his right! It is his duty! That is what it is to be a priest; that is what it always has been. By right, a priest holds the power of life and death in his hand, in trust from his god. Even kings and queens rule only by the priest's permission, and some day the barbarian Romans, with their crude manners and ignorant minds, would find that out. The long history of Egypt teaches one lesson, time and again: The soldier may rule for a day, now and then, but sooner or later all the power seeps back into the hands of the priest.

There was a loud and sudden thump on Serapion's door. He turned, startled.

The gull, frightened by the sudden noise and motion, took wing.

"Who is it?" Serapion called out.

"A messenger." By the gruffness of the voice and the Latin accent, Serapion recognized one of Hesperian's men. "The Centurion commands you to have breakfast with him in one hour!"

■ ■ ■

The sun had scarcely cleared the horizon, but already the streets of Alexandria, the white city, were filled with feverish activity.

All along the waterfront and particularly around the great obelisk in the main public square in front of the Temple of Augustus crowds of merchants, naked slaves, and linen-robed, shaven-headed priests hurried to and fro like frightened ants. Tomorrow was the Festival of the Ship of Isis. Everything must be ready! Later on, around noon, it would be too hot to work, so now everyone must work like a veritable Hercules in the Aegean stables.

Everyone worked, that is, but a few Jews, distinguished occasionally by their beards and more frequently by the blue trim about the edges of their tunics. These Jews stood around the edge of the square, some looking on with interest, others with frowning disapproval. The holidays of the *goyim* Greeks, Egyptians and Romans were not for them!

One of these clusters of Jews, catching sight of a Roman uniform, stepped aside to make way for a tall, cloaked, bare-headed centurion and a short, thin young woman in a white silk gown. The centurion held the girl by the elbow, gently but firmly guiding her forward.

"Gaius, won't you let go of my arm?" Hathor asked.

"No, my dear," Hesperian answered her.

"Perhaps you believe in my guilt after all?"

"Not at all."

"How can you be so sure?"

"Two things. First, as all the witnesses agreed, when your slave Rophos had tasted the poisoned soup, he began to sway, and you cried out a warning. That was after he'd tasted the soup, but before your father did."

"So?"

"So, if you'd known of the poison you might have, to save Rophos, called out before the slave took his taste, or somehow created a diversion, or even turned over the soup tureen."

"Perhaps."

"And if you had wanted your father dead, you would have waited. You would have let him take a sip, *then* cried out. An instant earlier, and you would have been guilty, because you would have had to know about the poison. An instant later, and you would have been guilty because you saw Rophos sway and said nothing. But no, you called out during that tiny fraction of an instant when only an innocent person would."

He smiled down on her with satisfaction.

"How clever of you," she said coldly.

"The second point, then. If you didn't do it; who did? That would have given me some trouble, perhaps, if it hadn't been for your false confession. There is only one person you would be willing to give your life for by making a false confession, and that is your brother Serapion. Isn't that true?"

She thought, *Yes, it's true.* Her brother—and her lover. And her painful secret, her hidden guilt. *If only I'd cut out my tongue . . .*

She said, "And now I suppose you'll arrest him?"

"Not yet. It is not enough to know a thing. One must also prove it."

They paused to allow two swearing Greeks to pass, dragging a wagon load of candy doves. When she spoke, her voice was weary, fatalistic. "You're so clever, Gaius. You'll find your proof."

"That Serapion is the murderer? Perhaps. But that is not what really needs proving."

"What else?"

"You're a remarkably virtuous woman in your perverse way, and you see others as being like yourself. They are not, my dear, and never were, not even in the fabled good old days of the Roman Republic. That includes your brother. What needs proving is that your brother is not worthy of the sacrifice you were ready to make for him."

"You'll never prove that!" She was angry now.

"We shall see."

"You're so Roman, so very Roman. So sure of yourself. So quick to pass judgement on what you don't understand. And you don't understand Serapion, and you don't understand me, and you don't understand Egypt. We know things here! We've been here a long time, longer than you Romans have called yourself a nation. We know things about the human spirit, about the gods, and about the truth behind the visible world! We know things about what happened in ages past, even before there was an Egypt! We know things, Roman! How can you pass judgement on us? You know nothing!"

"I can learn. There are things no man really knows . . . but everything else I can learn."

"Learn this, then!" She had raised her voice now, and a group of passing priests of Osiris turned to look at her, first with curiosity, then with approval. "There are laws higher than Roman laws, higher than any laws made by men, and by these laws Serapion is innocent! You may condemn him, but Osiris exalts him! Osiris praises him! He is the best of the Memnons, the only one of us who loves the gods more than money! You don't know him . . . his kindness, his gentleness, his strength! You don't know . . ."

"Do *you* know him?"

"Of course!"

"Did you know, ahead of time, that he was planning to murder your father?"

"No, but later . . ."

"How much later?"

"You wouldn't believe me if I told you. I can hardly believe it myself."

"If you had known what Serapion was planning before the murder, would you have let him do it?"

There was a long silence, then she answered uncertainly, "I . . . I don't know."

"This man you know so well . . . he planned a murder and carried it out, and you did not know it."

"Yes, but . . ."

"Then there may be other things he does and thinks that you do not know."

"No! I won't listen to you. It's not so!"

"Before I'm done, I'll prove it to you."

They had come to the foot of a flight of broad white marble steps and Hathor, recognizing where she was, looked around in surprise. "Gaius! This is the prison!"

"Yes, it is."

"You're not taking me here?"

"Yes, I am."

"But you told me I was innocent!"

"True. But all the same, I'm afraid I must place you under detention for a day or so—in only the most luxurious accommodations of course—so you won't warn your brother that I know about him."

■ ■ ■

"The breakfast is laid in the small dining room, Master."

"Very good, Wakar."

Wakar hobbled down the great staircase and Serapion followed.

Adrastia, who was already reclining at table, looked up with a frown as they entered. In the subdued and diffused sunlight that reflected in from the hall, he could see that in spite of her beautiful garments—she wore an ankle-length green silk tunic, loose-fitting but clinging, and over that a shorter, lighter-green wool palla embroidered in gold—and her high-piled Messalina coiffure, and her gold-bejeweled rings, bracelets and necklaces, she herself was no longer beautiful. There were lines around her eyes that makeup could not hide, hollows in her cheeks, a certain slackness in her flesh. Serapion thought, *You should take better care of yourself, Mother*, but he said nothing. It was obvious her serving women had been working on her since before dawn, but a little food and sleep would have done her more good.

"You may go, Wakar," she snapped.

The slave departed with a bow.

"Good morning, Mother." It had always given him an odd feeling to call someone almost his own age "Mother." "How lovely you look this morning." He settled himself on the couch to her right.

"Serapion." She looked at him with dark troubled eyes.

"Yes?"

"This trip you and Hathor are planning . . . Couldn't you put it off?"

"Why should we?"

"I need you. It's silly, I know, but I hadn't realized until now that it's up to me to manage it all, the whole Memnon financial empire, now that Demetrius has been arrested."

"I thought you were taking a trip yourself, to India."

She shook her head. "Not now. Don't you see? I have to stay here. I have to run things, do everything old Odysseus used to do . . . but I don't know how. I've never really even run this house. It's been Hathor who saw to everything. I don't know how to begin!" She seemed on the verge of tears.

"Well, you'll have to learn, won't you?"

She sat up with an angry jerk. "I might have known you'd say something like that! You're nothing but a dreamer, your head so full of the other world you can't see what's going on in this one! Well, go ahead and dream! You've never taken one decisive action in your life, and you never will!"

"Perhaps you're right." Serapion's voice held the merest touch of malicious amusement, too light a touch to be noticed by the furious Adrastia.

She leaned toward him, grasped his well-muscled wrist. "The money, the power . . . I'm willing to share it with you." Her anger was already fading, to be replaced once again by a kind of pleading anguish.

He shrugged. "Keep it."

"No, no. I'm serious."

"You have given so much for it . . . marrying an old man, an impotent old man if I'm not mistaken, and you've been faithful to him, haven't you?"

"Of course."

"Then it should be yours! You've paid for it many times over. I don't need it. I already have all I want."

"But, you have nothing!"

"That's what I want."

She was still talking, still begging him to share the Memnon empire with her, but he was no longer listening to her, though her fingers occasionally dug cruelly into his wrist. His thoughts had turned to the gods, particularly to Osiris-Serapis. So far they had protected him. So far they had kept the centurion baffled, after having totally defeated the earlier investigators. It must be, then, that the gods smiled on his actions. It must be that he had found favor in their eyes. And now that he had come this far without being captured, without making a mistake, certainly he would be able to continue to evade the law for one more day. The centurion was a fool!

"And why should we wait for a fool?" he said aloud, cutting Adrastia off in mid-sentence.

"What?" She was bewildered.

"Aren't you hungry?" he demanded.

"Well, yes, I suppose so."

"Then why don't you eat?"

"I'm waiting for Centurion Hesperian."

"Don't you understand how your life has changed? You must no longer wait on anyone. It is for others to wait on you!" He turned toward the door and raised his voice. "Wakar!"

The servant appeared in the doorway.

"Wakar," commanded Serapion. "Bring us bread and fruit."

"Right away, Master."

Serapion and Adrastia had almost finished their breakfasts when Wakar hobbled in to announce: "Centurion Gaius Hesperian is here."

■ ■ ■

Serapion did most of the talking, light, witty, bantering as always, often smiling as if at some private joke, while Hesperian, across the table from him, ate dates, nodded, and grunted politely in all the right places. Charming! But there was a deadly tension in the air, and Adrastia felt it. It made her very uncomfortable.

"I really must be going . . ." she began falteringly, her eyes darting back and forth from one expressionless masculine face to the other.

"Go then," said Serapion with a warm smile. "I'm sure our Roman friend here will keep me amused."

She turned to Hesperian, who nodded wordlessly, his mouth full.

She got up quickly and hurried out, not looking back.

Serapion said offhandedly, "I wonder if my sister will be breakfasting with us. She's usually up by this time."

Hesperian had to swallow before answering. "I think not."

"Oh? What makes you say that?"

"I've arrested her." The centurion seemed absorbed in the task of selecting the right nut from a bowl full of nuts. There was a long pause while Serapion studied Hesperian's face intently. *Is this a trick? Is the fool trying to trick me?*

At length Serapion said, quite calmly. "Oh, is she the guilty one?"

"What do *you* think?"

"Well . . . I don't know."

"She made a full confession." His blunt fingers finally found a nut that was exactly right and popped it into his mouth. There was another silence as Serapion thought, *She must be trying to protect me!*

Hesperian looked up. Their eyes met for the first time since Hesperian's arrival in the room. Hesperian spoke slowly, choosing his words with care. "I thought you might be able to tell me something."

"I..."

"Yes?"

"It may surprise you, Centurion, but I have nothing to say."

"It doesn't surprise me at all. I expected it. It confirms my theories exactly."

Serapion noticed an odd tone in the Roman's voice, a sad irony, a certain cynical wistfulness that seemed to say, "I have expected the worst, and I have not been disappointed." The slight warmth Hesperian had showed him up to now had vanished and been replaced with something almost like . . . contempt. There was no change in the weathered Roman face, but the deep voice was cold. Yes, it was all in the voice. "You have so much poise for such a young man, Serapion. Your sister confesses to the murder of your father, and you remain calm. Her life may be in danger, and yet you somehow remain unmoved. It is, no doubt, your religion that gives you this inner strength."

"Yes . . . perhaps."

"Hathor is more emotional. She has not yet learned your philosophical detachment. If she felt you were in danger, there's no telling what she might do . . . but then she's only a woman, right?"

Serapion, rattled at last, laughed nervously, but was unable to answer.

"Women are weak," continued Hesperian, almost absentmindedly. "They're slaves of emotion, aren't they? Not like men. Your sister's devotion to you, for instance. There are some who might call it extreme, even perverse, but you, of course, feel nothing like that for her, do you?"

"I feel toward her . . . just what a brother should."

"And nothing more. You see? A man feels what is fitting and proper, what is reasonable. That's why all the great philosophers are men."

Serapion was able to say only, "Whatever she did, I'm sure it was for . . . a good reason."

The centurion shook his head. "No, no, I can't agree with you there. I say she's been a poor naive idiot, a dupe! I say her actions were the product of nothing but silly childish illusions!" He paused, glancing at Serapion sharply. "Well, brother, aren't you going to leap to her defense?"

Serapion was speechless.

Chapter Two

DEMETRIUS MEMNON AND SIMON BAAL, under guard, emerged into the merciless morning sunlight from the relative darkness of the doorway of the Memnon mansion.

With a feeling of hopeless degradation, Demetrius noticed that all the slaves were lined up along the walkway, watching him, even little Sabella. Sabella was grinning openly, looking him fearlessly in the eye, and it was he, this time, who turned his head away. Then he saw Adrastia, standing a little apart.

He waved to her, forcing a smile. She turned away. *At least they could have spared me this*, he thought. *To be stared at by mere slaves . . . who would have dreamed the gods could be so cruel?*

"Move along there, you two," growled Daphnis, who was in charge of the detail.

A few moments later the nightmare worsened: The great gates of the villa grounds swung wide and Demetrius found himself being driven through the streets, surrounded on all sides by curious, unsympathetic eyes.

The crowds! Full of holiday gaiety! Lowborn dogs! Jews! Egyptian peasants and beggars! Sneering Roman soldiers and the round-blue-eyed northern barbarians in ragtag odds and ends of Roman armor. Even the camels, oxen, goats and donkeys they passed seemed to stare.

"Straighten up," hissed Simon Baal behind him.

"What for?" snapped Demetrius.

"Show them who you are!"

Demetrius glanced back and saw that Baal was strutting along as if he was the guest of honor, as if this was perhaps a parade of triumph for him.

"You look absurd," Demetrius told him bitterly.

"Not at all! Not at all! The crowd has more respect for a loser who walks proudly than for a winner who slouches. I tell you, my friend, there's many a gladiator owes his life to good posture." There was something obscene about the little Parthian's forced cheerfulness, about the way his necklaces and bracelets and braids bounced with every step.

Hawk-nosed, long-haired Daphnis noticed it too, because he called out to Simon: "Happy?"

Simon wilted somewhat as the Roman fell in step with him. "What a question, sir!" huffed the dark little man.

Daphnis reached out and toyed with the Parthian's braids. "I'd be happy if I were in your shoes."

"What? What?" cried Baal indignantly. "Happy to go to prison?"

Daphnis sighed. "I was in prison once, a soldier's prison in Rome. When I was in prison, I was always in love."

The soldiers broke into a gale of harsh laughter. Daphnis' homosexuality was no news to them.

"Leave me alone," protested Baal. "I'll report you to Hesperian."

"But," Daphnis said gleefully, "Hesperian is the very man who has set me to molesting you! He thinks you might not care for me. Imagine that! And he thinks you might even dislike me enough to tell me a few things about your employers, just to get rid of me." He gave one of Baal's braids a vicious tug. "Actually, I can see that you and I are going to get along." He favored the spy with a lewd wink. "With those braids and all, it's amazing how much you remind me of a certain whore I once knew, back in Rome on the Via Venus Verticordia. I'm not too clever, you know, and it's always been hard for me to tell the difference between a Parthian and a woman, particularly," he gave the braid another tug, "on the battlefield."

Once again the soldiers exploded with malevolent guffaws.

"You'll get nothing from us," said Demetrius, in a voice so low it could hardly be heard. Instantly, Daphnis turned his attention to the old man.

"A miracle!" crowed Daphnis, "It talks! So you're not dead after all. You certainly look like a corpse!"

I wish I were a corpse, thought Demetrius.

Daphnis slipped a brawny arm around the old man's narrow shoulders, saying, "I'll get nothing from you, eh? You're a brave man . . . or is it that you've reached the age when one forgets things?"

Demetrius tried unsuccessfully to shrug off the unwanted arm. "I've reached the age when I know better than to talk to scum like you!"

Daphnis had an ugly laugh. "What's this? Insulting a member of Nero's personal guard? Why, that's almost the same as insulting our emperor and god himself. I didn't realize you were an atheist." The Roman's grip became painfully tight.

"By all that's holy . . ." With a violent effort Demetrius pulled free.

"And a rebel too," added the Roman mockingly.

The old man crouched and picked up a loose brick from the pavement, then straightened up, brandishing it over his head. "I warn you!"

For a moment the two stood glaring at each other, then the Roman lunged forward. Demetrius swung the brick, but Daphnis danced easily out of the way. The force of the swing, however, turned the gaunt old man around, and Daphnis, seizing the opportunity, lashed out with a well-aimed kick in the rear that sent Demetrius sprawling in the gutter.

"One crime after another," Daphnis said, slowly shaking his head. "Now it's attempted murder!" Demetrius lay on his belly, resting his weight on his elbows, his bald head drooping.

"Get up!" snapped the Roman.

Demetrius didn't move. He was crying softly, tears streaming down his wrinkled, hollow cheeks.

Daphnis reached down, grasped Demetrius' wrist, and jerked him to his feet. "Stop that whimpering. It's disgusting!" He let go of the old man's wrist, and when he spoke again his voice was softer. "All right, all right. I'll leave you alone."

Neither man said another word the rest of the way to the prison.

■ ■ ■

The heavy wooden door was barred from the outside, and there were iron bars on the one small high window, but otherwise the room did not look at all like a cell.

Seated on the couch that did double duty as a bed, Demetrius took inventory of his surroundings, surprised at the degree of luxury allowed him. There were rich, heavy drapes on the walls, even a well-made little writing table, though without either pen or writing stylus. And everything was so clean!

He'd been so sure they would make him wallow in filth. But he was, after all, still a Memnon, not an ordinary bread-snatcher from the Diplostoon marketplace. A Memnon! He smiled. That name still meant something, even now.

He was alone in the room. Solitary confinement? It didn't matter. Demetrius was glad that at last there were no eyes upon him to witness his degradation.

The voice, when it came, was so unexpected that it startled him, making him spin around on the couch with a jerk.

"Is that you, Demetrius?"

"Why yes . . . yes, it is, but who . . ."

"It's Hathor. Praise Isis, someone's come at last to get me out of here."

The muffled voice came from the other side of the wall.

"Well, no," mumbled the old man. "I haven't come for that, exactly."

"I understand. Gaius wants to keep me here, so here I stay. But you can carry a message for me to Serapion!"

"Wait. Let me explain . . ."

"There's no time. You must go as fast as you can and tell Serapion that Hesperian knows everything, that Hesperian is setting a trap. Run, Demetrius!"

"I can't run. I can't even walk."

"But you must!"

"I'm a prisoner here too."

There was a long pause, then she said dejectedly, "Of course. Of course. You're a prisoner here too."

"But wait, Hathor. Are you saying that Serapion is the murderer?"

She didn't answer, but he knew it must be true. Serapion was the murderer, and running around free, while he, Demetrius, was in prison. "Typical," he muttered.

■ ■ ■

The water around Bubo's bare feet and legs was not unpleasantly cold—tepid rather—as he sloshed cheerfully through the absolute darkness. Bubo had no need of light; he had been underground many times before. All the slaves in the neighborhood knew how to slip quietly through the subterranean aqueducts. It was only their masters who comforted themselves with the illusion that once the gates were closed and the guards posted, no one could get in or out of the luxurious estates of this Alexandrian suburb.

The passages were restrictive—even Bubo the dwarf could reach up and touch the rough brick ceiling—but a normal-sized man could get through if he was willing to crawl. The aqueducts were fairly-well-traveled, but not sufficiently traveled to make the water taste bad. One might flee down here into the cool humid darkness to escape an irate master or the noonday sun, or to visit some pretty slave girl who lived in a different household. And if the passages smelled a bit earthy, and if an occasional spiderweb brushed one's face in the dark, what were such things to a slave?

Bubo paused to let his companions, Horus and Suchos, catch up. The sound of their splashing was so loud it was hard to believe that nothing could be heard above ground. "Ssh," hushed Bubo, half-angrily.

Out of the darkness came a stifled giggle.

"Have you still got the moneybags?" Bubo whispered.

"Listen." There was a reassuring jingle, another giggle; then Horus said in a low voice: "You're sure this isn't stealing?"

"Of course not!" Bubo was indignant. "We're not taking the Memnons' money for ourselves. We're taking it to help them."

"We might be punished . . ."

"Never! We'll be rewarded. You'll see. If we can help our Masters to escape, I wouldn't be surprised if they set us free."

"Set us free?" There was doubt in Horus' voice.

"Of course! And think about this, my friend. If the Romans cart the whole family off to prison, who knows where we might end? In the mines, perhaps, or even in the arena. When all's said and done, our lives could be a lot worse than they have been. But if we were free . . . with a little money... there's always a place for a few dwarfs in the theatre." He thought about a mime he'd once seen. Everyone had applauded, but to Bubo it hadn't seemed so wonderful... Everything would have looked twice as funny done by a dwarf!

"But do we have to take the money?" Horus persisted.

"Do you have a better idea?"

"No, but..."

"But what?"

"Couldn't we rescue just Hathor and leave old Demetrius in prison to rot?"

"We made the plan, and you both agreed to it," Bubo said. "Now we stick to it, no matter what happens." He turned his back on them and waded on.

■ ■ ■

The forged order, on a scroll of the finest Augustan papyrus, had cost them plenty. It was almost as if the one-eyed old Arab in the Egyptian quarter who had done the job for them had been able to see through the moneybags and count the coins inside, down to the last drachma.

But, thought Bubo, *it was worth it!*

The Arab had even been able to produce, from a vast collection of stolen Roman bric-a-brac, an authentic seal ring of the Praetorian Guard with which he pompously stamped the hot wax on the roll. That seal alone was worth something, the Arab had assured them, not to mention his risk...

And now Bubo held the precious scroll in his hand, and it was smooth against the palm of his hand, not rough like the poorer grades of papyrus, and they still had money enough left to bribe the gatekeeper at the prison to let them in to see the captain of the guard.

Now, as if in a dream, the tall, heavy-set Roman—a man named Captain Remus—was bending over, reaching down to take the forged order from Bubo's shaking fingers.

"Here it is, sir," Bubo said in a small voice. "From Centurion Gaius Hesperian of Nero's Praetorian Guard, sir."

"So I see." As Captain Remus took the document and straightened up, he examined the seal with interest.

Bubo glanced at Horus and Suchos, who were cowering close by. Their tunics were still a little damp from the trip through the aqueduct but, Bubo decided, the dampness could just as easily have come from sweat. It was hot outside, though here within the stone walls of the prison it was comfortable enough.

The Roman officer walked slowly over to the window, a narrow, barred rectangle through which came the beam of sunlight that was the room's only illumination.

Why doesn't he open the scroll? thought Bubo, trying not to show any outward sign of tension.

"Beautiful design," said Captain of the Guard Remus. Bubo had noticed the design too—a Roman eagle with every feather etched in detail, and the initials that stood for "The Senate and People of Rome."

Is there-something wrong with the seal? thought Bubo.

"Seems a shame to break it," said Captain Remus with a little laugh, then broke the seal and began unrolling the scroll. Bubo relaxed somewhat.

Remus held the scroll up to the light from the window and read it, frowning and moving his lips. He was, though an officer, not a very educated man, or so it seemed. Bubo watched his face, his moving lips, his heavy working jaw, the stubble of beard on his cheek.

The Roman grimaced.

"S-something wrong, sir?" Bubo ventured.

"I don't understand these Praetorians," the officer said, shaking his head slowly. "He wants us to release two prisoners we've just finished locking up for him. By Mithra, what is he up to now?"

"I'm sure I wouldn't know, sir. I just brought the message."

"Yes, of course. You wouldn't know anything about it. Still, it's strange. Where is this Centurion Hesperian now?"

"At the Memnon estate, sir, I guess."

"Hmm. Yes. I know the place. Gloomy old pile of rocks with a lot of statues. Yes, I know the place. Maybe I ought to send a runner out to the Memnons' to ask this centurion to confirm this order."

"No, you'd better not do that," broke in Horus.

"Why not?" demanded the Roman, still not really suspicious.

"Well . . ." Horus was tongue-tied.

"This centurion, sir," Bubo improvised. "He doesn't like delay. When he gives an order, he expects to be obeyed . . . instantly!"

"Instantly, sir," echoed Suchos.

Captain Remus laughed. "And if he isn't obeyed instantly, what does he do?"

"Oh, by the gods, don't ask!" cried Bubo.

"There are some things too horrible to talk about," added Horus.

"You don't really want to know," finished Suchos miserably.

"Come on, you little rascals, tell me." Grinning, Captain Remus walked over and set the scroll on a massive table in the center of the room. He seemed bored, in search of some sort of entertainment to put some life into his dull guard duty. An idea appeared in Bubo's mind;

there was no time to think it over, only time to act on it. He turned to Horus.

"This!" shouted Bubo, slapping Horus in the face. Horus was more astonished than really hurt: The dwarfs rough-housed like this all the time, but the slap was totally unexpected by Captain Remus who, after an instant of stunned amazement, exploded in laughter.

Thought Bubo, *Simple things for simple people.*

"And like this," added Bubo, kicking Suchos in the rear.

"And this," said Horus, tripping Bubo and, when he fell, jumping on his ribs. (*That* really hurt!)

In an instant the three little men were in a whirlwind of mock combat. Captain Remus was laughing so hard he could hardly stand up, and other guards, hearing the noise, appeared at the door and came crowding in to watch the show, sniggering and elbowing each other playfully in the ribs.

As the dwarfs went down in a writhing, squirming, kicking pile on the floor, Bubo whispered, "Give them a good show, boys," then pulled free.

All eyes were on struggling Horus and Suchos when Bubo picked up the forged scroll from the table and slipped it under his tunic. Then, a moment later, he quietly stepped out through the now-unguarded door into the hall.

Bubo had been to the prison several times before. He had never been arrested, but he had come down with old Odysseus when there had been a drunken sailor—or even a ship's captain—to bail out. Bubo knew there was only one part of the building fit for such honored guests as the Memnons, and now the little man was headed there, walking quickly but trying not to appear rushed.

There was a guard at the door of that wing. Bubo showed him the forged order.

"Is this all right with Captain Remus?" the guard asked suspiciously.

"If it wasn't, would he have let me get this far?"

"I suppose not." The guard let Bubo pass.

A second guard was similarly satisfied and even went so far as to unlock the cell doors for Bubo. The first cell was Hathor's.

"Come along," said Bubo. "You're free."

She asked no questions, but followed immediately.

Demetrius almost spoiled everything, when his turn came.

"What is this? Another trick?" demanded the gaunt old man, backing toward the far end of his cell.

"Don't be silly," Hathor told him in an undertone. "Come along now, you heard me."

"Leave him here," advised Bubo, and the guard, overhearing, laughed.

But Hathor seized Demetrius by a bony wrist and dragged him bodily out into the corridor.

As they hurried away the guard's voice came echoing after them. "Good luck with the old goat!"

The other guard let them out through the side exit into the street, but Bubo darted back, inside explaining to the surprised guard, "I forgot something."

"Bubo..." cried out Hathor.

"I'll meet you out front," said Bubo, as the heavy door swung shut, separating him from her.

A minute later Bubo re-entered Captain Remus' office, where Suchos and Horus were now keeping a crowd of about fifteen Roman soldiers howling with laughter. The dwarfs had progressed to an imitation of Nero in the gladiatorial arena ... with a bear.

Nobody noticed Bubo's return; nobody noticed him replacing the forged scroll on Remus's table. He might as well have been invisible until he suddenly shouted: "All right! That's enough."

There was a chorus of disappointed groans as the mock combat ceased.

Bubo turned to Captain Remus, saying, "I'm sorry if we've disturbed your work."

"That's all right." The captain had not yet altogether stopped laughing.

"But really, you won't have to send a runner to confirm that order, sir," Bubo continued blandly.

"No? Why not?" Remus was wiping tears of laughter from his eyes.

"Because we'll go get Hesperian for you!" cried Bubo, and scampered out, followed by his two companions. "We'll be right back!"

"You're welcome here any time," shouted Remus, between chuckles.

Hathor and Demetrius were waiting in the street, out of sight of the main entrance. The dwarfs almost passed without seeing them, but Hathor called out in a low voice, "Here, Bubo."

They held a hurried council in a narrow passage behind a statue of the goddess of justice.

"We'd better get out of here before Remus finds out you're gone," said Bubo.

"Not before I thank you ... thank you all," Hathor said.

"Never mind that," Bubo said, looking around worriedly. "Is there any place you and the old man can hide?"

"Serapion's ship is in the harbor. You know the place. Next to my father's principal grain warehouse. We can go there," she answered. Her body showed all too well through her white silk gown, and Bubo looked away, embarrassed, as she added anxiously, "But we can't leave Alexandria without Serapion."

"Your murderous brother," said Bubo bitterly.

"You know about that?" She was surprised.

"Of course. I've known for a long time, perhaps longer than you. You thought that because I was a dwarf and a slave I couldn't see anything, couldn't figure out anything, so you and your brother never bothered to hide from me the play of expression on your faces. I read your faces, and the whole story was there. And do you know something? I would have handed your brother over to the Romans if it hadn't been for you. I couldn't stand for you to know it was me who turned Serapion in."

She had turned quite pale. "Oh, Bubo . . ."

"And now," Bubo went on, "you want me to risk my life to save the man who murdered my Master . . . and he was a kind, fair master to me."

"I can't ask you . . . after all you've done already." Now Hathor was the embarrassed one.

"Why not, eh? What does my life matter when balanced against the life of a Memnon? What does the life of a dwarf and a slave matter? I've read the face of the centurion, too. The centurion knows. Your brother's secrets are secrets no longer." One glance at her face told him that he was right. "And now I'm to walk into the same trap your brother is in and try to snatch him out from under the very eyes of the Romans. Well of course I'll do it, my lady."

A burning anger seemed to transform the little man, to turn him into a giant. "I must humbly beg your pardon for not having done it already."

He turned on his heel and walked quickly away. Horus and Suchos trotted after him.

"Serapion is a priest, you know," called Hathor, before the dwarfs were out of earshot. "His magic will protect you."

"There is no magic!" Bubo snapped.

And then Hathor knew that Bubo had never really feared her, but only pretended to.

■ ■ ■

The terrible Egyptian sun had climbed almost to the zenith. Tall Serapion stood at the window of his second-floor bedroom and gazed moodily out over the broad expanse of the Memnon estate and at the jumble of bright white walls and red tile roofs beyond the wall.

Alexandria!

How he wished he could be out there now, in Alexandria's streets, joining the milling crowds that prepared for the great Festival of the Ship of Isis, the most important holiday of the year, a real *Egyptian* holiday, not an imported one like the birthdays of the various Roman emperors and gods, or the enigmatic celebrations of Alexandria's Jews and Greeks.

It was so hot!

Though he was clad only in a light white linen tunic and sandals, he was still drenched in sweat. Better even than being out in the streets of the White City would be to stand on the deck of his fighting ship, up front in the prow above the heavy gilt-iron hawk's head ram that had smashed through the side of so many pirate ships. Better to be far out at sea, beyond sight of land, on that ship that was like a living creature, with its eyes painted on the sides of the prow and its tail feathers turning up back in the stern . . . and its great square red sail catching the gale. At sea Serapion could cast off all his garments as he cast off all the polite restraints of "civilization" and, naked as a slave or a common sailor, let the wind, laced with cold salt spray, cool his body from head to toe.

He sighed.

Here in his room the wind was so feeble it hardly moved the green curtains on either side of him, let alone cooled his suffering flesh.

Hesperian's man, Optio Mannus, had just left, after giving Serapion an order—*An order, mind you!*—to lunch privately with the centurion this noon. At sea it would be he, Serapion, who gave the orders.

I wonder, he thought, *how much Hesperian knows.*

He must know something, or how would he dare be so bold as to command a Memnon to dine with him? But he had been bold, even impudent, from the beginning. Did he really think Hathor had committed the murder? Or was the arrest of Hathor a trick?

It may be his way of throwing me off my guard.

He turned from the window and began to pace the room, sandals slapping the marble floor.

If I can hold him off for just a few more hours!

There was a faint rustle outside the window.

His hand flew to his side, clutching for the handle of his sword, but it was gone. Hesperian, of course, had disarmed him, but the reflex, born of long training, was still there. He glanced around quickly, searching for some substitute weapon.

Ah, that heavy silver candle holder! That would have to do.

He grasped it like a club and, stepping softly, approached the window. A hand appeared, grasping the windowsill. Someone was coming in! Serapion thought, *So this is Roman Justice. One of Hesperian's men is going to kill me in exactly the same way I killed my father.* He raised the candle holder to strike.

An ugly little face appeared in the window, round-eyed with surprise. "Wait! It's me, Bubo!"

With a grunt of relief, Serapion lowered his makeshift weapon. The dwarf shifted his weight from the vines to the sill and scrambled into the room.

"By Serapis, what are you doing here?" began Serapion in a loud voice.

Bubo winced and, finger to lips, hissed, "Sssh, you fool. I've come to get you out of here."

"You?" Serapion almost burst out laughing, but he did lower his voice.

"Yes, me, but not for your sake. If it weren't for your sister, I wouldn't lift a finger to help you."

"I don't need your help, little man." There was the Memnon pride again.

"Oh no? Suppose I tell you that the centurion knows everything, that he's sure you're the murderer and is only waiting to arrest you when he's tricked you into some damaging admission. Do you still think you can afford to be so grand and independent?"

Serapion frowned. "How do I know this is true?"

"Your sister sent me. I got her and Demetrius out of jail. They're waiting for you on your ship down by the largest grain warehouse. Listen . . . there is a way out of here." He told Serapion about the underground aqueduct, then finished with: "Now do you believe me?"

"It could be Hesperian that sent you, not my sister."

There was a moment of silence, then Bubo said, "That's true, but you'll have to trust me. Make up your mind."

Serapion considered, rubbing his lean jaw with a muscular finger. Hesperian knew. Serapion had felt that for some time now, but had not wanted to believe it, yet now . . .

"I believe you, Bubo."

"Good! Now we wait for the right moment and slip out the window and down the wall. The Roman guard passes here only about every five minutes . . . they are so sure you can't get beyond the outer walls of the estate that they're not guarding your window very well. Then it's down the back stairs to the aqueduct and . . ."

"Not so fast, little man. There's one thing I have to do before I leave."

"What's that?" Bubo was exasperated.

"Kill Hesperian." Serapion said it very calmly, almost indifferently. Of course. What could be more logical? Most of the Romans were stupid, easily outwitted; but Hesperian, it seemed, was different. Hesperian might follow him, sniff him out like a bloodhound, stop him somehow. No, the centurion was too clever to live.

"You really are a madman," said Bubo, taking a step backward. "They're watching you now. You couldn't possibly..."

"But *you* could." Serapion's voice was still cool and detached.

Bubo shook his head violently. "No! I never killed anyone, and I never will."

"Would you like to stay here when I leave? The Romans might change their minds about torturing you if they are angry enough, and you couldn't tell them where I was, could you? That would be betraying Hathor. You'd die before betraying her, wouldn't you?" He looked down at the little humpbacked man with a cold, calculating eye.

When there was no reply, Serapion strode to the far corner of the room, knelt, and with his fingertips pried up a loose bit of red mosaic tile from the Greek key design in the floor's border. Below the bit of tile was a small hole from which he gingerly extracted a tiny bottle made of blue-green translucent glass.

He handed the bottle to Bubo, saying casually, "Here's a bit of very special seasoning. I'm sure it will improve the centurion's wine."

■ ■ ■

In the Memnon household lunch, like breakfast, had never been an elaborate affair: Bread, cheese, a bit of cold meat, some vegetables, and fruit washed down with cool, spiced and watered wine. Simple but nourishing.

Even this food was not yet on the table when Serapion came into the smaller dining room and reclined on his couch. There was nobody else in the room; only a fly buzzed lethargically around the ceiling from time to time.

Serapion, resting on one elbow, watched the fly and frowned. It was cool and dim in the room, and very quiet. Quite comfortable in every way. *But where was Hesperian?*

The Roman was usually the soul of punctuality. Was he late this time on purpose, to make Serapion nervous? Indeed, what better way to soften up a guilty suspect?

Forcing himself to concentrate, Serapion began his calculations. Let's see. When the Roman collapsed from the effects of the poison, there would be time for a quick walk through the kitchen to the back stairs and down to the furnace room, which opened onto the cisterns and the underground aqueduct. Very good.

But what if Hesperian was on his guard? Serapion pursed his lips. *I'm younger than he is... quicker... probably stronger.* And there would certainly be a knife on the table. One unguarded moment and the Roman would be dead before he knew what had happened. And suppose

Hesperian had posted a guard outside the door? Well, with Hesperian's sword, he could finish off the guard quickly enough, particularly with the element of surprise in his favor.

But if Hesperian did not come in alone? What then?

Serapion bit his lip. Things were happening too fast now. There was no time for that careful planning that makes success a certainty. Perhaps it would have been better not to try to kill Hesperian, when so much was in the hands of the Fates.

He heard footsteps in the hall. One person? Two? Three? There was an echo: it was hard to tell at first.

It was one! He was sure of it. He breathed a deep sigh of relief.

Gaius Hesperian, smiling and genial, entered.

"Ave Caesar," said the Roman, with a vague salute.

"Ave Caesar." Serapion gave no outward sign of his tension.

Hesperian reclined on the couch across the table from him.

Serapion thought: *He hasn't even posted a guard outside the door.*

In the dim light that found its way in from the courtyard, Hesperian's clean-shaven, square-cut face seemed to have lost its lines of age and worry, and in spite of the gray in his thick, bushy eyebrows and receding hair, he seemed somehow young, innocent and . . . trusting. When he laid down on the marble top table the swagger stick of twisted vine that was the symbol of his centurion's authority, it was with a gesture that, to Serapion's feverish eyes, seemed to say more clearly than words, "I am no more than a man. I too can die."

The impression was strengthened by the fact that, though he wore shortsword and dagger, he had no helmet or armor, only a short red linen tunic and a pair of open-toed leather boots. By the gods, he looked as defenseless as a baby!

"You're a clever fellow, my friend," began Hesperian.

"I? Oh, no, it's you who are famous for your keen mind."

Hesperian regarded him seriously. "I know I have a certain reputation, but I must honestly confess that I don't deserve it. I'm actually rather slow-witted—no, really I am—but persistent. It's my belief that even a slow-witted man can understand anything if he tries long enough."

"You don't say?"

"Ah, but I do . . . now, where is our lunch?"

"It will be ready in a moment, I'm sure."

"They fuss over food too much, don't you think, Serapion? A simple lunch like this, but they must put in a little of this and a little of that . . . You know what I mean?"

Serapion nodded, feeling slightly ill.

At that moment Wakar appeared, bowed almost imperceptibly, and shuffled in with the food on a tray. As the slave set one dish after another on the table, Serapion burst into a flood of talk, saying anything that happened to come into his head, all the time thinking, *Pour the wine, Wakar. Pour the wine!*

"Ah, my friend Hesperian, have you ever tasted Jewish food? There are so many rules to follow in its preparation you'd think it would be dull and tasteless . . . but it isn't! Here in Alexandria there are eating places in the Jewish quarter where you can get food that would be the envy of the gods. Sometimes I think it isn't what you put into food that makes it good, but what you leave out . . ."

Wakar was pouring the wine from a small, perhaps one-quart, amphora, into the two white, glazed-pottery, goblets. Serapion thought, *What if he insists that I drink first? The host is supposed to drink first, but am I the host, or is he? Do I dare hold the poison in my mouth? No. I'd just pretend to drink. But wouldn't he notice?*

But as he thought these things, his mouth, as if it was someone else's, went on talking, just a little too fast. "The best food is what you get at sea. I don't mean the garbage you bring along. I mean fish, fresh-caught and fried right there on deck over a crackling brazier of live coals."

Neither man had touched the food or the wine. Serapion rattled on.

Hesperian raised a hand to stem the flow. "What's wrong, Serapion? Aren't you hungry?"

"Frankly, no. There's so much tension . . ."

"Well, I am! And thirsty, too."

Hesperian reached for his wine.

Chapter Three

CAPTAIN OF THE GUARD REMUS was horror-struck.

"Demetrius and Hathor Memnon escaped? But that's impossible!"

"They're not in their cells," said the guard.

"You mentioned that there were some dwarfs here," Optio Mannus prompted.

Captain Remus threw himself down in a chair behind the heavy table in the center of the guardroom, pale in the reflected light from the single sunbeam that entered through the room's small and only window.

"Yes, that's right," Remus said. "But I didn't let them past. They played tricks for a while to amuse us, then went on . . . they said they'd be right back with a confirmation of their order." He held up the scroll.

"It seems they played one trick more than you thought." Optio Mannus stood before the table, glaring down at him.

"It wasn't my fault . . ."

"I hope you can prove that. Soldiers have died for lesser mistakes." Mannus turned to leave, face flushed with anger.

Behind him Remus was muttering, "They were only slaves . . . and dwarfs even. How was I to know . . ."

Mannus paused in the doorway. "Don't just sit there like an idiot! Organize a search!"

"Yes . . . yes, sir."

■ ■ ■

Mannus' first thought, as he emerged into the street and the blazing sun, was *This could ruin everything!* He glanced around, saw one of Remus' troops walking toward him, leading a handsome brown horse by the bridle.

"Give me that," Mannus commanded.

The soldier opened his mouth to argue, but noticed Mannus' rank and saluted instead, then bent over slightly to hold his foot as the optio swung into the saddle. With a clatter of hooves on the paving stones and a jingle of bridle chain, Mannus was on his way, whipping the horse to a gallop.

It was only moments before he was forced to slow almost to a walk. The street was narrower a little ways from the prison, though, like all the streets in the city, it was straight as a rule and met all side streets at a perfect right angle. The crowds of tourists, street merchants, and devout pilgrims here for the Isis Festival made progress slow even on horseback. Again and again he found his way blocked by a wagon full of wildly colorful flowers or delicious-smelling cakes or candy statuettes of the goddess in the shape of a dove. Again and again some idiot, already drunk though the festivities had not yet begun, staggered into the Roman's path and, in spite of shouted threats and even an occasional crack of the whip, would make way only with the most maddening slowness. Repeatedly some pack of filthy children and dogs ran almost under the hooves of the horse, making the poor animal balk or lurch sideways, once almost dumping Mannus into the street.

The festivals of the elder gods and goddesses were always riots, reflected Mannus grimly. It's as if the deities begrudged man even that shaky semblance of order he'd managed, over the centuries, to achieve. Chaos! That's what the High Immortals loved!

The road grew wider and the crowd thinner after he had passed through the Gate of the Sun and was beyond the walls of the Inner City, and he was able to once more break into a full gallop as the buildings of the Jewish Outer City, luxurious, half-asleep, and undulating gently in the shimmering heat, flashed by.

With an exchange of salutes at the Gate of Canopus he passed outside the walls of the Outer City and swung southward into the suburb of Eleusis, where the streets, for the first time, curved and branched at odd angles instead of being laid out straight as a spear, for here, where the estates of the rich were located, property lines, not the dreams of city planners, determined everything.

In a moment he reined up outside the gates of the Memnon villa and dismounted.

"See to my horse," he commanded the Praetorian who stood guard there, then pushed open the heavy gate and ran in, head down, puffing and panting.

It was at the door of the Memnon mansion that his headlong rush was finally checked. "Stop," said Daphnis, stepping forward out of the shadows to block the entrance. "Hesperian left orders he was not to be disturbed . . . for any reason."

"What's this? Let me by," wheezed Mannus.

"Of course, if you're a good enough swordsman . . ." The scribe's handsome face wore a mocking smile. The smile vanished when Mannus, at the end of his patience, drew his shortsword.

Daphnis stepped aside with a low bow, saying only, "My, aren't we masculine today!"

In the great hall, Mannus shouted at a startled Wakar, "Where's Hesperian?" The slave, speechless, could only point. Mannus dashed by him, pounded down the long, echoing hallway, and burst into the smaller dining room.

Hesperian and Serapion were reclining at table. Hesperian had a cup of wine at his lips. Slowly he lowered the cup, without drinking, and turned toward Mannus, one eyebrow raised questioningly.

Serapion, too, turned toward Mannus, but there was a look of thinly-disguised dismay in the young man's eyes.

Mannus saluted, then gasped out, "Hathor and Demetrius, sir! They've ... escaped!"

Hesperian's face was an emotionless mask, but Mannus, who knew him well, could detect faint traces of anxiety: The flicker of an eyelid, a slight trembling in the big hands.

The cup now rested on the table.

Hesperian sprang to his feet. "And Simon Baal?"

"He's still under lock and key, sir."

"And did you order a search?"

"Yes, sir!"

"Good! But wait ... Did you also give orders that Hathor must, under no circumstances, be harmed?"

"Why, no, sir."

"Why not?"

"I saw no need ..."

"Damn you, Mannus! You know what bloodthirsty fools these local troops are! If they find her, they may kill her on the spot and expect a reward for it. I swear, if they do harm her, I'll hold you personally responsible."

"I'm ... sorry, sir."

Hesperian turned to Serapion. "Pardon me, my friend, but I must leave you. You'll have to finish the lunch without me, but don't worry. I'll post two guards to see that you are not disturbed at your meal."

Serapion ate nothing, but he spent several minutes, after Hesperian and Mannus had gone, staring gloomily at Hesperian's wine.

■ ■ ■

Adrastia Memnon, beautiful in the way a slightly wilted flower is beautiful, and clad in sweeping green silks and glittering rings, bracelets, and necklaces like a princess, strode grandly down the great staircase, paused a moment at the foot of the steps, delicate fingertips touching the base of her throat, practiced smiling, then set off in the general direction of the smaller dining room.

Centurion Gaius Hesperian and his man Mannus passed her in the dim hallway. She wished them a good afternoon, but they were so engrossed in their muttered conversation they hardly noticed her.

She shrugged. What could one expect from the Roman boors?

As she reached the entrance to the smaller dining room, Serapion was just coming out, a soldier on either side of him. She wished him, too, a good afternoon, but he did not say a word, only glanced at her with such a wild-eyed look that she gave a little gasp.

She watched him and his guards as they continued on up the hallway, a puzzled frown on her fine-cut features, then turned and entered the dining room.

It appeared that Serapion and Hesperian had not touched a morsel, but all the same Wakar—faithful Wakar—was there, starting to clear the table.

She was thirsty; she reached for a cup of wine.

Wakar's hand shot out and caught her wrist as he said, very quickly, one word. "No."

She turned on him, amazed. "How dare you say 'No' to me?"

"That is the Centurion's wine."

"What do I care? Wine is wine." She tried to get free, but his grip was strong.

"I'll brine you a cup of your own."

"That will take time, and I'm thirsty now. I warn you! Let go of my wrist or I'll have you whipped. I want that wine, and I shall have it!"

He looked at her with anguish but did not let go. "No, no, beloved Mistress. That wine is poisoned."

"What?" She stopped struggling and took a step back from the table. His grip relaxed, but she could see on his face the evidence of some great inner conflict.

"Who?" she asked him. "Who poisoned it?"

"The dwarf Bubo." His voice was low, almost a whisper.

Adrastia prided herself on her kindness to her slaves. In her way she loved them, and thought they loved her. The dwarfs in particular loved her; she was sure of it. "Impossible!" she said. "Not *my* Bubo!"

"It was not you, Mistress, that he was trying to poison. It was the Centurion. Bubo is a good slave. He would give his life for the Memnon family." He released her wrist and she stood rubbing it, bewildered.

"But this poison . . ." she began.

"He was only obeying his Master, Serapion."

She sat down abruptly on one of the couches around the low table. "I see. I see." And she did indeed see. She saw and understood everything, all in a flash. Serapion! Yes, of course. Who else? "And you saw him? You saw Bubo put in the poison?"

He nodded. "Yes."

"And you did nothing to stop him or to warn the Roman?"

"Nothing."

"Because of your loyalty to the Memnons?"

"Yes."

Now it was she who reached out and took him by the wrist. "I'll never have you whipped, Wakar. Never again."

"No promises, Lady. Please. This thing is heavy on me. It is easy enough to be loyal to you, or to Hathor . . . even to Demetrius, who thinks of slaves as being lower than animals. But now I don't know . . . I don't know if I can still be loyal to Serapion."

"Because he murdered your master?"

His wild laugh startled and frightened her. "My Master? No, Lady. Because I realize now Serapion must have killed Rophos, and I loved Rophos. I loved him, Lady!"

Tears had begun to trickle down his cheeks.

"Hush now. Hush, Wakar. That was long ago." She gave his wrist a little squeeze, looking up into his anguished face. "Sit down here." She patted the place beside her on the couch. He obeyed, slumping slowly into a sitting position. Old slave and young mistress, they leaned together as if for warmth, though the room was not cold.

"Now listen to me, Wakar. Please control yourself and try to answer my questions."

"Yes. All right."

"Where is Bubo now?"

"I don't know. He was in the kitchen . . ."

"Come, Wakar. We must find him." *But when I find* him, she thought, *should I punish him . . . or reward him?*

■ ■ ■

Adrastia had always known there was some place on the estate where slaves could hide and not be found, but she had never been able to figure out where, mainly because she had never tried very hard. It had not seemed important.

But now, suddenly, it had become important, for, she was convinced, this secret place was where Bubo must be hiding. She and Wakar had searched everywhere else. Neither Bubo nor the other dwarfs seemed to be anywhere around the house or grounds, yet she could not imagine how they could have gotten beyond the wall that went around the Memnon estate on all sides and was guarded both by the Memnons' personal guard and the Romans.

As she and Wakar returned to the smaller dining room (where the meal remained undisturbed on the table), a suspicion crossed her mind. "Wakar, are you telling me all you know?"

"What do you mean, Mistress?"

"I think you know where the dwarfs are, but some sort of misplaced loyalty prevents you from telling me."

The eunuch turned away from her. *So I'm right*, she thought triumphantly.

"Tell me," she commanded.

He said nothing.

"I can have you whipped."

"After your promise?" said the slave.

Damn. How can one whip someone who has just saved one's life?

"I must know, Wakar." It was as if she was begging him. That wasn't right. A mistress does not beg a slave for anything.

"Why?" he asked her, quite simply.

She gripped his arm. "I must hear from Bubo's own lips that Serapion is the murderer. It seems so unbelievable. I mean, I always took Serapion for a harmless dreamer, a weak child in the body of a man. The Serapion I knew—or thought I knew—could never have made the decision, let alone formed the plan and carried it out."

"Hush." Wakar held up his hand for silence. "Someone's coming."

There were indeed the sounds of hurrying footsteps, and the Roman scribe Daphnis stuck his head in the door. "Have either of you seen the dwarfs recently?" he demanded.

"Why no," Adrastia answered. *They're looking for them, too*, she thought, slightly puzzled.

"I'm not surprised," Daphnis said off-handedly. "They'd be fools to come back here after helping Hathor and Demetrius to escape." The Roman had continued on his way before Adrastia could recover enough from this new bit of information to ask an intelligent question.

Wakar said softly, "Serapion is proud. If you confront him face to face and ask him, perhaps he himself will tell you what he's done."

She nodded slowly, thoughtfully. "Yes. Yes. Perhaps you're right. Come, let's go up to his room and see if we'll be allowed to speak to him."

Hesperian and Mannus met them as they came out into the hall. "Wait, Wakar. I want to have a word with you," said the centurion. Wakar stopped, but Adrastia, since no one attempted to stop her, continued on down the hall.

■ ■ ■

"I suppose you can go in," said the guard outside Serapion's bedroom door. "I have no orders to the contrary." He stood aside and she entered.

Serapion, seated dejectedly on the edge of his bed, looked up at her with suspicion. "Adrastia! What do you want?"

She closed the door behind her carefully. She knew that with the door closed the guard would not be able to eavesdrop so long as she and Serapion kept their voices down.

Finger to her lips, she quickly crossed the room and seated herself beside him. "You did it, didn't you?" she whispered.

"Did what?" He was on his guard.

"Killed my husband, of course."

"Don't be silly. Why would I do . . ."

"Ah, I see in your face that I'm right. Until this moment I wouldn't have believed it."

"You're making a big mistake."

"No, you are. You think I'm angry about it. You think I might tell the Romans. How little you understand me! Don't you see? I'm glad you did it! I admire you for it! Oh, how I underestimated you, just because you wouldn't help me run the Memnon financial empire. But of course you wouldn't want to get mixed up in business! You'd find such things dull . . . and they *are* dull."

She edged closer to him, continuing in a low, breathless voice, "But I could handle the dull parts of it. You could spend your time sailing. You could be commander of your father's fleet of grain ships and fighting ships. If you and I were to marry—oh it's not so insane as it sounds—we'd hold the whole Memnon empire together, build it up bigger than ever. You've never been comfortable calling me your mother, I know that, because we're almost the same age, and because there's more between us—it's unspoken but it's there—than there could be between son and stepmother."

"No, by Serapis. No!"

"I offer you everything, and you still say 'No'?"

"I can't marry you!"

"There's someone else? Ah, Hathor. Of course. Well, I'm not jealous. Every man has his other woman. At least we'd keep it in the family."

"I can't marry anyone. Tomorrow I may be in prison . . ."

"No, no. I can help you."

He turned to face her at last, and she shrank back from the desperation in his eyes. "I don't need your help," he said so loudly that she glanced involuntarily toward the door. Up to this point they had been speaking in whispers and near-whispers, but she was sure the guard could not have failed to overhear that last remark.

She stood up, murmuring, "I see. You have other help, eh? The dwarfs? You don't need to answer. But if you need me, I am with you, remember that."

As she went out she could feel his feverish eyes burning into her back, and she thought, *You murderer. You magnificent murderer! Why won't you believe me?*

∎ ∎ ∎

The afternoon sunlight, hot and bright, streamed in the open kitchen door. Wakar stared numbly at the sunlight, and as he did the Roman centurion and his aide, who stood on either side of him, seemed to fade out of his consciousness, and a strange feeling came over the slave, a feeling that at any moment he would see his old friend, cheerful, foolish Rophos, step through that door again, as he had done so many times in years past.

But Rophos was dead.

With a jerk, Wakar once again became aware of those around him. The centurion was saying: "This doorway, Mannus, may be the most important one in the house, for our purposes. Through this doorway someone could slip out, climb up the vines on the outside wall, and spear old Odysseus like a fish in a barrel, and through this doorway someone might also slip into the kitchen to poison the soup. It's one of the few doors that open to the outside of the house rather than to the courtyard."

Mannus nodded and said something Wakar couldn't make out. The Romans were fading out again, and suddenly, with feverish hallucinatory clarity, there was the smiling face of Rophos peering out from the shadows behind the great brick oven where the bread was baked.

Wakar did not fear the dead. To him, as to almost everyone else, it was not uncommon for the dead to visit the living, in dreams or, more rarely, when one was wide awake. The dead were his friends. They could tell him where riches were hidden, or predict the future. It was the living one must fear! And this ghost in particular was his friend. Good old Rophos! But now the face had vanished.

Hesperian called, "Wakar! Come here."

Like a sleepwalker, the slave obeyed.

"You're in the kitchen a lot, aren't you?" the centurion asked.

Wakar nodded. "Yes. Most of the time."

"On the night when your master was murdered, were you on duty here?"

"During the meal. After that I went back to the slaves' quarters."

"Then if someone had come through here and gone out that door . . ."

"I didn't see anyone, Sir."

"No, no, how could you?" Hesperian seemed angry, but more at himself than at anyone else. He turned to Mannus and muttered, "The case is crumbling, Mannus. I had it all right here in my hand, but now it's crumbling." His gaze returned to Wakar. "But you were here when the soup was poisoned?"

"So they say, but I saw nothing."

"You said some of the Memnons were here in the kitchen."

"Yes. Hathor. Demetrius."

With a sigh Hesperian gazed at the bright doorway, as if expecting it to answer him. "And Serapion, Wakar."

The motion was quick and furtive, but, out of the corner of his eye, Hesperian saw it. "Wakar! What was that you did just now?"

"Nothing, Sir."

"You crossed yourself."

"I suppose so. A meaningless gesture . . ."

"Meaningless? It means you're a Christian! That's what it means. Isn't that right?"

Wakar, after a pause, nodded. "Yes, Sir."

"You crossed yourself when I mentioned the name of Serapion. Why?"

Wakar, eyes downcast, remained silent.

"I know your religion. You're sworn to tell the truth. Tell me the truth, then, about Serapion." Hesperian waited expectantly.

Wakar thought, *But the Christ also tells us that a slave must not disobey his masters. God places these men in authority over us. If we disobey them, we disobey God.* Wakar could neither speak nor meet the Roman's gaze.

Then he felt once again the presence of Rophos, though this time Rophos was invisible. Wakar thought (for he believed the dead could read thoughts), *Rophos! What should I do?*

But it was only at certain times that the dead could actually speak to the living, and this was not one of them. *Rophos! Speak! By the living Christ, speak!* These were his thoughts, but his lips were motionless.

He felt a hand on his shoulder, strong but gentle. The centurion was saying, "Rophos was your friend. Will you allow . . ."

Why didn't Hesperian leave him alone? The other time had been easier. The other time the Romans had tortured only Wakar's body.

Rophos! Come to me! By the risen Jesus! By eternal Yahweh! By the Holy Spirit! Come!

But the presence of Rophos was fading, fading away. And now, through the drone of the centurion's urgent voice, Wakar heard something else, the sound of some of the servants in the smaller dining room, laughing together as they worked. It was a soothing, familiar sound, except for . . . Wakar straightened. Except for the poisoned wine, which was still in there on the table!

What was that? Sabella's giggle. Sabella, he knew, was in the habit of eating a bit of the leftovers as she cleared a table, and of taking an occasional sip of the leftover wine.

"Excuse me, Sir," Wakar said awkwardly to Hesperian. "Excuse me."

Wakar caught a glimpse of the Roman's amazed face as he turned and lurched toward the smaller dining room as fast as his crippled leg would allow.

There was the hallway, long and dim.

And there was the doorway to the dining room.

And there was Sabella by the table, cup in hand.

"No!" shouted Wakar wildly. The little black girl turned a defiant eye in his direction and raised the cup to her lips. He threw himself forward and slapped the cup from her fingers, spattering the floor and walls with wine.

The girl howled with dismay and anger and kicked him in the shins. (Fortunately her feet were bare.)

Behind him Wakar could hear the footsteps of the Romans, then the voice of Hesperian boomed out, "That was poison, wasn't it? Poison meant for me!"

Wakar was tongue-tied.

The centurion continued, more loudly, "Is this what your barbarian religion means, Christian? That you stand by silently and allow men to be murdered?"

"No! No! You don't understand!"

"Do you think your God, if there is a God, will forgive you if you go on protecting the man who murdered not only your master, but your closest friend? If that's true, then your God must be worse than men!"

The face of Rophos appeared and disappeared abruptly, again and again, first near the table, then near the door, then over by the walls that glistened with trickling wine. There it was, smiling, behind the furious Sabella. There it was above the heads of the cowering serving maids. Then, suddenly, Rophos was gone. There had been no words, but somehow the specter had spoken.

Wakar collapsed on one of the couches next to the table. "Yes," he whispered. "Yes, it's Serapion. I can't let this go on. It's Serapion."

There was silence only for a moment, then the deep voice of Hesperian roared out triumphantly: "On your feet, Wakar! I want you to repeat those words to my officers and men, to the whole world!"

Wakar stood up and limped slowly toward the door. He felt a great peace coming over him, a feeling of infinite relief.

There were running footsteps in the hall ahead of him, then Daphnis burst into the room, panting and sweating, and thrust him roughly to one side. The handsome scribe stood swaying, trying to get his breath. Hesperian said impatiently, "What now?"

"Trouble, sir." Daphnis glanced at the serving maids and Wakar questioningly, as if to ask if it was all right to speak in front of them.

"Out with it!" commanded the centurion.

"Basileides, a former freedman of the Emperor Claudius and a rich and powerful friend of the Memnon family . . ." He paused to suck in a lung full of air. "He's here with a signed order from the Praefectus of Egypt, Tiberius Julius Alexander. Sir, he is demanding that we stop the investigation and set everyone free!"

Hesperian was the first into the hallway, but Wakar was close behind him. The centurion turned and said softly, "Stick close to me, Wakar. I'm going to need you."

A richly-dressed fat old man with dark mottled skin was waddling toward them, shaking a pudgy fist and bellowing, "I want to see the commanding officer here. I want . . . ah, there you are, Centurion!" He thumped his bloated chest and gave a flabby salute. "Ave Caesar!"

"Ave Caesar," echoed Hesperian, Daphnis and Mannus.

"Ave Caesar," chorused the crowd of well-dressed but decadent-looking Greek-Egyptian aristocrats who followed the fat man. Wakar noticed that several of the aristocrats wore the toga of Roman citizenship . . . a distinguished company indeed.

And there among them, smirking, was the Parthian, Simon Baal.

"My name may mean something to you," said the fat man, with a slight bow. "Basileides."

"I've heard of you," answered Hesperian crisply.

"And I, sir, have heard of you. Everyone is amazed at the stories of the evildoers you have brought to justice. You and I know, of course, that there's never much truth in these stories, but the people must have heroes." He smiled. "What's really remarkable is that someone as low-born as you could rise so high in the ranks of the army, and so young, too. You and I . . ." He winked. "We know how little birth matters these days, fortunately for us. But . . ." He frowned, almost pouted. ". . . really, Gaius—may I call you Gaius?—this time you and Nero have gone too far. He has no authority to send in his private troops on a purely local matter like this, arresting people right and left without evidence, without even charges. As soon as I heard you had ordered a manhunt for members of such a fine and universally-respected family as the Memnons, I had no choice but to instantly bring the matter to the attention of my good friend, Alex—Tiberius Julius Alexander—who agreed with me that this harassment of innocent people, undertaken without his knowledge or consent, must stop at once."

Hesperian leaned forward. "But sir, what would you say if I told you I now know who it was that killed Odysseus Memnon?"

"Lies!" cried out Simon Baal, his head snapping up so violently it set his braids bouncing.

Basileides ignored the interruption. "Do you have proof?"

"The testimony of one of his slaves . . ." began Hesperian.

"The word of a slave? What's that worth?" sneered Simon. Some of the Greek-Egyptian nobles laughed outright.

"Together with a chain of simple, logical reasoning . . ." Hesperian said.

Basileides broke in, "After all this time, no possible chain of reasoning could be convincing enough to justify holding a Memnon. No, nothing short of a freely-given confession before unimpeachable witnesses would convince us." The nobles nodded their agreement. "Do you have that?"

"No," admitted Hesperian, after a baffled pause.

The fat man brandished a scroll. "Then you have no choice but to obey this order from Praefectus Alexander himself!" He turned and caught sight of Adrastia coming down the hall, a puzzled expression on her face. "Adrastia! Don't worry, my sweet. I'll have you out of this man's power in no time." He turned back to Hesperian. "And now where's Serapion? I have no intention of leaving here without him."

This can't actually be happening, thought Wakar, dazed. He stepped forward and said, "May I speak?"

"No!" called out Simon Baal.

There was a murmur of accord from among the nobles.

Wakar turned toward Hesperian, thinking, *The Roman is clever. He'll think of something.*

But the centurion just stood there helplessly, arms dangling at his sides. After a long pause, Hesperian exhaled softly and said, "Follow me."

He led them all through the hallway, out into the great front hall, up the marble staircase and finally to the door of Serapion's bedroom. The guard at the door looked at him questioningly.

"Wait here," said Hesperian, his voice heavy with defeat. "I'll bring him out."

"We'll wait all right," said Basileides, glancing at Adrastia, Simon Baal, and the rest of his friends. "Not that we don't trust you . . ."

The guard stepped aside and Hesperian opened the bedroom door.

■ ■ ■

Mannus knew that in every battle there comes a time when the action goes beyond anything that either general had planned for, a time when planning is replaced by improvisation and chance, but even then there is an advantage to the commander who has prepared himself for such a moment, who is ready to act in the midst of chaos.

But Mannus was as surprised as any of the others who waited there outside the door (which Hesperian had only half closed) at the centurion's first words to Serapion. That wasn't the voice of a defeated man, but of the victor!

"They've come for you, Serapion."

There was a long silence before Serapion's reply. "I expected as much."

Hesperian's voice was crisp and commanding now, as if he was speaking to one of his troops. "Get your things together." There was a sound of shuffling feet, then Hesperian added, "Are you still proud, Serapion?"

Suddenly Mannus understood. Without actually saying so, Hesperian was giving Serapion the impression that he was under arrest!

Serapion's voice, when it came, was defiant. "Of killing the old man? Yes, damn you! I had my reasons, good reasons, but reasons I could never expect a Roman to understand!"

Mannus glanced around at the stunned faces of Basileides and his friends. They wanted a freely-given confession before unimpeachable witnesses? Well, here it was!

There was another pause, then the sound of a sudden blow, a grunt, and the thud of a falling body. Mannus was the first to leap through the doorway, shortsword in hand.

Hesperian was sprawled on the floor, still conscious, but with blood running down his forehead. "The window..." he groaned as he pulled himself into a sitting position. Outside Mannus heard the sound of a man landing on the lawn, then running footsteps.

Hesperian, shaking his head slowly, dragged himself to a kneeling position and reached out to pick up a heavy silver candle holder that lay on the marble floor beside him, then grinned sheepishly at the small crowd gathering around him and said, "I thought it would be more convincing if I let him take a crack at me." He rubbed his forehead, then examined the blood on his fingers. "Don't worry about Serapion. My men are all over the villa. He can't get far."

"Let me help you, sir," Mannus said, stooping and extending a hand. With a grunt and a heave he had the centurion on his feet.

Hesperian blinked and swayed as Mannus continued to hold him erect. "Sorry. I guess I'm still a little dizzy." With an effort he steadied himself. "And now my friends..." His slightly unfocused gaze swept around the circle of Greek-Egyptian aristocrats. "Now I am issuing an order for Serapion's arrest. Do any of you gentlemen wish to object?"

Not one of them, including Simon Baal, dared to say a word.

Hesperian continued, "Then Daphnis, spread the word. I want this estate sealed ... nobody goes in, and nobody goes out. Then I want every corner of the house and grounds searched, and searched again, until Serapion is found."

Daphnis saluted. "Yes, sir!"

Hesperian seated himself on the edge of the bed. "Mannus, will you oversee the search? I'd like to lie down for a few minutes." He stretched out and closed his eyes. "If I'm asleep when you catch him, wake me, eh? Show me no mercy." He touched his forehead and winced.

"Yes, sir," Mannus said uncertainly, backing away from the bed to join the others, who were filing out of the room, murmuring excitedly to each other.

In the hallway Mannus felt a hand tug at his elbow. It was the slave Wakar limping along, trying to keep up. "Master Mannus, I have something to tell you."

"Later, slave, later," Mannus growled, brushing the eunuch impatiently to one side.

Mannus was sure that everything depended on speed. There was no way for Serapion to leave the estate, so all he had to do was move quickly enough to flush Serapion out before nightfall. After dark it might not be so easy.

But as the afternoon faded away and he found himself in the kitchen, watching the red glare of the setting sun stream in through the open doorway, his certainty began to waver. When Daphnis appeared in the doorway, Mannus shouted at him, "Have you found him yet?"

Daphnis shrugged. "No, but he must be somewhere on the estate. There's no way he could get out of here unless he actually has magical powers." The sardonic smile on the scribe's face said quite plainly that he had no faith in magic of any kind. Mannus, however, was not so sure. In Roman Britain he'd seen things no man could explain or, having seen them, forget.

There was a rustle behind him and Mannus turned, startled. It was Hesperian, a bandage on his forehead, doubtless put there by one of the serving maids.

"Are you all right, sir?" asked Mannus with concern.

"Damned headache, that's all. But you ... haven't you found Serapion yet?"

"No sir, but we're sure he's around here somewhere."

"You are? Then tell me, how did those dwarfs get out of here when they went to get Hathor and Demetrius out of prison?"

"Well ... I don't know exactly, sir."

"Neither do I, but I'll tell you this. There's some way out of this place, some way we don't know about. There's got to be!"

"Sir . . ." It was Wakar, emerging from the darkness behind the huge brick oven near the door.

"Do *you* know?" demanded Hesperian.

"I . . . I think I do."

"Then why didn't you tell us?"

"I tried to tell your man Mannus, but he wouldn't listen."

"Tell me then!" Hesperian shot a look of exasperation in Mannus' direction.

"There's a way all the slaves use," said Wakar nervously. "There are underground aqueducts connecting all the estates together . . ."

"Of course!" cried Hesperian. Sabella had just come in carrying an earthenware oil lamp in which a smoky little flame was burning. Hesperian snatched the lamp from her fingers and led the way downstairs. "Look there," he said, pointing, as the others caught up with him.

On the brick rim of the cistern, near where the aqueduct pipe protruded from the wall, there were muddy footprints, some small and some normal-sized.

"By the gods," whispered Mannus.

"Now we'll never catch him," added Daphnis.

As Hesperian turned his face toward him, Mannus could see every dark line of anger and frustration outlined in light and shadow from the lamp.

"We must!" shouted the centurion, and the shout echoed for a long time before it faded away.

"He could be anywhere . . ." began Daphnis.

"Not anywhere. Somewhere special. Somewhere that someone like him would go and someone else wouldn't. Think, man, think!"

Daphnis and Mannus looked stupidly at each other.

"Wait . . ." said Hesperian. "Serapion's a sailor. A sailor must have a ship! And that's how he'd get out of Alexandria. He's got a ship!"

"That's right, Sir," said Wakar.

"Quick, Wakar," demanded Hesperian. "Tell me where it's moored."

"In the harbor somewhere. I don't know where."

"Does anyone in this house know?"

"Adrastia perhaps."

"She'll never tell us anything. She's a Memnon!" Hesperian started back up the stairs. "Mannus! Daphnis! Get the men together. Get some fast horses from the stables. We're heading for the harbor!"

Chapter Four

THE MUMMY OF ALEXANDER THE GREAT LAY, on public display, in a looming square marble tomb at the intersection of Alexandria's two main streets. The tomb was closed now, silent in the gathering twilight. The streets that, only an hour before, had been filled with noisy holiday throngs, were now all but empty, so that those few who remained—street vendors and an occasional prostitute—could hear from a long way off the rumble of approaching hoofbeats, and had plenty of time to step back against the walls of the tomb, out of harm's way.

Because of the straightness and breadth of the streets, they could also see, some distance away, the galloping horses and their cloaked riders, a bare-headed, powerfully-built centurion followed by his second-in-command and scribe and, a little further back, eight Roman soldiers in full armor wearing the black tunics and cloaks of Nero's dreaded Praetorian Guard.

The prostitutes shouted obscene invitations at the riders as they thundered past, but not one soldier so much as turned an eye in their direction.

Instead, the column wheeled and set off down the intersecting street, the street that led to the harbor, while the prostitutes dashed into the center of the roadway and shrieked insults at the Praetorians' retreating backs.

A moment later the soldiers streamed into the wide city square in front of the huge Greek-style temple of Antony and, passing between the two towering hieroglyph-studded obelisks that stood in the center of the square, reined up on the quay, near the water's edge.

Mannus stared in dismay at the maze of masts, yardarms and rigging that stretched out before him, moving and rocking in the faint breeze that came in off the Mediterranean. "There are hundreds, maybe thousands, of ships at anchor here. How will we know which one belongs to Serapion?"

Hesperian called over to him, "Don't forget, the port is sealed until tomorrow. Serapion, if he puts to sea tonight, will be the only ship that does, and he *must* put to sea tonight if he hopes to escape at all. Without the cover of darkness he wouldn't stand a chance of evading us." The centurion thumped his heels into the ribs of his horse and set off at a canter toward the dimly-seen, pierced travertine blocks further down the quays where his own ship was moored.

Valuable time was lost rousting out the crew of rowers from a dockside inn—some of them were drunk, and two or three were nowhere to be found—so that the last glimmer of day had faded before Hesperian and his men were able to clamber on board and cast off their long slender fighting bireme with its heavy iron bull's-head ram.

The stars supplied the only light; the moon had not yet risen and the lights of the lamps and torches of the city did little more than cast flickering reflections on the smooth waters of the harbor. The great light in the Alexandrian lighthouse would not be lit until tomorrow, and Mannus realized that there was a real danger that Serapion's ship could slip by them in the gloom. He could hardly see his own hand, let alone the ships at anchor around them; once or twice, in spite of their slow speed and careful steering, they bumped into some nearly invisible craft, but without damage to any vessel.

When they had cleared the mooring area and were in open water, Mannus turned to Hesperian, whom he could now see fairly well, since his eyes had adjusted to the dark, and said: "By the gods, sir, we'll never find him if we don't get a little more light somehow."

In a low voice Hesperian replied, "When the eye fails, we use the ear. Row and wait, row and wait. Sooner or later we'll hear him."

They glided on, past cluster after cluster of silent anchored ships, but there was no telltale sound, not a whisper, to reveal the location of Serapion.

■ ■ ■

Serapion's ship was built more for combat than for speed, and it was heavier though not much larger than Hesperian's. The massive gilt-iron hawk's-head ram on the prow was sturdily braced by thick belts, or wales, that ran from the ram all the way back to the tail-feather-like wooden aplustre that rose from the stern, so that the ram, with the whole length of the keel behind it, and stayed on each side by the heavy wales, had a rock-like solidity quite out of proportion to that of the other parts of the galley. Both wales and keel were considerably heavier than was customary for a fighting bireme.

He had designed the ship himself, and trained its crew, so that it was as much a part of him as his own body.

He had named it *Ra-Harakhti*, after the sun god Ra, in an incarnation as a bird of prey.

Now, as the *Ra-Harakhti* drifted slowly away from the quay, Serapion, bare-headed but clad in a heavy purple cape, stood on the afterdeck with Demetrius and Hathor and, in the faint light that still reached them from the torches and lamps of central Alexandria, commanded his galley slaves by hand signals, and though they could hardly see him they responded as if they could read his thoughts. The great square sail amidships had not been spread; there was too little wind and the ship was more agile under oar.

The three dwarfs crouched nearby against the gunwales. One of them whispered something, and the other two giggled; Serapion silenced them with an angry throat-cutting gesture.

Hesperian, he thought, *will be listening.*

A little earlier, in the last dim light of day, he had been crouching belowdecks when he'd heard hoofbeats and peered out through the oarport to see the centurion and his men gallop by on the quay, so close he could see the bandage on Hesperian's head. He had watched and done nothing, just continued on, quietly waiting for the cover of darkness.

And now the darkness had come!

As they drifted clear of the other ships on oar strokes so gentle one might have thought the oars were swinging free and unattended in their locks, the faint breeze grew a little stronger and took a definite direction. It was coming from landward, carrying them away from shore and the Romans.

Serapion thought, *You're still with me, Serapis.*

Grinning with silent exultation, he threw his arm roughly around his sister Hathor's shoulders and gave her a clumsy kiss on the cheek. To his surprise she did not melt against him, as she had done so many times before, but grew stiff and resisting.

Perhaps, he thought, *this is not the moment for such thinking.*

He leaned close to old Demetrius and saw a strained expression, as if the man was seasick. He murmured, "Come, come. We've faced worse than this before." He gave Demetrius a playful punch in the arm, then added, "Why don't you climb up into the forward watchtower and keep an eye out for the Romans?"

Demetrius seemed to understand he was being "kept busy," but he reluctantly obeyed. (If the Romans had been as close as a ship's-length away, he couldn't have seen them.)

It was too dark for hand-signals now: Serapion removed his sandals—even the faint slap and scrape of a sandal-sole on the deck would have been too loud—and padded barefoot back and forth the length of the ship, kneeling occasionally to whisper to one of his rowers, even to convey his meaning by reaching down through the openings in the deck that ran along the sides amidships and touching one of his men on the shoulder.

The rowing grew stronger, though the oars still rose and fell with almost total silence. The only sound was the hiss of the wake and the drip from the oars as they swung back for a stroke, and these sounds were so faint Serapion could hear the sound of his own breathing over them.

Even in the dark Serapion knew this harbor . . . he could not count the number of times he'd sailed in and out of it, under every imaginable condition of weather and light. With the aid of the stars and the distant lamps of the city, he could calculate his position as easily as if it had been broad daylight.

Now, for instance, he knew that he was nearing the tip of Pharos Island, a long narrow ridge of almost bare limestone that broke the force of the Mediterranean waves and provided a natural shelter for Alexandria's harbor. There were reefs there, just beyond the island's tip, but Serapion knew where they were.

And now, exactly when he expected, the glass-smooth harbor waters gave way to gentle ocean swells, and he knew he had entered a narrow, sandbar-lined channel called "The Entrance of the Bull."

At the forwardmost point on the ship, the mighty hawk's-head ram rose and fell with a steady hiss and splash, hiss and splash, as he thought, *Hesperian does not know these waters. He will have to move slowly . . . or run aground on the sandbars.*

And now the Entrance of the Bull was behind him and he was beyond Pharos Island, pitching and rolling in the open sea. He kept his balance easily on the heaving afterdeck, standing between the two Nubian giants who manned his steering oars, and stared back over the faintly glowing wake behind the ship. There was the famous lighthouse. He could hear the surf booming on the rocks at its base, but could see it only as a towering blackness where no stars could be seen.

The wind shifted and grew stronger; it was blowing steadily out of the southwest. When he raised his sail he'd have the wind behind him as he headed east toward Judea . . . Judea where, in the confusion of the war, he'd be able to make his way along the camel routes to safety in the Parthian Empire.

Light as a dancer he glided along the deck openings; a touch here, a muffled word there . . . that was all that was needed to command his slaves to ship the oars and begin slowly and carefully raising the mainsail. He was chuckling softly with exhilaration when he returned to Hathor on the afterdeck.

"Feel that wind?" he whispered to her.

She nodded, and though he could not see her face clearly enough to make out her expression, he sensed a coldness in her that he'd never known before.

Still speaking softly, he said, "All the gods are with me tonight, even Father Neptune."

Hathor murmured, "And if Hesperian catches up with you?"

"So much the better! Anyone who stands in my way . . . I cut them down!" He whipped out his shortsword and made a few practice thrusts.

"Even me?"

"Even you," he answered teasingly.

He reached out and grabbed her arm, but she angrily pulled away from him and ran toward the foredeck.

"Come back!" he shouted after her.

■ ■ ■

"Did you hear that?" whispered Mannus. "Serapion."

"I heard," said Hesperian quietly. Serapion's shout had been faint, but clearly audible above the rush of the wind and the breathing roar of the distant surf.

The centurion had already shipped oars and raised his great square mainsail, so on board his ship not even the sound of rowing broke the silence; even his little steering sail, jutting out in front of the ship, held full, not flapping. There was the slapping splash of the bulls-head ram cutting through the wavetops, nothing more.

"Amazing," whispered Mannus with awe. "How did you know which way he'd go?"

"There's an old proverb, Mannus. 'A fleeing man always sails with the wind.'"

A moment later the moon began appearing on the horizon, only a sliver at first. Wordlessly Hesperian pointed, and the pale light revealed that his lips were curled in a satisfied smile.

Serapion's sail, still quite distant, could be plainly seen silhouetted against the moon.

The others saw it too, and Mannus heard a rustle behind him as the eight Praetorians checked their weapons.

For a while Mannus lost sight of the other ship, then, as the moon rose higher and became a full round globe ahead of them, he caught sight of the sail again, closer.

"We're gaining, sir," he told Hesperian.

Daphnis remarked, "We must be lighter and shallower-drafted than he is, praise the gods."

"It's an advantage in the chase," said Hesperian, worried. "But if we get into a ramming duel, that extra weight may win the battle for Serapion."

"Do you suppose he's seen us yet?" asked Mannus.

"No. When he sees us, he won't take long to realize it's useless to try and outrun us. Then, if he's half the captain we've been told he is, he'll reef his sails, come about, and fight."

Several minutes passed, then Mannus broke the silence. "Look there!

He's seen us all right. He's not only reefing the sails, he's dropping them to the deck and—by the gods—he's knocked over his own mainmast!"

"Clever," Hesperian muttered. "He's not taking any chances on us ripping away his rigging so he'd be slowed down after the battle. He's thinking ahead, I'll say that for him."

Curtly Hesperian ordered his own sails reefed, then commanded his rowers to get back on their oars. A few minutes later Mannus could make out figures on the deck of the other ship, which had, by this time, come about to face them and stood, rising and falling on the swells, waiting. Hesperian signaled a stop.

Serapion's voice rang out over the black waters. "Hey, Roman!"

"Yes?" bellowed Hesperian in answer.

"The goddess Fortuna has intervened with me on your behalf." Serapion broke off to laugh recklessly. "You have a friend on my ship. My little sister is pleading with me to let you live. You know I can't say 'No' to that bitch, so stand clear and let me go. You'll have another chance at me some other day."

Hesperian cupped his hands around his mouth and shouted, "Surrender, Serapion! For your sister's sake, surrender!"

"Not on your life, Roman! Look at my ship, then look at yours, and think, man, think. No one will call you brave if you throw your life away for nothing!"

In the light of the full moon the hawk's-head ram on Serapion's ship appeared and disappeared rhythmically in the waves. It was painfully obvious that Serapion's ship was stronger and heavier than Hesperian's. Hesperian licked his lips but did not answer.

Angry voices drifted over from the other ship, then Serapion added: "Hey, Roman! You wouldn't believe what a fancy my poor sister has taken to you. Look at it this way. Suppose you win, eh? Suppose you sink us. Do you want it on your conscience that you drowned a girl who was madly in love with you?" Under Serapion's bantering, teasing tone there was an undertone of bitterness, anguish.

"Set her adrift in a lifeboat," countered Hesperian. "Whichever one of us lives through this can pick her up after the battle."

"Never, Roman! Hathor and I . . ." He faltered. "We've always been together!"

Mannus saw an expression of inner conflict on his commanding officer's face that was almost inhuman, an expression one might imagine on the face of a dumb animal caught in a trap. The cool, calculating gentleman soldier had been replaced by a madman who now screamed out, "So be it, damn you!"

At a gesture from the centurion, the rowers on the Roman ship stood up, leaned back, and pulled on their oars with a great groan of effort. The bireme moved forward, slowly at first, then faster.

The *Ra-Harakhti* surged forward to meet it.

■ ■ ■

Hathor felt a sharp pain in her wrist. "Serapion," she cried. "You're hurting me!"

He did not reply or loosen his grip on her wrist, only dragged her roughly after him as he lunged across the deck to crouch with her against the gunwales.

"Ship oars," he shouted. "Brace for impact!"

There was a clatter of wood on wood as the oars were hastily shipped. She could hear the same sound, like a distant echo, coming from Hesperian's ship.

They were on the afterdeck, and across from her, against the opposite gunwale, she could see the dwarfs also crouching and hanging on. The two Nubian giants stood erect, feet placed wide apart and hands firmly gripping their heavy steering paddles, their powerful naked bodies bathed in moonlight, as if they were too proud to take cover, but even they, at the last moment, dropped into a crouch and braced themselves.

But the expected impact did not come.

Instead a shower of arrows, with a sinister swishing sound, came raining down on the unoccupied deck and Hathor, looking up, saw the yardarm of Hesperian's ship pass overhead.

"Unship oars!" shouted Serapion.

There was a second wooden clatter, together with some excited shouts in languages she could not understand, and a loud splashing as the oars struck the water.

"He veered off," he told her with satisfaction. "He's afraid to meet the *Ra-Harakhti* head on, and if he's shooting arrows, that means he hasn't got any heavier weapons—like catapults or balistas—aboard. He didn't try to board us either, which means he probably has only his eight-man squad of Praetorians able to fight hand to hand, and probably knows or suspects that all my rowers are trained fighting men. What do you say, little sister? Do you want to bet on the fight?"

Hathor was about to answer, but her gaze wandered toward the little watchtower on the foredeck and the words froze in her throat. Demetrius was sprawling, half in and half out of the tower, an arrow through his head, his arm and the upper part of his body dangling down and swinging with every movement of the ship.

Serapion followed her line of sight and went on, almost without a pause, his voice swelling with a kind of ecstasy, "And that Roman, with all his shooting, has managed to inflict only one casualty!" He stood up and shouted to his rowers, "Turn to starboard, you swine! Hard starboard! Get your backs into it!"

The ship turned so sharply the deck tilted steeply. The rowers on the starboard side were rowing backward while the rowers on the port side rowed forward, and the giant Nubians swung their tiller oars over as far as they would go. On either side of the ship the sea turned white with swirling water.

Hathor could not take her eyes off Demetrius' corpse, but she could hear Serapion muttering, "If he turns faster than we do, we may be in trouble." He fell silent a moment, then shouted delightedly, "It's too late! He's starting his turn too late!" His grip on her wrist grew still tighter.

"Serapion, please," she pleaded, but he seemed not to hear her.

"That's it, you idiots!" he screamed at his crew. "Enough! Now, full ahead! Pull, you scum! Pull those oars! We'll get him this time!"

Hesperian's commands could also be heard across the narrowing gap between the ships, but there was a note of dismay in the Roman's voice. "Break the turn! Veer out! Full ahead there!" There was a cracking sound of oar against oar. Serapion burst into a maniacal laugh.

"Get up!" he shouted, dragging Hathor to her feet. "You see that? His oarsmen can't change rhythm quickly without getting confused. Look at that! Look at that!" He was laughing hysterically.

Now the rowers on Hesperian's ship had picked up the new rhythm from the steady dull thump of the oarmaster's drum, but the ship had already lost valuable momentum. The *Ra-Harakhti*, whose crew, even during the difficult turning maneuver, had moved as one man at all times, was now moving at full ramming speed, and bearing down relentlessly.

Serapion's crew needed no oarmaster's drum: They kept together as the musicians in a fine orchestra keep together, almost by instinct.

"We've got him!" Serapion shouted exultantly. "Stand by for the shock!"

A volley of arrows whistled overhead and Hathor, in the instant before she ducked below the gunwales, caught a glimpse in the bright moonlight of Hesperian's agonized face, then there was a heavy splintering crash and a shock that sent her sprawling as Serapion's ship rammed into the side of Hesperian's, just forward of the stern.

■ ■ ■

In the instant after the impact, the two ships were locked together in a terrible silence broken only by a creaking, scraping sound and the snap of an occasional breaking plank, as the vessels rose and fell with the sea, each movement increasing the damage to Hesperian's ship, while Serapion's remained virtually unharmed.

The centurion, by keeping a firm grip on the rail, had managed to remain on his feet, and as he looked down the long sweep of his opponent's deck, he could see nobody looking in his direction. Time seemed to pass more slowly; there was ample time to estimate the damage to his ship, realize the ship was finished, and make the decision to attempt one last desperate move.

He vaulted the rail and landed on the curved upper face of the heavily-braced prow that supported Serapion's hawk's-head ram and clung there as the ships separated. The prow was only slightly damp, not dangerously slippery; this part of it was well above the water line. He took a deep breath and clambered forward until he reached the dangling anchor chain, tested it to see if it was secure and, finding that it was, climbed up it hand over hand and, a moment later, swung a leg over the rail and found himself on the forward deck of the *Ra-Harakhti*.

Behind him, moving steadily further away, he could hear the panicked screams of his own rowers, but he did not so much as glance in their direction; there was nothing more he could do for them. If they kept their wits and clung to the ship, they wouldn't drown. The bireme was made of wood and it would float . . . though rather low in the water, of course . . . and they were not far from shore.

Ahead of him, as he had hoped, there was nobody on deck but Serapion, Hathor and the two Nubian tillermen. All the slaves, including the dwarfs, were belowdecks, and Demetrius . . . that old man's troubles were over.

Hesperian thought, *Surprise is with me. If I can reach Serapion before he can call for help . . .*

He drew his shortsword and sprinted for the afterdeck, cape streaming behind him. But one of the naked black giants cried out in surprise and pointed, and now Serapion looked up, astonished, and called out, "Hesperian!" Instantly he let go his sister's wrist, drew his own shortsword, and crouched, ready.

Hesperian slowed to a walk. He reflected, *We're equally matched. We have the same weapons, and are both without shield or helmet.*

But Serapion was younger, and probably quicker, more nimble.

Hathor screamed, "No!" and rushed forward to try to stop her brother, but he threw her aside with such force that she fell and seemed stunned, perhaps unconscious. Hesperian gripped his sword a little tighter, a sudden irrational anger welling up inside him.

They were face to face now.

Hesperian stopped.

The two men stood like statues a moment, then began to circle each other warily, each waiting to catch the other off guard. Out of the corner of his eye Hesperian could see the Nubian giants waiting for a sign from their master and, through the openings in the deck next to the gunwales, the heads of astonished rowers appearing.

A high piping voice called out, "Need help, Master?"

It was Bubo, the dwarf.

The crew laughed, but Serapion said nothing, he just kept circling, a trace of a contemptuous smile on his thin lips. In another moment there was nothing to be heard but the creak of the ship and the faint rush of the wind and the distant breakers on the shore.

It is, Hesperian thought, *a beautiful night.* The breeze was warm, and the moonlight was, by now, almost as bright as day. The pitch and roll of the ship was gentle, soothing. To be on this ship, on such a night, with Hathor, under different circumstances . . . Hesperian's blade lowered a hair's breadth.

Serapion lunged.

Sword blades clanged together.

The two men parted, unhurt, and continued to circle.

"Very good," murmured Serapion. "My compliments, Roman." He lunged again.

There was a lightning exchange of thrusts and parries, but this time as they separated Hesperian was bleeding freely from a cut in his right leg.

"You're getting old, Roman," Serapion remarked, then smiled faintly and added, "But don't worry. I'll see you don't get any older."

He lunged again, but it was only a feint. All the same, Hesperian was forced to take a step backward.

Serapion attacked again, this time in earnest, and Hesperian found himself retreating steadily. Laughing recklessly, Serapion advanced behind a blade that flicked and darted like a serpent's tongue, so light on his feet he seemed more a ghost than a swordsman, while the centurion, limping badly, could only stumble back along the deck until he found himself amidships.

There he tried to counter-attack, but only succeeded in picking up a deep cut on his left arm. He managed to stand firm for a while, but he was getting dizzy from pain and loss of blood. He had to see, but his eyes had begun to go out of focus, and every time he moved his wounded leg it hurt as if cut again. His left arm hung useless at his side . . . there was no feeling in it. But the worst pain was in his mind, the humiliating realization that Serapion was just playing with him, tormenting him . . . for sport!

And then Hesperian slipped.

He slipped in his own blood and went down on one knee, and Serapion, with a sweep of the cloak, caught the Roman's sword in its folds and jerked it from his hand.

Before Hesperian could draw his dagger, Serapion was standing over him, sword at his throat, panting and laughing.

"Lie down on the deck, face down, Roman," Serapion commanded, grinning.

Hesperian hesitated.

"Now!" shouted Serapion.

Hesperian obeyed.

"Now," went on Serapion, "pull out your dagger very slowly and throw it away. Ah, that's it."

Hesperian did as he was told.

Hathor, who had dragged herself into a sitting position some distance away, called out, "Serapion, please! Please! You can't kill him when he's helpless like that!"

Serapion answered scornfully, "I suppose not, little sister. There's no sport in it. I'll let my slaves do the cleaning up." He turned to the crowd of rowers who had come up on deck to watch the fight. "All right, you there. Finish him off!"

■ ■ ■

As he looked down at the Roman who lay, face down, spread-eagle on the deck, Serapion thought with a kind of awe, *This is the moment of victory.*

It was hard to believe that the terrible game was over, and that he had won.

But what could stop him now? The only ship that had pursued him had been wrecked, and the only man who had come close to catching him now lay helpless at his feet. With Hesperian dead, the way would be clear to freedom and perhaps honor and wealth in Parthia at the court of King Vologases, perhaps an overland trip to India to exploit the Memnon business holdings there.

He wiped his shortsword clean, returning it to its sheath.

And he thought, *I have been faithful to my god, Osiris-Serapis, and now my god is rewarding me. Success is the sign of the favor of the gods. So the gods approve all I've done! They approve the way I saved my father from the Second Death. They approve the way I love my sister, so like the way the god Osiris-Serapis loves his sister, Isis. They approve the way I rid myself of this Roman pig, Hesperian! He and his kind should never have come to Egypt! My ways may not please the Romans, with their rigid and alien morality, but the ancient gods of Egypt not only forgive me, they applaud!*

He could almost hear the gods cheering, like the mob in an arena at a gladiatorial spectacle, cheering Serapion the Victor and turning thumbs down on Hesperian the Vanquished.

Serapion glanced around, and frowned. The crew was hanging back. Were they afraid to attack a helpless, unarmed man?

He glared at them. What a mixed, ragtag crew they were, but he'd made real sailors, real fighting men, of them . . . blue-eyed, yellow-bearded Northerners, giant black Africans, tough, wiry, brown little Jews and Arabs, tall native Egyptians, stocky brown-bearded Britons . . . he'd melded them all together into a fighting machine that could beat, it seemed, even the much-feared Praetorian Guard.

"What's wrong?" he shouted at them. "Didn't you hear what I said?"

"He's an important Roman official," said one of the big Greeks apologetically.

"This could mean trouble . . ." added one of the giant black tillermen.

Serapion shouted: "A hundred drachmas to the first man who gets in a cut!"

Before any of the slaves could respond, Hesperian, still flat on the deck, called out, "Is that all he'll bid for the life of a Centurion of the Imperial Praetorian Guard? I can top that!"

The slaves hesitated.

Some lowered their weapons: knives, shortswords, clubs, boat hooks.

Jeeringly, Bubo, the dwarf piped: "Make your bid, Roman!"

"Give me my life," shouted Hesperian, "and I'll give you your freedom . . . every one of you!"

"Kill him! Kill him! Kill him!" shrieked Serapion, as he saw them glancing at each other curiously, considering Hesperian's offer. "Two hundred drachmas!" screamed Serapion. "Three!"

But it was too late.

The slaves were turning away from Hesperian and advancing on Serapion.

Serapion drew his shortsword, went into a fighting crouch. There were so many, and he was only one.

He retreated a step, then another.

Hathor screamed.

He half-turned, but the attack came low, lower than he had any reason to expect. Bubo hurled himself at the back of Serapion's legs, knocking his feet from under him.

Serapion thought, *I don't understand.*

The foot of a Nubian giant stepped on his sword hand. He could feel the crunch of broken bones. His sword tumbled on the deck. Hands ripped away his dagger. Knives and shortswords penetrated his flesh in a dozen places at once. There was pain, but it was not unbearable. He looked past the snarling faces that pressed in on him, looked into the eyes of his sister Hathor, and in the midst of the pain a part of him, which did not share the agony of the body, savored the love and concern he saw there.

He thought, *It will only be a little while before we meet again. But in what different time and place? In what different bodies? And will we remember? A little, yes. You always remember a little . . . a feeling, when you see someone for the first time, that you have known her for centuries.*

Serapion was not yet dead, but his body no longer obeyed him. They were dragging him along the deck, lifting him into the air, and now he was falling. The water, when he struck it, was cool and good.

He went down, down, and it seemed . . .

It seemed someone, a dark man with the head of a dog, was waiting there under the sea to take him somewhere.

END OF BOOK THREE

Coda

IN THE HARBOR OF OSTIA the *Ra-Harakhti* dropped anchor one hot summer morning, under a cloudless sapphire sky filled with wheeling squadrons of white seagulls.

A small boat rowed out to meet the bireme, threading its way among the other ships that lay at anchor there, rocking gently on the swells.

A naked Greek slave held the small boat as steady as he could while a small group of friends, laughing and joking together, transferred one at a time from the larger vessel to the smaller.

In the lead was Centurion Gaius Hesperian, limping slightly. He jumped down from the *Ra-Harakhti* quickly and easily, like a man who'd spent his life at sea. His wounds were almost healed; soon they would be no more than a few more old scars, a few more fading memories of pain. He wore a short red tunic and sandals, a dagger and a sword.

Next came Hathor, dark with the tan she had cultivated on the long Mediterranean cruise from Alexandria. She was barefoot and wore a pale blue linen shift that clung to her supple body with the dampness of sweat or sea spray; her light brown hair had grown long and tangled during the voyage, and it streamed out behind her as she leaped down into the small boat. Hesperian caught her and steadied her and they both laughed, but there was in the laughter an undertone of sadness.

Third came Mannus, his short-cropped brown hair perhaps just a little grayer, his thick hard body perhaps a little more weary than it had been when he left for Alexandria. Like his commanding officer, he wore neither helmet nor armor, but a short black linen tunic, sandals, dagger and shortsword. From his dagger-belt hung a small leather moneybag. And, like his commanding officer, he made the jump from the larger vessel with the careless ease of a true sailor.

Last came the scribe, Librarius Daphnis, handsome, muscular, hawk-nosed and arrogant as ever, his clothing identical to Mannus'. Daphnis' leap was made self-consciously, as if showing off his gracefulness.

When the four were seated, the Greek shoved off, and the little boat headed back toward the quays.

Hesperian shaded his eyes with his hand and made out the figure of a Roman soldier, a Praetorian, waiting near the small-boat dock. The soldier had four horses with him, saddled and bridled. Hesperian's message, sent ahead when he'd docked overnight at Neapolis, had apparently gotten through on time.

"Ave Caesar!" snapped the soldier as they mounted the stone steps toward him, and the crispness of the straight-arm salute would have been in itself enough to tell them that they were home.

Hesperian, Mannus and Daphnis returned the greeting and the salute with an unaccustomed precision. On the long sea voyage they had fallen into the habit of hardly saluting at all.

"Your horses, sir," barked the soldier.

"Thank you, soldier," answered the centurion.

The soldier cupped his hands and Hesperian stepped into them and swung a leg over the nearest horse, as fine a black stallion as a man could want.

When Mannus, Daphnis and Hathor had been similarly helped into the saddle, Hesperian told the soldier, "We're riding to Rome. I should be back by nightfall."

"Yes, sir. Ave Caesar!" The soldier thumped his breast and once again gave the straight-arm salute.

"Ave Caesar," returned Hesperian gruffly, but as the four turned their horses and rode away, he asked Mannus, "Do you think you can get used to 'Ave Caesar' both coming and going?"

Mannus answered ruefully. "I suppose I'll have to." They rode at a brisk easy canter, past the long rectangular brick warehouses with the booths set into the walls behind mosaic walkways portraying grain ships, lighthouses, dolphins, gods—a maze of trademarks interspersed with the names, usually in Greek characters, of the distant ports with which the different corporations traded. There were merchants in those booths, standing behind tables and arguing—as they would spend the rest of their lives arguing—over prices.

At the first cross-street they swung away from the waterfront and, slowing, picked their way through a crowd of slaves, merchants and seamen to the less commercial part of town.

At one point Hathor's horse—a powerful brown mare—reared up as a barking dog dashed across its path.

"You're all right there?" asked Hesperian with concern.

She laughed and tossed her head. "I can ride as well as any man. You want to race?"

Hesperian grinned and shook his head.

"Sir," called out Mannus.

They reined up.

"Yes, Mannus?"

"With your permission, sir, Daphnis and I would like to leave you here. As I remember, there's a certain inn not far away where they serve only the finest wines, including, so it's said, the very best vintage Falernian. Daphnis has kindly volunteered to treat me."

Daphnis scowled, but it was obvious he wasn't really angry.

"Very well," Hesperian said, giving Mannus a light, playful punch in the arm. "But aren't you forgetting something?"

Mannus was puzzled. "Forgetting something?"

"The salute."

Laughing, they exchanged salutes and Mannus and Daphnis galloped off.

"Where to now?" asked Hathor, looking around at the almost identical five- and six-story red brick apartment buildings filled with noisy, squalling humanity that surrounded them.

"Follow me," Hesperian answered.

Their horses' hooves clattered on the paving stones as they set off, Hesperian in the lead.

A few minutes later they had left Ostia behind them and were pounding down the Ostian Way. It was almost like open country here, with the straight lines of willows spaced evenly along the road's edge, the occasional clump of umbrella pines, and the little farmhouses set back from the road, with their white walls and red tile roofs.

The highway was divided into three lanes: the center lane was wide enough for oxcarts and donkeys and horses to move past each other in both directions; then, separated by a footwalk on either side, there were two narrow lanes for rapid one-way traffic, and it was down one of these outside lanes that Hesperian and Hathor were riding.

Hesperian slowed slightly to allow Hathor to come up beside him.

Above the drumming of the hoofbeats, Hathor called over, "You've been so kind, Gaius. I'm afraid I must have bored you with my weeping and hysterics at the Festival of the Ship of Isis."

Not looking at her, he answered, "You made up for it later."

"And now all the questions are answered, eh, Gaius?"

"There's one thing. Tell me, when did you learn that Serapion . . . ?"

"Killed my father? I thought you knew. It was when I was eavesdropping on you the first time you questioned him. You knew too, didn't you?"

"Yes, but then you threw me off, you little fox."

They laughed.

On their left the Tiber River came into view and began running parallel to the highway. It was flat country along here, flat as a tabletop.

After a pause Hesperian began. "I'm glad you can laugh now. I was afraid . . ."

"That I'd pine away for love?" On the ship she'd gotten into the habit of finishing his sentences for him. "Oh Gaius, you're so old-fashioned. Women may have done things like that in the days of the Roman

Republic, but not any more. Besides, now that I look back on it, I'm not sure I really loved Serapion after all."

"What?" Hesperian was surprised and slightly scandalized.

"I think if I'd really loved him I could have turned him in. It was because I didn't love him, only wished to believe I did, that I was ready to sacrifice my life. I wanted—you know—to prove a beautiful lie, a lie that was like poetry. Beware, Gaius, anyone who has something to prove!"

After another silence, Hesperian said uncertainly, "When you asked me if I was married . . . ?"

"Oh Gaius, not now. I've lost my taste for poetry. I can see things more clearly now. For instance, you're awfully old, you know."

"That's true." This time his laugh was nervous, forced.

They rode on in silence for a long time.

The buildings along the road were taller and closer together. That was Rome up ahead, spots of white marble showing in a mass of green trees. Rome could be seen from some distance away, as the famous seven hills on which it was built were almost the only hills in the area.

And now they were entering the outskirts.

The streets were still wide, but so crowded they had to slow their horses to a walk.

They passed under a towering two-tiered aqueduct, passed alongside the vast bulk of the Circus Maximus, and heard the cheering crowds. All around them the sweating mobs milled and pushed, heedless of anything but their own immediate business. Hesperian, who knew his way, rode in the lead; Hathor rode behind him, too far away for conversation.

The crowds thinned.

Ahead of them lay the gates of a sumptuous villa protected by high walls. Hesperian reined up before its heavy wooden gate and dismounted. Hathor sprang off her horse and followed him.

He spoke briefly to a slave who peered out at him through a little window in the door, then waited in the sun and buzzing flies.

She took his hand.

"Gaius, won't you stay for supper? I'm sure my mother would be honored."

He turned away. "What would be the point?"

She was about to answer when the villa gate burst open and an older woman ran out; she was not beautiful, but very slender and dignified, a woman who looked like Hathor would look some day.

"It's been so long," murmured Octavia Memnon.

She looked at Hathor for a moment, as if afraid someone was playing a cruel joke on her; then the two women embraced. There were tears in Octavia Memnon's eyes.

Hathor pulled free saying, "Mother..." The word sounded awkward on her lips. "Mother, I want you to meet..."

But Hesperian had stepped quickly away and now sprang into the saddle of the stallion and, clutching the bridle of the brown mare, thumped his heels into the ribs of his horse and galloped away, head down, shoulders hunched.

Octavia said, "Well, he's certainly very rude!"

Hathor answered defensively, "You just don't understand him!"

The women talked together in low voices for a while before going into the house.

Late that summer the garden party to celebrate Hathor's debut in Roman society was the event of the season, but Centurion Hesperian did not attend.

THE END